The Blind Do See

Philip W Lawrence

Books by PW Lawrence

Looking on Darkness   Book 1 Detective Toni Webb

The Blind do See   Book 2 Detective Toni Webb

The Eight (Decades in the life of an English boy)
                              Book in process

With thanks to my family and friends for their comments and the time they gave to read my work.

To Gupta who inspired me to write, although I did not realise how much time it took, not the writing, that came fairly quickly, but in my personal editing and the constant adjustments needed to make everything fit together, which it never really does.

I like spell-checking software; my dyslexic fingers never match my thoughts or it is the other way around?

To my lovely Margaret who allowed me the space and time, when time is now so precious.

All the locations in this story are based on real places I know. The characters and plot in this tale however are fictional; any similarity to real persons or events is purely coincidental.

I do not believe in coincidences.

For my super wife
Margaret

The Blind Do See

Philip W Lawrence

Weary with toil, I haste me to my bed,
The dear repose for limbs with travel tired;
But then begins a journey in my head,
To work my mind, when body's work's expired:
For then my thoughts, from far where I abide,
Intend a zealous pilgrimage to thee,
And keep my drooping eyelids open wide,
Looking on darkness which <u>the blind do see:</u>

From Shakespeare's Sonnet Number 27

Prologue

He pulled into the layby on the A33, unloaded the lead lined van of its contents placing them into a compartment hidden in the boot of his specially prepared car. His dark long protective suit with its attached hood covered his head and face, the special glasses his eyes and the thick gloves his hands. He separated the file and books, memory chips and jewels taken from the safe into separate piles. The experimental rack from the laboratory he carefully lifted out with tongs and placed it in the specially constructed lead container. He checked everything was now safe with a Geiger counter. He closed the boot locking away the danger. He removed his protective clothing and threw it into the back of the van closing its door. He turned to his partners who were standing well away a safe distance from the offending objects.

"Jim, everything is secure now, you and George take the van to dump and burn it, collect the car from the station likewise. Give them their down payment now, they will get the rest later when I've sold the stuff, arrange the pick up as we said".

Jim Quarrel had been his friend and partner in crime for some years. They had worked together on many jobs, some legitimate and some not. Jim was the only one who had contact with him and although they had never met him, all Jim's team were aware of his presence and the danger of even thinking about crossing this unforgiving man.

"Okay, I'll wait for your call, after the clear up I'm going to stay with my Dad. I have collected all the mobiles, which I will destroy. I'll get a new pay as you go and text you later as arranged, so in a couple of hours it will be done and dusted".

Jim was organiser, enforcer and paymaster, he the planner and financier. Jim thought the precious stones were a great catch but had no idea why he wanted the other things and a crappy piece of apparatus. Jim had been instructed to find some new guys to go in and take the stuff out and not the regular team. The entry was easy, except that he had not been able to get into the lab, so had no choice but to break it open. The night watchman was a small problem that the brothers quickly resolved. Once the new lads had loaded the van and had left, he was to take it to the A33 layby and wait. He was very clear about the lab being a dangerous place, so did exactly as he was ordered. He watched him drive off leaving Jim to dispose of the van and later the car.

Jim was looking forward to seeing his Dad, then having a pint in their local, before spending a week in front of channel four racing on the T.V.

Chapter 1

Toni Webb woke to the sound of her mobile buzzing. It was almost dark outside, the embryonic daylight only just showing itself through the crack in her curtains. She hadn't set her alarm, for she had enjoyed a late night at her favourite pub and today was her first Saturday off in three weeks. The phone insisted she pick it off the bedside table before it shook itself onto the floor. Her slowly focusing eyes studied the number as one she knew but couldn't immediately place with her blurred vision and even blurrier mind.

"Hello, Webb".

She almost mumbled half awake and not really wanting to be so.

"Sorry to call you so early Ma'am and on your day off too".

She recognised the voice straight away her brain now coming to its normal functioning level.

"Oh, hello Peter, that's okay what's the problem?"

Toni was now fully alert. Detective Constable Peter Andrews continued.

"There has been a robbery Ma'am, at Westfields Laboratories. The night watchman has been badly hurt and is on his way to hospital. They by-passed the alarm system somehow and have emptied the safe. I don't know what's been taken yet we are waiting for one of the directors to arrive. The reason I'm calling you now is there has been a serious breach of one of their research laboratories, it's where highly dangerous materials have been disturbed".

Peter paused to gather his thoughts before continuing. Toni interrupted him, she being fully aware of the dangerous nature of Westfields research, was immediately very concerned for the well being of her officers and the people in the area.

"What have you done to secure the situation?"

"We were called in by one of the researchers who came to work very early, he also called the Environment Agency who immediately dispatched a team to help contain the problem. I've closed the road entering the estate and have checked the premises of other businesses. We have two cars here and four uniformed officers who have cordoned off the estate and are controlling things. Only a few people were at work in nearby premises, they have been taken to the roadway just outside the estate entrance into the cordoned off area. The Environment Agency guys are here Ma'am all suited up, they are going in to seal off the building. I don't know the nature or extent of contamination, we were asked to keep well away by the researcher and were told to wait for the Environment Agency decontamination unit to arrive".

"You do that Peter keep well clear, did you go inside the building and where is sergeant Musgrove?"

"No Ma'am, only the research technician a Mathew Walker; he pulled out the night watchman. The ambulance people took him away from outside they didn't go in, I've already called Sergeant Musgrove he's on his way here".

"That's good, I'll be with you as soon as I can" Newly promoted DCI Webb was half dressed before finishing the phone call. She had grabbed her favourite grey slacks, a cream blouse and a warm zip up sweater. Half slipping into her tan flat shoes on over black socks she hobbled down the hall to her front door. Checking to see that she had her car keys, warrant card and purse, was out of her house two minutes later. The slim tall woman, with the thin nose and facial features typical of some tribes descended from the Igbo people of Nigeria, moved to her car. Her hair was curly and still mostly dark with the odd fleck of grey, kept short and unstyled when brushed quickly took on a neat shape of its own, it was a little dishevelled at this moment. Her eyebrows narrow and arched over large black and shiny eyes. Her smile revealed even white teeth that had been braced as a child and obviously well cared for.

Her first major case as Chief Inspector was not going to be what she expected. Normally her rank would seldom be involved directly on the ground, but Basingstoke CID was so short-handed, at both Sergeant and Detective Inspector level that she was obliged to assist when they were busy. Regardless of her senior officer status she had no choice today, as this dangerous and serious event required her personal on-site attention.

She sent a text message of the situation to Superintendent Munroe, he was no doubt sleeping but would pick up the message soon enough. With an incident of this nature there may well be some political repercussions, he was the one to deal with that and would want to control the liaison between the police and the media. He was welcome to that.

She sat in her car, waiting for the misted windscreen to clear, wondering what had brought her to this moment; five in the morning no breakfast and worse still no coffee, her teeth uncleaned and with unbrushed hair, she felt a mess. Her mind drifted back two years, where at this time of day she would have been tucked up in bed in her Southampton house with her husband Larry. Now separated, by a few miles and some considerable time, she was still unsure how she felt. Toni was the one who had left and came to work here in Basingstoke; even so she did miss him but not enough to go back yet. The 'yet' was her sticking point not his, she had no idea when she would feel differently, their trial separation had stretched to more than a year. She had become used to her new home and although a lonelier life, one more acceptable than living in the tense, silent atmosphere that had become the norm for the childless Webb household. Larry spoke to her on the phone every now and then, a very limited conversation.

"Hi Toni, just seeing if you're okay".

He would say, her reply being the same each time.

"Fine, how are you?"

They never discussed any subject of consequence although it seemed that Larry was waiting for her to react positively to his enquiries, a response she was not yet prepared to give. Their almost forced friendly exchanges at least showed no animosity. One unexpected bonus from her departure was the move to Basingstoke. The transfer had been a real boost to her career, the promotion to Chief Inspector had come out of the blue when DCI Bean retired, this would never have happened in Southampton. Her luck, in that respect at least, had changed for the better; being in the right place at the right time was not normally one of her fortes.

Toni rented a house in Chineham, a small suburb of Basingstoke. A wooded area known as Great Oaks Grove. Hers was the end house of a twenty-five-home development nestling in a small valley with many of the oaks still undisturbed. Some of the larger trees had been felled to make room for the houses but the area continued to retain that country feel. A small brook ran through the valley with a parallel path amongst the trees and shrubs. A micro haven that supported some wild life not normally seen so close to a town centre. She had been pleasantly surprised to spot several deer over her back fence devouring the heads of wild flowers that had sprung up amongst the grasses. The modern houses had been a bit of an eyesore in such an environment at first, but the new owners had planted wisely, even if accidently, so that the shrubs, climbing roses, clematis and ivy among others had softened their building's sharp features making them more acceptable. How planning had been given to build on such a site was beyond Toni, she was not party to that, but pleased that it had been. She was very taken with her new rented home to the extent that she was now considering trying to buy it.

Toni Abakoba was born in Nigeria; her once affluent parents were from the mid-west who had been at starvation point during the Biafra war. At the first opportunity the Abakoba family Joseph, Maru, Dan and the baby Toni had immigrated to England living in London initially.

Clever and hard working her parents provided young Dan and later Toni the finest education they could afford.

The family eventually moved to Southampton where Toni, met and married Larry Web. Toni fell pregnant soon after but miscarried at month four.

With her loss came an unacceptable void that was filled by becoming a part time community police officer near her home. After some full time years in the force proper she rose from being a beat copper to the rank of Detective Constable on through Detective Sergeant and eventually Detective Inspector four years before this current transfer to Basingstoke. Her mathematics degree and she suspected her ethnic background, had put her on the fast track for promotion. There were very few ranking officers of African origin on the force and the hierarchy were keen to redress the balance. She did not feel she had been unfairly privileged because of her black skin, as others might, for she had worked herself into the ground from the beginning, with an exceptional clear up rate second to none, she deserved every promotional advance on merit.

The transfer away from Southampton was at her request as her marriage had suffered partly due to the long hours she worked as a police officer, but more because of the strain of her husband wanting a family that would probably never materialise. Being childless in this marriage was totally depressing from which she had to have some respite. The respite continued.

She woke from her reverie; the car's heater having cleared her windscreen several minutes before and set off with little or no traffic this early; it took only ten minutes to arrive at the gate of the estate.

Chapter 2

Westfields was sited at the far end of a small industrial complex on the southern outskirts of Basingstoke. There was a recessed entrance from the main road more than wide enough to allow two large lorries to pass. A pair of chest high, wheeled, iron gates led on to a straight road though the main part of the estate that had a mixture of large and small units with parking spaces at the front of each unit. There were twenty-six in all along this section. At the end was a Tee junction with Westfields occupying all the space from left of centre to the extreme right, the rest of the left section being a box shaped carpet warehouse.

Westfields was by far the largest of the buildings on the complex but unlike the standard units it had been custom built. It was wide and extended back to just short of the rear fencing. The building had three floors with parking to the front. The ground floor was slightly raised; two wide and deep steps approached a glass double door entrance leading to a foyer, in the centre of which was a reception desk with an office behind. To the right was a long room with shelves and cupboards used for storage at the end of which was another containing the electric fuse panels, the heating and hot water system. To the left a canteen style kitchen with some basic dining tables, a rest room with several armchairs and a large bookshelf. There were lockers, toilets and shower facilities at the extreme end. There were no windows to the rear of the building, just a few ventilation grills. To the right of the reception were two lifts and an emergency stairway behind a closed fire door. The first floor consisted of nine offices and a security control room. The second floor was divided into five laboratories and three storage rooms.

A pedestrian pavement ran the length of the estate on both sides, broken every so often by vehicle crossovers. A few of the units had some shrubbery planted in various tubs but most were sadly neglected.

On her approached she saw two police vehicles blocking the entrance and the usual striped orange and yellow 'keep out' tape. There was a very large white van parked on the inside of the gate partially blocking the road. Obviously, the Environment Agency vehicle with its circular logo on the doors and side panel. There were several white suited men close by the van huddled in discussion. Four police officers conspicuous in yellow safety jackets were standing around outside the gate. Inside a taped off area was a group Toni assumed to be personnel from the estate businesses. Peter Andrews emerged from the cluster as she parked her car some twenty yards from the gate. A few moments later Detective Sergeant Jonny Musgrove pulled up and parked behind her.

Detective Constable Peter Andrews walked over to the two cars.

"Morning Ma'am".

Peter made an exaggerated mouthed "sir" with a nod to the sergeant who was still sitting in his car talking into his phone.

"Not so good constable it seems. What's been happening so far?"

"You are right there, at least for some of those here. The environment agency guy says that anyone one of us who were within twenty yards of the open door of the building will need to be checked, he didn't say what for though, although he reassured us that it was unlikely that we had been exposed to any significant level, whatever that means. We are to be called three at a time into the Mobile Decontamination Unit due here any minute. That fellow over there is the technician Mathew Walker".

Peter was looking at his notes for the name and pointing out a short be-speckled young man in the grey topcoat. He then moved over indicating another group.

"There are four men who were working a night shift in the carpet place next door who will have to be checked as will I and Mr Walker, the paramedics and their patient too I suppose but they have gone to the hospital. No one else was anywhere near. Only two other firms had manned security and I'm told they were well outside the dangerous area. I've kept them all here though just in case, and they will need to be interviewed anyway".

By then D.S. Jonny Musgrove had joined them and was listening in.

Toni was aware that the type of contamination was from radioactive material and the fact that the E.A vehicle arrived after the ambulance had left meant that she needed to take immediate action.

"Right first you need to contact the hospital and the ambulance crew tell them that there is radiation contamination, the hospital will need to take precautions. Phone them now Peter"

"Yes Ma'am".

Peter was taken aback at the news of a probable radiation leak but immediately started the call on his mobile.

"Now I must talk to the E.A. team leader and make him aware that there are exposed personnel at the hospital. He will know what to do".

Peter pointed inside the gate.

"The guy in charge is in the back of that white van"

"Right Peter, start interviewing everyone, use the uniforms to help, Jonny come with me".

"Ma'am".

Jonny followed as Toni hurried towards the van with her warrant card in hand. The officer at the gate opened it just enough for them to walk through. She knocked on the side door that opened immediately.

"Please go outside the gate this is a controlled area".

The young dark-haired man in jeans and denim top seemed not to notice Toni holding out her warrant card, as he was about to shut the van door in her face. Toni reached out with her hand to prevent him from doing so.

"I'm Detective Chief Inspector Webb and must talk to you".

"I don't care who you are you must leave at once".

Toni did something she would not normally do; she raised her voice to such a pitch that he had no option but to comply.

"Young man please stop what you are doing and listen to what I have to say".

Jonny took a step forward one foot over the threshold and held onto the door handle. The young man looked at him with screwed up eyes, obviously not used to being disobeyed.

"What do you want"?

"You have three people who are probably the most contaminated who have left the site".

"Why…. How the hell did that happen"?

"Before you or anyone else arrived the ambulance crew took the injured night watchman from the steps by the doorway of the building and are now at or very close to North Hants. Hospital. My officer has just informed the hospital that they have probably been exposed to radiation and must be isolated, I expect you will need to get a decontamination unit over to there as well as here".

"Sorry, Detectives I was pre-occupied with a major problem, please note this is a quite serious event, I'm Frank Jones a Chief Technician with the Environment Agency and need to make sure everyone is okay, I don't have time for interference from outside that's why I was a little short with you. Sorry once again".

Toni nodded her acceptance of his apology, the name of Jones triggering some unsavoury thoughts not needed at this time. He continued.

"How come you know that there has been a radiation accident?"

"Not a difficult conclusion seeing you here. This facility is one of our responsibilities and we are fully informed of the nature of all the business concerns here, especially ones like Westfields, which could be a potential hazard. How serious is the breach?"

"My men are inside now and have sealed the area containing the radioactive material. We believe most if not all the material is still inside and has not been removed".

"How can you know that?"

"We can't for certain until the Westfields' technicians do a full inventory, but the levels traced just outside the lab and in the corridors are low enough to indicate that, although radioactive source material has passed through those areas, it was there for such a short time to be of no harm now. Of course, the persons who broke in may have carried some away in special sealed containers although what use it would have, I cannot fathom".

Just then another large white vehicle arrived. "That's the decontamination unit, please go outside the gates now as my priority is to check everyone here and get them cleaned up if necessary, I'll also deal with those at the hospital. To put your mind at rest first indications are that the initial levels found are not too high, but we still need to deal with it as a class A high level incident until we have it confirmed otherwise".

Toni nodded her agreement as she and Jonny left him to his task and moved back to their cars.

"As soon as I received Andrews call Ma'am, I searched out the company emergency numbers and spoke with director William Grimm, who is on his way here now, and told him what had happened. He already knew from another director, a Mr James, whom his technician had contacted earlier, James lives closest, so he shouldn't be long. William Grimm lives a fair distance away, so it may be some time before he gets here".

"That's good Jonny, as soon as the technician has been checked I want to talk to him. If either of the directors arrive before I've finished leave me with the technician and keep the directors away from their employees, we'll try and find out just what they think might be missing and why, let's get it down in your note book before they can think of better answers, I don't want them in contact with each other before they have been interviewed separately. It's not out of the question they might start putting a story together to cover their arses. With the state of the night watchman this could become a more serious enquiry and I don't want self-interest from witnesses clouding the issue".

"Right Ma'am I'll keep an eye out for them".

Jonny relished the idea of tying Mr James and William Grimm down at first interview; before suspects had time to think, those initial answers were always very revealing. William Grimm's manner on the phone was not of concern for the watchman or the technician but for what may have been stolen from his precious company, Jonny didn't like that.

Toni and Jonny were waiting outside the decontamination van; they were told it would not take long to check everyone out, a little longer to clean their clothing if necessary. The technician Matt Walker had gone in first as being the most exposed of those needing to be checked followed by Peter Andrews. They could treat three at a time. First, they took all your clothes measured the radiation level around your body and the clothing you had on. Next you entered a shower unit to wash with this special 'soap' followed by a high- power scrubbing spray for ten minutes. You were then dried by a high-speed blower and finally put on a white coverall suit. You were then checked again. If your level was above a certain reading you would have a blood sample taken and be hospitalised in a special unit. Fortunately, the levels were very low in all cases, the technician was the highest on entry, but the decontamination had removed all the material which had absorbed the deadly radiation from his body, his clothes carried too much residue to be cleaned easily so were taken away in a sealed container to be decontaminated. Peter and the others although exposed, were well below dangerous levels but still went through the cleansing process for their safety. A further precaution meant their clothes and possessions were to be thoroughly cleaned in a special facility not available in the mobile unit and would be returned later, in the meantime the white coveralls were sufficient to protect their modesty if not very warm.

As they emerged one at a time from the van looking a little odd in their new white suits, all silently thanking heaven the it was not winter, Toni stepped forward.

"Mathew isn't it"?

"Err....yes...I". The technician, his brow furrowed and eyes squinting, without his glasses, was bewildered coming from the darkish van into the bright light to be confronted by a black woman holding out a warrant card in front of his face. Toni wanted to catch him with no warning, not giving him time to think of excuses to cover up any mistakes or wrong doings by him or any colleagues he may wish to protect

"I'm Detective Chief Inspector Webb sir, and this is Sergeant Jonny Musgrove, a brave thing you did there going into that place and pulling out the watchman like that".

She paused waiting for a response. None came he just shook his head, seeming like he had never heard.

"Please will you tell me exactly what happened as far as you can remember"?

Again, no response.

"Take your time young man you have had a bit of a shock, but I need to know what happened here".

"Sorry yes, I understand, I feel a bit odd and I can't see very well without my glasses. I was miles away wondering about Horace, it was awful you know just coming across him like that and all that blood, I thought he was dead. I don't suppose you know if he will be okay, do you"?

"Not yet, he's in the best place my constable will enquire for you, what is Horace's full name"?

"Horace Peables I'm not sure how you spell it".

He replied slowly as he observed the Sergeant was writing it down in his notebook.

"That's okay, please continue".

"Well, I came to work as usual I'm always the first in, I can't stay in bed, don't sleep much when we have something good going on, I wanted to see the results of last night's run. Anyway, I parked in my spot and walked to the main door, I had my key-card ready to get in but found the door was already wide open. I knew something was wrong the door should never be like that, it is only opened to go in or out. I could just hear an alarm from one of the labs beeping. It was then I saw Horace was not behind the reception desk and the office door was open too. I didn't want to go up with that alarm going off so went to look for Horace; I thought maybe he was dealing with the problem. I had no idea what had happened, I tried the storeroom first in case there was an electrical fault he may have been looking for, then the kitchen, as there was nowhere else that he could go apart from the upper floors. I pushed open the swing doors and saw him lying there with lots of blood round his head. It had dried a bit but there was a lot of it on the floor. At first, I thought he was dead, but he was still breathing, thank goodness, and I knew if a lab door was open then there could be contamination too, so I lifted him under his arms and dragged him to the steps outside. I phoned 999 on my mobile and asked for an ambulance, the police and then The E.A. emergency number….Oh.. then I called Mr James".

"You did fine there, did the watchman have specific duties do you know"?

"He always sat at reception during the night, he could see and be seen. He had rounds to do but only on the ground floor. The stores and the rest rooms really there's not much down there. The lifts were shut down at night and the emergency stairwell door locks automatically when the last person has left the building, it is done electronically from the entry cards we all carry. Horace was officially here until seven, he and David do twelve-hour shifts, they provide continuous cover by working two days on and two off. We have to have someone here at all times for the insurance I think. Normally he would come and say hello to me, and we would have a chat for a few minutes before I went up. He would often stay on after his time until one of the girls arrived to take over the desk about eight usually. Although he could have left before I think he liked to see everyone come in, made him feel part of the team. A nice man I do hope he is alright".

"I'm sure he is being well looked after. I already know the type of research you do here but what can you tell me about what has been taken. What was in the safe and what was in the laboratory"?

"I'm not sure if I'm allowed to talk about the work, but I'm sure they must have been after the precious stones that were kept in the safe, there were some in the main laboratory too, these are set up as part of the experiment. You say you know what we do so you understand how close we are to treating some cancers that are inoperable by conventional means. We use rubies, diamonds, emeralds as well as many other crystal structures to produce laser light streams at different frequencies. We are trying to direct radiation to sit beside the light in a narrow beam so that we can target minute tumours that lie deep within the brain".

"How close are you to achieving this"?

"A way to go yet, we have had some promising results recently but are unable to reproduce them on a reliable and regular basis. A year maybe, but you never know with luck we could hit on the right combination at any time".

"So, what do you really think the thieves were after, the equipment or the jewels"?

"Oh, the precious stones of course we have over twenty thousand pounds worth of diamonds alone and probably the same in rubies plus all the others, fifty grand I'd say at a guess. The ones in the safe are okay but the ones in the laboratory are housed close to a source of radiation. If the thieves took them from the lab they could be in some serious trouble. We have to wear protective clothing whenever we work in the main laboratories. I've not been inside so I don't know what's missing".

"Where is the safe"?

"In the office behind reception, I didn't go in, but I could see it was wide open through the door just before I went to look for Horace".

"You have been very helpful in your report here Mathew, probably your scientific mind eh. So, you don't you think information about you experiments would have some value"?

"Well they must have a value of some kind but stealing it is near impossible as it is irradiated, and the related technical information is spread all over the place, in any case we have no real results yet. No, no it's the jewels they were after for sure".

"I'm inclined to think that too, but I had to ask just in case. We might need to talk to you again. Thank you for your help so far".

Chapter 3

Toni was well aware that industrial espionage was big business and couldn't rule it out just yet in spite of what she had just been told. The director may not be as forthcoming as his technician although much of what he had told her Toni was already aware of, this through reading the police bulletin on local companies with special requirements from a public safety viewpoint. What it didn't say was that there was a considerable quantity of precious stones stored on site.

The directors, her next target, had still not arrived, so she went back to her car as tiredness suddenly made her feel a little lightheaded.

"Missed my coffee; I bet these buggers James and Grimm have stopped for theirs and a bit of toast too I'll wager".

She spoke aloud to no one in particular as she sat half in, half out, with the door wide open.

Jonny just smiled at his new senior officer's moan to herself, as he walked back to his car to wait. He was still unsure how well they would work together, having a black woman boss was not something he had envisioned in his future. He had been with DI Colin Dale for a long time and had built up a relationship, which produced good results, even though Colin's methods were not as straight as he would have liked. An old-fashioned copper with old-fashioned ideas who got results. Jonny often found himself covering up mistakes and altering reports to hide deliberate procedural transgressions. Illegal searches and suspect intimidation were not alien to DI Dale. His new boss seemed straight in this respect always by the book, so far anyway. She was a clever detective with ways of questioning that put her suspects at ease, so they revealed much more than they intended. Not the bully tactics of Colin, which often led to the suspect saying what you wanted to hear and far from the truth. He'd reserve judgment but liked what he'd seen up to now.

A Mercedes saloon pulled up just behind the two police cars that were blocking the entrance to the estate. The officer on duty leaned towards the window, spoke to the driver and looked up pointing to where Toni was parked. The car reversed to park just in front of Jonny Musgrove's Ford Focus. The driver climbed out walked round and opened the rear door. His passenger exited slowly and stood by the door looking towards Toni waiting. Toni waited too stubbornly determined that she wasn't going to move first. The driver closed his door went around the rear of the car took his passenger's arm and walked him over to where Toni still sat.

"Sorry if I kept you waiting miss, but I had to wait for Henry here to bring me, I can't drive any more you know my eyes have gone, old age they say bloody nuisance but mustn't grumble eh, I can still see a tiny bit with one eye and a big magnifying glass but not good enough to get around without help. Any way I'm James Grimm director of Westfields. Matt called me out first as I live nearest, but he didn't say much, can you tell me what's happened so far and is Horace okay"?

Toni was quite taken aback, not what she expected at all. A short well-proportioned man of seventy odd with a full head of grey hair, in jeans and baggy maroon jumper, which looked like it had been hand knitted. His soft London accented voice and furrowed brow of genuine concern made Toni feel more than a little ashamed that she had jumped to conclusions attaching negative characteristics to someone she had never even met. 'I bet he hasn't had his breakfast either', she thought giving herself a mental slap on the wrist.

Toni got up from her seat and seeing her rise was quickly joined by her Sergeant.

"Good morning sir I'm DCI Toni Webb and this is Detective Sergeant Musgrove sorry you've a problem getting here but we do need to talk to someone in charge. Horace has been taken to hospital I'm afraid I don't know his condition yet. Your technician Mathew Walker has kindly put us in the picture, but we cannot enter the estate until it is cleared by the E.A. boss. I need you to tell us what was in the safe if you can".

Jonny was puzzled by his boss's more than pleasant tone, but he had missed the first part of their conversation. He looked sideways pointedly at Toni who returned his silent question with a slight smile and a 'leave it' shake of her head.

"That is something I can do; however, I've called my son William who lives out Hurstbourne way, he will be here soon, he kind of runs things now and will have an up to date list of the contents. I just come in now and again to know what's going on and I get bored sitting at home on my own".

The old man paused a moment, to get his breath and to think.

"I get out of puff lately, all that smoking when I was young, I expect. Gave it up ten years ago but it is catching up with me now. Let me see, I believe the safe contains a quantity of precious stones and crystals. There will be some files and memory sticks containing the results from experiments conducted over the past year or so. Company chequebooks maybe and our

34

accounts ledger. I don't know the details, as I said William could give you exact descriptions of the stones when he gets here. I know we keep copies of most things in the office upstairs".

Toni went on to explain what had occurred, thanked him for his help and left him to go to his car. She walked over to the group of people in white where she was about to task DS Jonny to begin interviews.

"What was that all about guv why so nice when he kept us waiting so long, he only lives five minutes away"?

"Shush there Jonny, the guys virtually blind so had to wait for his driver to get up and fetch him so he couldn't have got here any sooner. He's more than concerned, we got the names mixed up too they are both named Grimm, the father is James and the son William. The old guy is known affectionately by the staff as Mr James".

"Sorry Guv we got that wrong, or at least I did. One thing strikes me, from what Walker said, it may not be just the jewels they were after; the technical secret stuff may provide a much bigger payday".

Toni just smiled and nodded, the two detective's minds were in tune.

"I'm thinking the jewels being stolen were a diversion away from the real target".

"Nice bonus though eh"? Toni voiced aloud.

"Aren't we getting ahead of ourselves Guv we don't know what's missing yet"?

"You're right, I'm fed up hanging around doing nothing, go and see when we can get inside and chase up the other Grimm".

Jonny moved towards the white van as Toni sat sideways on her driver's seat again.

Jonny knocked on the door of the van and walked straight in.

"Mr Jones please call me as soon as we can have access to the building. Anytime, day or night".

He said handing him his card. Jones took the card forced a smile and nodded without a word. Jonny smiled back turned on his heels and left to go back to Toni.

"I've given him my number he will call as soon as he knows".

"Good, you and D.C. Andrews stay here and finish the staff interviews, there will be people arriving for work who will have to be sent home. Sort out who they are, take names addresses of those that work at Westfields ask about their colleagues, see if someone who is expected to come to work does not turn up, chances are that if the alarm was bypassed someone inside might have lent a hand there, use the uniformed officers to help with the interviews or you may be swamped. Check especially with the guys who were working in the carpet place next door they may have seen something. I want you to take on the interview of William Grimm when he finally arrives. If possible, a list of all employees would be nice but may not be possible until we can get into the building. When you have finished leave a couple of uniforms to keep watch before you go. You'll also need to nip Peter to the staff house to get some clothes and a phone; they have taken everything of his for decontamination, even his car keys. I'll wait here till you get back you shouldn't be long, then I'm going back to the station".

Toni had some research to do and needed to get more officers on this task. The day was flying by she wanted to get inside and start the process of finding the men who did this.

Whilst she waited for her detectives to return from the station the name of Jones played on her mind, not for the first time by a long shot.

"I must get on to Colin to see if he had come up with anything recently".

She said this aloud, not directed at anyone, but to re-enforce her resolve to do so.

Detective Inspector Colin Dale had joined her on a case, when she was Senior Investigating Officer and then a Detective Inspector on the first day she arrived at Basingstoke from Southampton.

The case involved the abduction of a young girl, the murder of an accomplice and the wounding of D.C. Andrews. The murderer and psychopath Sandra Cooper escaped but died by her own hand accidentally before she could be charged. Jonny Musgrove was then the Detective Sergeant working with Colin before he left to go to London. The true instigator of these crimes they knew was 'Toby' David Charles Jones. He managed and controlled these events through Sandra and all those involved without ever getting his hands dirty. He left the Country with shed loads of cash and diamonds before they could question him. *'The Powers That Be'* closed the case putting all the blame on Cooper for having killed her lover, torturing the girl and finally shooting Peter. The senior officers ignored Toby's motive of a huge financial gain and the fact that he had inside information from someone on the force.

"There is not enough evidence for the CPS to prosecute Jones so close the case now".

This was the order from The Assistant Chief Constable. He was only interested in results with the minimum of expense. Colin and Toni had to concede and officially accepted the order but together they vowed to keep looking for Jones in their own time and bring him to justice regardless of the decree from above.

DI Colin Dale operating in London again was able to trace the private investigator Joseph Mallard who was in the employ of Jones. He had gone missing at the same time as Jones but had resurfaced a month later. He said he had been on holiday and denied any connection to the events in question, even though Colin had witnessed him with Jones around the time. Just routine enquiries concerning a property deal he said. This being a non-official investigation Colin could not officially use the warrant to search his office, one that he had obtained whilst he worked at Basingstoke. He had however put an under the counter watch on him through friends in London. Once Colin had some evidence of wrongdoing, he would put the pressure on but so far nothing had come to light. Toni thought once she cleared this case, she would devote some real time to tracking Jones. Colin's transfer to London later led to his promotion to Chief Inspector, this gave him much more freedom to carry out his own enquiries.

Chapter 4

Toby, or should I now say Alan set his alarm to wake earlier than usual. This was to be a special day, the first of many that would see the disappearance of David Charles Jones and the emergence of Alan Mortimer. He rose, even before the alarm, to a warm day with the sun already well on the rise; it was always warm here in Busios, always Summer. He longed for an English Spring day or a bit of snow and Father Christmas. He had been here for almost a year now and had established himself in this unique Brazilian community. He had left England to escape the chance of arrest and prosecution for conspiracy at least and more likely retribution from a group of less than savoury investors whom he had caused to lose a few million pounds whilst feathering his own nest.

He had callously left behind, his one-time friend, Sandra to face the music but found out later that she had died through her own stupidity soon after he had gone. His property empire had been sold to a group of investors who were to find later that this empire was on the verge of collapse and were now after his blood. It had been some time since then, so perhaps they had given up looking, who knows, soon it would make no difference. There were still several properties in London that he had purchased years before in the name of a Company owned under his new name of Alan Mortimer. They had been bringing in good rental income paid to this small legitimate Limited Company. A well-paid manager whom Toby had deliberately never met ran the company. Alan took a small salary, paid his taxes and had thereby established an official 'honest' identity and place to come home to.

The driver arrived on time ready to take him to the clinic in Macaiay, a town two hours drive north. Macaiay was once a small fishing village, with a large natural deep-water harbour, but had since grown into a new town with the discovery of oil off the coast. It was busy with English, Portuguese and American engineers and had all the facilities that came with this influx.

The Estaban Clinic was a private hospital catering to the wealthy, and more recently oil company personnel and their wives; run by a Doctor Ramos Estaban whose father had funded the building of this facility. It was a sound investment as its services didn't come cheap and over the past three years had flourished to become the best facility for a thousand miles. Alan had researched the best hospitals for him to have his features altered, it seemed Rio was not a safe place and as the oil money had attracted the best people further north that was where he went. Doctor Ramos

Estaban was a plastic surgeon of some skill that had been studying Alan's x-rays and scans planning the structural changes that would transform Toby into Alan.

"Good morning Alan".

The doctor was unaware of his real name and background, his only interest was in the large sum of money he was being paid to carry out the transforming surgery, after all this was Brazil where everyone had a price, no one asked questions and never remembered anything when asked.

"Morning Doc are we ready to go"?

"Today is the first of six procedures we will carry out over the next several weeks, I hope you are strong".

"No worries, what's the first job"?

"We are going to start with the ears as this will be the least invasive. We will remove a small section of hard tissue from behind each ear and re-attach the skin in the natural crease with fine stitches that will become almost invisible when healed. You will need to wear a large supporting bandage for a short time whilst the flap section of the ear settles to its new flat position. We must take care not to disturb the area of the join, as a tear would be serious, so you will need to be patient. Two weeks should see it healed enough for us to move on to the next stage. We will have a look and change the dressing in a day or two".

"I don't care how much time you need as long as it works".

'David', as was his given name at birth, thought back to his childhood where his ears stuck out so much that he gained the nickname 'Toby' after the famously made pottery figures or Toby Jugs whose ears were often used as handles. He was quite proud of the name and he never worried too much about his appearance. He always thought of himself as special and his ears were part of that notion. The good doctor interrupted his reverie again.

"As we discussed before we will start work on the other features when your ears have healed. I will learn a lot about your skin reactions to surgery and your rate of recovery, which will help with the more difficult procedures. The next operation will be re-shaping your nose and tightening your cheeks, which can be done at the same time. After that the chin and the eyes will complete the surgery. We can do the teeth and coloured contacts at any time between. Two or three months should see it all complete. You'll be a new man.

"Alan Mortimer the 'New Man', that's what I want to see. Shall we get on with it then".

He came around from the anaesthetic a little groggy, dressed in a helmet like bandage fitting over his head, under his chin and covering his ears. It was not uncomfortable and didn't hurt much. A young nurse was checking his pulse looking at him with a big smile on her face. Although he had learnt a little Portuguese, enough to order a beer and a restaurant meal with a few phrases to use socially, however it didn't stretch to asking about his operation. He started with a few disjointed words and was pleased when she interrupted him in English.

"You good, you rest please, doctor come soon okay".

Although the bandage completely covered his ears, he could hear well enough to understand her stilted English even if a little muffled. He smiled back with a thank you "Obrigado, what is your name?"

"I Juanita you rest please".

"Nice name".

He replied and promptly fell asleep.

The next time he woke Doctor Ramos Estaban was shaking him gently.

"Welcome back Alan, the procedure went very well with no complications and you are recovering as expected. You must stay here a few days to rest after which I will check the incision sites; there is always a risk of infection, so you will be on a course of antibiotics more as a prevention you understand. If all is in order, we will change to a more comfortable dressing and you can go home. Are you in pain"?

"No not really a little sore maybe".

"That is normal, if it begins to pain you or itch the nurse will give you something to help. Please whatever you do keep your hands away from the bandages, we must not disturb the stitches at this early stage".

Three days later Doctor Estaban removed the 'helmet' and carefully checked the healing was going well, no sign of infection and although the area was swollen and bruised the ear position was better than expected. When the swelling went down, they would lie as flat as any he had done before. He gave Alan a mirror who was shocked at the difference it made. Just this one alteration made him look like a different person, he thought. 'Once all the other things are done no one will recognise me; Toby Jones will be gone for good'.

Chapter 5

Once back at the station Toni sat next to Constable Compton Busion both looking intently at Compton's computer screen.

"Please print that off for me will you".

Toni said.

"Yes Ma'am, shall I carry on looking"?

"If you will please Compton, I want as much information on Westfields and their personnel also find out the effects of short-term exposure to radiation from different isotopes".

"Do you know what they were using"?

"Not at the moment, DS Musgrove will know soon, he should be interviewing their MD as we speak. Also, can you find out if we have a radiation expert on the force in Hampshire, it could save us some time and the possibility of getting it wrong. This stuff can be deadly, but it may also become less dangerous as time passes, we just don't know yet".

"Good idea I'll see what I can find"

Constable Compton Busion was the computer whizz who had helped to solve many a puzzle for Toni and other officers in Basingstoke. Her ability to analyse financial data was second to none. She could find her way round the mysteries of the WEB and had a knack of 'guessing' passwords, guessing being a word mostly used by those less gifted that didn't have that special skill acquired by hard work. This girl was a real asset to any police force.

Toni took the printed sheets, a breakdown of the management and senior personnel and staff at Westfields with a brief description of their functions within the Company. She noted that the technician Mark Walker's name was not on sheet one, too low down to be included in the top ten. Interesting that he was the first one on the scene, keen to see the results of his experiment is what he said. Toni wondered and noted to herself to find out if that was his normal behaviour. Someone let them in for sure, he was close by, just maybe he was too close. She would reserve judgment, ideas like that, without facts, can cloud the issue whereby you miss the truth.

Her phone buzzed her from her thoughts.

"Andrews here Ma'am this is my new number, all staff accounted for except a Verity Pargiter. According to the staff who have arrived, she should have been in today, although she may have tried to call in sick or something, we can't check as we still are shut out and can't get access to the phones. She's a personal assistant who was at work yesterday with no problem. I have her mobile number, from a colleague, which goes straight to voicemail, do you want me to find out where she lives and go around, there's nothing much we can do here until we get clearance from EA guys?"

"No Peter you stay there, I want you to see what's been done by the clean-up team and to check with William Grimm exactly what is missing and whatever else you can glean from the scene. Get SOCO to do a sweep, although everything will have been compromised as far as viable evidence is concerned, we may still get a lead if there are prints or DNA. Is Sergeant Musgrove with you?"

"He's interviewing the Director William at the moment Ma'am".

"Tell him to call me the moment he's finished".

She hung up and went back to the computer screen print out, familiarising herself with the names and positions of the staff. She was looking at Verity Pargiter's name and details when Jonny called.

"You want me guv?" Jonny said "I've just finished with William Grimm, nothing much different from what we heard from his old man, we have to wait till we can get inside to see exactly what's been taken. He was very nervous about some papers though he said he couldn't, or more likely wouldn't tell me what they were. I didn't press him as I thought you may want to interview him in depth when we have a handle on what has gone down here".

"That's good Jonny any negative vibe from anyone there is food for thought. Now though I want you to go and find this Verity Pargiter who didn't come in as usual, I'll text her address and details, take a WPC with you, find out why she was not at work".

"Yes, guv I'll call you as soon as I have found out anything".

Toni wanted to get stuck in and have hands on, but the job of a DCI was supposed to be more one of administration and guidance than direct detective work. Still they were short at least one DI and a sergeant at the station, as she had not been replaced. Neither had Sergeants Jonny Musgrove or Melanie Frazer been promoted yet. In fact, Mel was unattached to any senior officer and was really under used. The Super said he was dealing with it and asked Toni to use everyone as best she could. Some local politics to which she was not party no doubt. She resolved to find out why if nothing changed soon.

Chapter 6

Jonny was glad he could get away from the site. He wasn't unduly worried about the contamination, although he knew it could be deadly even in small exposures, he just felt safer that's all. In any case hanging around waiting just was not his thing, he needed to be busy. He called the station as there were no women police officers on duty at the site and requested the desk sergeant send a WPC to the address of Verity Pargiter in Rotherwick village just six miles east of Basingstoke. 'Thank God for satnavs', he thought as he came upon the house tucked up a lane banked either side with amazing rhododendrons unfortunately no longer in bloom. A late flowering border led to the house, it was large, very large and old too. You could tell there was money here. Well-kept lawns, flowerbeds to die for and two black Labradors who ran to greet you as if you were a long-lost friend. No sign of the WPC, but Jonny exited his car anyway and walked towards the imposing oak porch with its wide-open front door, the dogs demanding attention by nudging his hands. He bent a little and stroked one of the dogs to be greeted by a female voice coming from the doorway.

"Can I help you?"

Jonny didn't know what to make of the lady who approached him with a smile as glorious as her flowers. She was in her late forties, greyish hair, almost blond, long tresses that fell naturally to each side of a mature and beautiful face. Obviously dressed for gardening carrying a small basket and a pair of clippers he could not respond at once as he was mesmerised by her deep blue eyes and that smile. He stood still for it seem an age but at last he gathered himself and showed his warrant card embarrassed by his lack of control.

"Good afternoon I'm Detective Sergeant Musgrove madam, I'm looking for a miss Verity Pargiter".

"Oh, that's my daughter, she'll be at work right now, back about six, it's almost that now she won't be long".

She didn't seem at all worried that a policeman was on her doorstep enquiring after her daughter.

"Have you found her stolen handbag? She has already stopped her cards and had the phone blocked, so apart from a bit of cash and having to replace everything no great harm done. I hope you have caught the blighter that took it is that why you are here"?

He now knew why she was so unconcerned he did not want to alarm her so played along a little.

"No news there I'm afraid Mrs err..."

"Oh, sorry I'm Margaret Pargiter"

"As I said nothing yet Mrs Pargiter we are still looking, however I do need to speak to her about something related that happened at Westfields, what time did she leave for work this morning?"

"I don't know, she stayed with her friend Julie last night and went straight to work from there, do you think someone at work took her bag, it seems unlikely they all so nice"?

"These days anything's possible we try to keep an open mind. Do you have Julie's address"?

He tried to keep his voice calm and casual with a smile forced out of concern.

"Oh, sure that's Julie Wells Hawk cottage, it's just half a mile on the left as you leave the lane, you can't miss it, names on the gate. I don't think anyone will be there as Julie works too, but why......"?

Jonny could see that she was getting worried, so he interjected before she could ask the question.

"It's just a routine enquiry madam I'm sure I'll find her at work or her friends, I'll ask her to give you a call to put your mind at rest when I see her there".

Jonny said goodbye and climbed into his car, the smile and bright eyes that greeted him were no longer shining, and there was doubt in that frown.

He immediately called the desk sergeant, who told him the WPC was lost, Jonny understood why; these places are really tucked away. He asked the Sergeant to pass on Julie's address by radio and said his car would be parked in the lane outside, so she could more easily find it. He then made his way to Hawk Cottage.

A more modest residence with a rustic wooden gate, its name burnt in to the top crosspiece. A short path led to a front door set back in a tiny porch covered in a pale lilac clematis. He parked and waited. Five minutes later the police car pulled in front of his. He was glad to see WPC June Owens emerge front the front seat.

"Sorry Sarge, got a bit lost back there what's up?"

Jonny quickly put her in the picture whereupon they approached the front door together. The bell was a physical old-fashioned type with a clanger and a piece of thick string. Jonny waggled the string and the sound, which ensued, would have woken the dead. No answer he tried again a little less exuberantly this time but still no response. He then took to banging on the door with his fist.

"There's no one in Sarge".

"Maybe. I'm going around the back, you wait here".

Jonny went to the side where a tall wrought iron gate blocked his path to the rear of the cottage. He was preparing to climb over when he happily found the gate unlocked, it swung open with a slight push. He moved down the side where just one small window quite high up was visible. He moved to the rear on a small garden the path to the left leading to the back door, a door that stood wide open. He looked inside, saw no one, entered slowly keeping as quiet as he could. He moved through the kitchen into a small dining room the door of which led into the hall. Nothing so far but why the open door. He went into the hall and opened the front door to admit June Owens. He put his index finger to his lips to indicate silence as she entered. He was listening and was sure he could hear movement and some small noises from upstairs. He glanced into a neat but unoccupied sitting room off the opposite side of the hall as he approached the stairs. He indicated to June for her to stay put. He climbed the stairs not as silently as he wished as the boards creaked like an old ship at sea; his presence in the house was sure to be known.

The rustling noise was obvious now it was coming from the room on the left. He pushed the door open quickly anticipating a response from an intruder but saw only the figure of a young woman on the bed trussed up by her hands and feet. These had been lashed together behind her making it impossible to escape. Her face was hidden inside a black bag secured over her head with duct tape. The girl was screaming but only a weak sound emitted past whatever was covering her mouth.

"Don't be alarmed I'm a police officer, we'll have you free in a moment".

He yelled down the stairs.

"June call an ambulance then get up here pronto"!

Jonny tried carefully to remove the black bag; he unwound the tape a little trying to tear it. He tugged at the edges again trying not to crush it bearing in mind he may be destroying prints. He needed to relieve the girl of her bonds at the same time preserving evidence. June arrived at the door he turned to her.

"Find some scissors or a sharp knife June, try the kitchen be as quick as you can".

The well being of the girl was uppermost in his mind. Trying to rip the tape was difficult if not impossible. The cloth bag did rip and was free now hanging round her neck. He could see the girls face she was terrified. The darkness gone her eyes were now streaming with tears partly through fear and from the sudden influx of light. Her mouth was covered in the same duct tape wound several times round her head. He needed the scissors now. June arrived with a kitchen knife and a pair of small kitchen scissors. He grabbed them and slipped the points behind the tape behind her ear, once under, the small blades easily sliced through the several layers that his fingers were unable to break. He removed the tape round her mouth and passed the scissors under the tape on her neck to fully remove the black bag mask. In the meantime, June was sawing through the ropes binding her arms and legs. All this time he was soothing the girl with reassuring words to calm her from the trauma that was at the forefront of her mind.

"Its Julie Wells isn't it you'll be safe now. We are police officers, I'm Jonny and this is June, it's going to be all right, just relax".

The girl nodded confirmation of her name and repeatedly asking.

"Where's Vera"?

She whispered, between sobs, which slowly subsided. Jonny rose leaving June sitting on the bed with her arms around the young woman's shoulders continuing with the reassuring words. Jonny went down stairs pulled out his phone just as the ambulance arrived. He pointed up stairs. They knew what he meant.

"Boss we have an incident here, we need someone to help with forensics".

He explained what they'd found and what he feared may have happened.

"This girl Julie Wells was well and truly bound; if we hadn't found her, she may have suffocated. God knows what her mental state will be after being trussed up like that in total darkness. The ambulance crew and WPC June Owens are with her at the moment. It will be easier to question her after she has been looked at and has calmed down a little. It may be better coming from June".

"You are right there Jonny, good job you found her now, another few hours and it may have been too late. Finding Verity Pargiter is now our priority, I don't like the way this is going, do the usual, question the neighbours you know what to do but if necessary, you must find out from Julie Wells what happened a soon as you can. I'll send a 'Scene Of Crime' team over".

"We've trashed it a bit but had no choice, SOCO will sort it out. Any news on the Westfields front"?

"I haven't heard from Andrews yet, so no. With her going missing like this it looks like Verity Pargiter may have been their means of entry do what you can then go to the hospital, leave June with the girl she'll know what to do, I'm going back to Westfields, I need to have some answers now, I'll call you when I get there and have some information".

Toni was hoping they've just tied her up somewhere like her friend Julie, the alternative she didn't want to think about but that uneasy feeling was ever present. Why did they take her? Was she needed to gain entry? What did they do with her after? All these questions and many more were building up in Toni's mind not least, how they knew she was not at home that night and would be an easy target.

Chapter 7

Toni's mood was sombre. She awoke to the memory of what was in the letter she found when she arrived home yesterday, it all came flooding back. She retrieved it from the back pocket of her yesterday's slacks as she threw them in the washing basket. Folded almost flat now, recovered from the waste bin after having been screwed up and tossed away in anger. 'How could he do this' she thought, near to tears. The trial separation was just that. In her eyes a period of adjustment before reconciliation but for Larry it was different. The weekly phone calls were pleasant with still the hint of intimacy that Toni thought would lead to a new beginning. She had been fooling herself, reading more into the regular contact than was there. She almost spoke out loud chiding herself.

'A fine detective I am, can't even see what's in front of my bloody face'

It was clear now the marriage had ended the day she left to come to Basingstoke. The letter was not from Larry but from his solicitor, the first step in divorce proceedings. She put the letter in her bedside cabinet drawer out of sight and out of mind as she had serious work in hand that needed her full attention.

Today she dressed ready for work in a skirt of grey fine tweed. A beige silky blouse and a short-sleeved darker grey body warmer along with a moderately heeled leather shoe, a red cashmere scarf completed the ensemble. She normally wore trousers, sweatshirts and trainers but felt the need for a softer approach, which more feminine wear would support.

A coffee would be nice before she left but that would make her late.   Coffee would have to wait. Westfields her next stop.

DC Peter Andrews looked knackered and probably was, for he had been up most of the night. Toni had no time for sympathy yet as things were coming to a head.

"Ma'am I'm glad you're here I was about to call you with an update. I have gleaned some information from the director William Grimm and I've had the all clear from the EVA man, there is no danger any more, I and the uniform officers have taken statements from the staff and everyone who was here, I then sent them home. Before he would release the building, the EVA man went in with the technician to check if any dangerous materials were unaccounted for. He told me that the risks were minimal as they were using something called ..." he paused to look at his notes.

"Samarium 153. The test sample is used in breast cancer apparently and decays quite quickly. Its half-life is 47h, which they say, means its strength reduces by half every 47 hours. It will still be dangerous for some time, several days he said. None of the locked up radioactive material was taken away although a piece of experimental radioactive apparatus was removed, including three large rubies. Oh, and a small white crystal not part of the equipment. There should be no ill effects for anyone here. If the thieves weren't wearing protective clothing they will have been exposed to a dangerous level. How bad the effects on them are, will depend on the time they spent in the lab, how close they got and if they touched the material directly. The rubies and apparatus will be irradiated but the level will have decayed to be of little harm in four to five days. Jones has sent out a bulletin to hospitals in the south including London for any signs of patients with radiation sickness, it's part of their containment protocol. He said they would inform us of any hits, if anyone reads the bulletin that is, so don't count on it".

"Good job Peter anything else before you leave. Can we go in now?"

"Yes, Ma'am all clear I called SOCO earlier to be on standby, they will check everything, the entrance, the safe area, canteen and the lab, they are in there now.

When they have finished, I will go in with William Grimm to do an inventory of what has been taken from the safe and elsewhere. He went home for a couple of hours but has come back now. I also called the security firm who look after this place; a Mr Bernard Dumbar is their engineer for this site, he is waiting in his car, he will be able to access the security logs to see how they got in and can download any CCTV footage which may help us".

"Well done Peter go and have a break and leave him to me you can come back to the station later. I will need you in good form, tired officers make mistakes so go home for a couple of hours, do you have spare keys for your car till you get yours back from the E.A. decontamination?"

She deliberately didn't tell him about the missing girl as she knew he would not rest with that problem on his mind, she would fill him in later, maybe it would be happily resolved by then.

"Yes, Ma'am thank you I have spares at home, I'll pick my car up this afternoon".

Peter left, glad to be going home.

Toni walked towards the security man's car. He saw her approach in his mirror and climbed out to meet her. Good morning, Mr Dumbar isn't it; I'm Detective

Chief Inspector Webb showing him her warrant card. We can't go in for a while yet so can I have a word out here please".

"Hello Detective, yes I'm Bernie Dumbar what's been going on here then? The Constable wouldn't tell me much just that I was needed to verify how the security system was breached".

Toni was not going to hold back on this guy, straight to the point, she did not want waffle and excuses him blaming everyone except a weakness in his companies' system.

"That's just it Bernie, we find it hard to believe that the security was bypassed somehow, no alarms sounded, people injured, goods stolen and nothing to warn us anything was amiss. Can you tell me about your system and what would allow that to happen"?

Bernie went white and opened his mouth, but nothing came out at first. "I ..I'll need to examine the log to see what went on. I can't guess without that".

"You must have some idea, run me through the sequence for someone entering who has a legitimate reason to do so".

"Well, first of all you must have a key card. All cards gain entry to the foyer, simply by swiping the card through the reader on the door. Cards are specific for each person and are programmed to allow entry into the area where they work. The more secure areas need a voiceprint as well as the card. You just swipe your card and state your name. The stair doorways are always closed and lock when the last person leaves at night. In case of fire they unlock automatically but remain shut, except by the security officer opening them from the front desk. Everyone uses the lift to gain access to the labs and upstairs offices, again the same card operates the lift".

Bernie was more confident now as he was expounding the merits of their system.

"Can the watchman gain access to the lifts and upper floors?"

"No, his card only gives him access to the foyer and ground floor".

"What about the lifts and stairs"?

"No..oh... except as I said before he can open the stairs by pressing the emergency button. He will need to use his card to do that. This will unlock the stairwell doors and return the lifts to the ground floor and shut them down. Any of the laboratory fire detectors will do the same".

"Why two lifts?"

"One goes to the first-floor offices the other to the second-floor laboratory areas, this one has a radiation detector and a local alarm if levels in the lift are unsafe. Only certain personnel have access to these".

"Now what about the office behind reception?"

"Ah that has the safe ..Yes.. The door is locked with both card and voice recognition the safe has a combination lock. I don't know who has access, but the company will have a list. The cameras are in the foyer and in the hallways of both floors. When we get in, I can download the log and see just what has happened".

"Where do they keep the radioactive material"?

"There is a special lead lined safe in Lab one. It has several compartments for the different materials again the company will have a list of what is current, we are not party to that information, There is a radiation detector in the upper hallways that will sound a special alarm at any time, if safe levels are breached ".

Toni could see the flaws in the system, which Bernie Dumbar thought, were secure so she now had a good idea of what may have happened.

"Well thank you Mr Dunbar, please wait here, I'll call you when we can enter".

Toni now wanted to speak to the younger director William Grimm. She moved to the area still cordoned off by the gate where some of the uniformed officers were standing. She saw that most of the personnel had gone, however the technician Mathew Walker was leaning against the fence talking to a tall well-dressed man in his thirties whom Toni assumed was William Grimm. This was confirmed when she approached as Matt turned to her and immediately introduced his boss "Hello Detective this is Mr Grimm the company Managing Director".

William Grimm turned and held out his hand, which Toni took briefly.

"Good morning sir I'm Detective Chief Inspector Webb of Basingstoke CID, I need to ask a couple of questions whilst we are waiting for the scene of crime officers to finish".

"Fire away how can I help"?

"Firstly, who is Verity Pargiter?"

"Vera! Why do you ask, is she all right?"

"Who is she sir?"

"She's my P.A. why what has happened?"

"I'm sorry sir but it seems she may have been abducted. I believe she was used to gain entry to your company secure areas. She is missing at the moment we are searching as we speak".

At that moment Toni's phone interrupted the questioning. "Webb what is it"?

Chapter 8

"Sergeant Max Treddle here Ma'am SOCO leader, we have just found a young woman locked in a cupboard on the second floor, she has been bound and gagged close to suffocation I have called an ambulance. We have finished here now so you can come in when you like".

"Thank you, sergeant, I'll be there at once please wait with the girl".

She turned to the two men trying to listen in to her conversation.

"Please follow me Mr Grimm and wait by reception".

She called to Bernie Dumbar to do the same.

Toni explained to the uniform officers that an ambulance was on its way and to open the gate ready, she then hurried down the roadway up the steps and into the foyer of Westfields closely followed by the director and the security man. Both lifts were open as were the stairwell doors. Toni indicated to the men to wait she then bounded up the stairs two at a time to the second floor. Out of puff to such an extent that she promised herself to do more exercise. There were three men in whites packing up their equipment. The Sergeant came over as she entered the hallway.

"This way Ma'am".

Leading her down the hall where a young woman was laying in the recovery position near the far wall.

"I am very concerned that she has suffered severe oxygen deprivation and needs immediate attention, I cannot get any response, she may have been drugged I don't know, have you seen the ambulance? She was not awake when we found her. We removed the bonds at once but no change since. Her respiration is very shallow, and her pulse is very weak and erratic".

The paramedics appeared at the top of the stairs at the same time as the sergeant was explaining the situation. Jane Thornby and Joe Felix ran the length of the hall. Toni recognised her at once as she was the girlfriend of her DC Peter Andrews and had also met her on another case. She stepped back confident that Verity, for she was sure it was the missing girl, was in good hands.

The sergeant turned to his team and instructed them to depart along with the bags of evidence collected including the bindings used to subdue Verity. He remained behind, as he wanted to update the DCI on his findings.

"Ma'am We have collected a multitude of finger prints but suspect these are from the employees, we need to eliminate all of these before we can know if we have any that should not be here. The laboratory that was broken into had two glass doors, which were jemmied open; the second door would have normally created an airlock, as both doors should never be open together. This second door was wide open when we came in. The equipment was scattered all over the floor. The EAU officer removed any exposed radiation sources and has checked the residual levels as being safe. The sources in the lead lockers are still in there and appear not to have been disturbed. You will need someone who was working here to tell you if anything is missing. The safe downstairs was opened using the combination no sign of a break in either. I'll send you a full report".

"Thank you, sergeant very thorough as usual".

She turned back to where the paramedics were working on the girl, it didn't look good. Toni was distraught her mind racing with frustration. She has been in that dam cupboard all night and we couldn't get in because of the bloody radiation.

Praying that they had still found her in time. Jane had attached an oxygen mask to her face, Joe was pumping her chest. Jane was applying the portable defibrillator paddles, Joe stood back as Jane shocked her then returned to his task. Four times they tried and then they both stopped. Jane turned to look at Toni a shake of her head told a terrible story.

Toni felt sick, her thoughts were that this young lady had been seriously let down. 'Bloody hell there we were standing about all day and half the night waiting to get in here, we could have released her hours ago she should be alive'.

"Sergeant will you please wait, this is now the scene of a suspicious death, I want you to recheck everything in this area. I know you have already finished but in light of what has just happened I must be sure we have everything covered".

Sergeant Treddle complied without question thinking he should have done more, if only he had found her earlier maybe checked the cupboard first instead of at the end.

Jane rose from the body leaving Joe sitting on the floor head in hands.

"Hello Detective. Sorry we couldn't help, it looks like she had a massive heart attack, her blood oxygen level was so low I think it must have happened some hours ago, it's a wonder she was still alive at all, nothing anyone could have done at this late stage".

"Thank you Jane, I'll call the pathologist to confirm, I'll get your statement later if you like".

"Shall we wait?"

"No need Jane, the Coroner will deal with it from now I'm going to call this in as a suspicious death".

Jane professional to the end helped Joe to his feet packed up their gear and headed towards the stairs. They saw death and trauma every week. Often, they were able to help and would save a life, which is what kept her going with this sometimes, sad job. Today they were too late.

On her way out, she looked about to see if her fiancée DC Peter Andrews was on duty. Joe stopped the ambulance at the gate for Jane to ask after him from the uniformed officers, to learn that he had left more than an hour before.

"Back to the hospital Joe we need a cuppa eh"?

Toni padded slowly down the stairs with a heavy heart, not relishing delivering the news she was carrying first to William Grimm her boss and friend, secondly to her family which she would have to do very soon. First things first confirm her identity for which there was little doubt. William Grimm was pacing in the foyer as she exited the stairwell; Dunbar was seated on the window ledge by the entrance doorway. William was at her side in an instant. Dumbar just stood up rooted to the spot.

"What is going on the medics left without saying anything is someone hurt?"

"Please come with me Mr Grimm, Mr Dumbar wait here a little longer if you wouldn't mind".

On the way up the stairs Toni walked beside William Grimm. She halted at the first-floor landing and turned.

"Sir, I'm sorry to tell you that we have found a young woman on the next floor who died just a few minutes ago, we believe it may be Verity Pargiter".

"Oh my God.... What happened are you sure it's her?"

"We believe so but need you to identify her if you wouldn't mind before I go to the family with the sad news".

He did not say anything else just nodded and hung his head as they continued their climb to the second floor. Toni was hoping that they could get the lifts working soon maybe Mr Dumbar could help there. Jane had covered the body leaving the face visible, William Grimm held his breath as he approached. He could see it was her before he had walked a few paces across the hallway.

"Oh, my Lord what have they done to you Vera?" He looked at Toni tears running down his face nodding that it was her, his hands held open questioning anyone for an answer.

"You called her Vera?"

"She didn't like Verity much, it came from her Grandmother I think. I always call her Vera she prefers that".

He paused and wiped his face with the back of his hand.

"How did she die?"

"We don't know yet, it may have been her heart; we have to wait for the doctor and probably the autopsy before we find out for sure".

Toni then called Sergeant Jonny Musgrove.

"Where are you Jonny?"

"I'm still at the hospital Ma'am why what's up?"

"We have found Verity at Westfields, we were too damn late Jonny, I'm afraid she has just died".

Toni then went on to explain what had happened.

"Get back here as soon as you can, I need to go and break the news to the family".

Toni hesitated but needed to ask the next question hoping that she didn't have two deaths on her hands.

"How are the watchman and Julie Wells?"

"He is out of danger but still unconscious, I was hoping to question him but that won't happen until tomorrow at the earliest. June came with Julie to the hospital to have her checked out and is still with her now. She seems to be fine but very agitated about her friend. Do I tell her about Verity Ma'am?"

"No, not until I have spoken to the family. Thank goodness they are both okay, I'd better go to the Pargiter's now. See you later you know what to do".

"Wait up Guv, I can do that for you I've already met them you see, the mother I mean, it may make it easier having met me before".

"If you're sure, that would be a great help, I'm up to my eyes in it here. I'll call for a family liaison officer to meet you there. Tell June what has happened and call her when you have seen the family. We will leave telling Julie till later, when she has recovered from the shock of her ordeal. Come back here when you've done. Thanks Jonny".

Chapter 9

No one liked the job of giving bad news to relatives, Toni was no exception and she suspected that Jonny didn't either. The fact that he had taken on the unwelcome task, on her behalf, would not be forgotten. With June Owens looking after Julie she knew her gentle approach would find out more that any formal questioning by herself or Jonny.

Toni turned to William Grimm.

"I'm so sorry Mr Grimm but I must ask you to stay with me for a while I have many questions which only you can probably answer. Let's go back down stairs, sir".

On the way down, they met the pathologist on the way up.

"Hello Chief Inspector".

"Ah. Doctor Taylor, I'm glad it's you; the young woman is on the second floor, SOCO are re-visiting the areas where she was found but that shouldn't interfere with you. Her name is Verity Pargiter I'll see you before you go okay".

Debbie Taylor thanked her and moved on up as Toni and William moved down.

At the foyer Mr Dunbar was still waiting patiently.

"Please Mr Dunbar would you now examine the security systems, our forensic officers have finished work on the first floor. Download a time log of everyone's movements for up to a week back, if you can, along with any CCTV footage for the same period. Oh, and would it be possible to enable both lifts without the use of a card".

"Yes, detective I can do that, the lifts I will do straight away. The system control centre is on the first floor I'll be there if you need me".

She indicated to a uniformed constable to accompany him and to keep his eyes open.

Toni and William moved to the small office behind reception where the safe was kept. The windowless room was about three meters square. There were two filing cabinets side by side a desk with a computer screen and several scattered open files. The single chair was turned away facing the back wall. On the back wall, behind the desk, facing the door was a large wall safe the size of a small fridge, the door was wide open and completely empty. A hinged picture, which had covered the safe when closed, had been ripped away and flung in the corner.

"Can you tell me what was kept in here?"

"Our stock of stones and crystals, our accounts ledger, two company cheque books, some files of our customers records, files with our test results. Some hand-written notes of our technicians too and flash drives with the computer tracking results. The notes are gone as is the accounts ledger".

He said pointing to the scattered files.

"Can I touch these?"

"Yes, SOCO has finished here have a look through and tell me if anything is missing"

Grimm gathered the files together looking through them as he did so. "All the precious stones have gone as well as the flash drives and cheque books.

"All the files are here, I think. No, there should be seventeen but one of them is missing".

"Is that file special"?

"I don't know which one it is or its significance, I will have to consult the computers upstairs and our senior engineers".

"Now who has access to the safe and this office?"

"Well there's is myself of course, my father, the accountant Bob Chaney and Verity".

"Where else does Verity's card give her access?"

James Grimm went white and put his hand on the doorframe to steady himself, what Toni suspected had finally sunk in.

"My God you know she is the only one apart from me that has access to everywhere, the bastards have used her to gain entry and have callously killed her without a second thought".

He looked at Toni, again with tears in his eyes unable to say any more.

"Please sir go to your office and look to see if there is anything significant on that missing file, I'll find you later".

He left silent and stunned.

Toni felt sad for him; the realisation that Verity having overall access to all departments, had led to her death would haunt him for years to come. It would be up to her to provide some closure by securing an arrest and conviction of the perpetrators.

Chapter 10

Toni wanted to speak with Debbie Taylor so gave the director time to get to his office before trudging up the stairs again to the second floor. The lifts were still not working despite, Dunbar's assurance. Debbie was suited up in her whites and was bent over the body of Verity Pargiter. Toni waited whilst she finished.

Debbie Taylor was five feet five inches tall with shoulder length brown hair greying a little, which she kept mostly in a ponytail when working. Married to Terry, ten years her senior, now retired, she looked younger than her fifty something years by keeping slim and healthy through cycling and running on a regular basis, hobbies she shared with her very fit husband. She drank wine on occasions never smoked, and with a naturally high metabolic rate, could eat most anything without fear of putting on a pound. Not a trait shared by Toni who had to work hard and eat carefully as she tended to put on weight just thinking about food. Debbie's clothes were always practical, loose fitting trouser suits and crisp cotton, usually light coloured blouses with flat slip-on leather shoes. Efficient, methodical and exceptionally perceptive she was the best pathologist that Toni had met by far.

Forensic pathology was a path that Debbie had not deliberately chosen but following her initial medical training and some years in St Thomas Hospital as an intern and later as resident and finally senior surgeon specialising in coronary disease. Following an unusual death her medical ideas shifted whereby she spent three years in the study of pathology and particularly forensics. Finally, she was appointed as a forensic pathologist with the Metropolitan Police. Debbie was on call to several different authorities; today it was the Hampshire Coroner.

Debbie turned and rose slowly looking Toni in the eye whilst she did so. "Too young this one what happened?"

"We found her in that cupboard, she'd been in there more than twenty four hours, trussed up like a chicken with tape over her mouth she was still alive but barely, there were signs of suffocation, so we removed the tape and bindings before the paramedics arrived. They applied oxygen via a mask but soon after her heart stopped. They tried to revive her for some minutes but to no avail. It was Jane Thornby and Joe Felix, out of Northhants Hospital, Basingstoke if you want to talk to them to find out exactly what they did. They were both very upset that they could not help her, I saw no point in

80

keeping them hanging about so I sent them back to the hospital".

Debbie opened her hands face up in resignation "It is what it is, I think there was nothing that anyone could have done, even if found straight away, there is evidence of long-term severe oxygen deprivation that would have caused almost total brain dysfunction, it was amazing that she was still alive when she was found. I'm sure the damage was done long before then, the autopsy will reveal more. I'll call you when that will be, will you attend?"

Debbie removed her coveralls booties and gloves and placed them in an evidence bag.

"Of course, one of us will be there. How are you coping with the cutbacks"?

"I'm lucky they chose my department at Richmond as the main base, some of the other pathologists have a long journey now to complete the job, they are not happy I can tell you, although we have the best facilities, they are now too small. Two police surgeons who live on the south coast have de-registered, as they don't have the time to continue with their practices, deal with police call outs and travel to Richmond. The result is the backlog can extend to a week or longer when we are busy. They are building an extension and installing more fridges, so it can only get better. I have already called my people to remove the body they shouldn't be long now so SOCO can check the cupboard and this floor area again".

Each County used to have its supply of police surgeons based locally with nearby mortuaries where they could perform the autopsies, but last year, financial changes in Hampshire closed four of these local facilities and moved them to Richmond. The exceptions being the offices on the Isle of Wight and Winchester. The Winchester facility was small and could only handle a very limited caseload, it meant that many of the doctors based in the south had to travel to Richmond to complete the work started sometimes many miles away. It made financial sense but was sometimes very impractical, like now where the transfer of Verity had to be done by a vehicle based nearly forty miles away.

"Thanks Doctor Taylor I'll attend this one myself if I can".

Chapter 11

Detective Chief Inspector Toni Webb's hands on approach was not looked upon with much favour by Superintendent Walter Munroe, he had hoped when agreeing to her promotion that she would share the load imposed on senior officers by dealing with the endless paperwork and meetings brought about by legislation protecting the public. It also protected criminals from the very officers who were there to keep the peace. Self-regulation was no longer acceptable there was now large department of officers who were there to police the police. Making sure that his team followed the safe and acceptable path was more than a full-time task for Superintendent Munroe.

Foul-ups and mistakes were not going to happen on his watch, his promotion depended on keeping a clean sheet and that's how it was going to remain. He accepted that they were under-staffed, and that DCI Webb needed to continue at least in some ways to follow on with the work she did as a DI. He hoped to woo her away from the field and with that in mind he resolved to recruit another DI and was looking at his current officers to expand their horizons. His restricted budget would enable him to promote rather than recruit; this morning he was going to devote his time to setting that in motion.

The knock on his door heralded the first of his visitors.

"Ah, come in June sit down please, don't worry this is just an informal chat".

"Thank you, Sir".

WPC June Owens was still apprehensive his words only slightly mollified her feelings. The Super did not normally call on lowly constables unless they had done something wrong.

"I've been studying your progress of late where you have been of considerable help to CID, reports from DCI Webb and particularly DS Musgrove made me wonder if you were interested in moving to work permanently with plain clothes?"

June was relieved she was not on the carpet; she'd enjoyed working with the detectives but never considered changing out of uniform. Without thinking she replied.

"I have been happy to assist when asked sir, but my mind has been on promotion within the uniform branch. I have been studying for my sergeant's exam that I hoped to do next year. A sideways step has not been on my mind at all".

"Look I know this is sudden, but I feel you have an aptitude for detective work, any transfer to that branch would not necessarily slow your promotion chances, indeed I would encourage you to continue your studies and sit the sergeant's exam. By transferring, it would be to the rank of Detective Constable that is a promotion in itself. I don't need an answer now think about it and let me know, say, in a couple of days".

"Yes Sir, I will thank you" June rose, turned and left, her mind in a bit of a whirl, she knew she wouldn't have to think long, it never dawned on her that this chance would be given to her just like that. Excitement was her overwhelming emotion, knowing already that she would take up the offer without question.

Superintendent Munroe felt that she was almost certain to accept, now to move on.

DC Melanie Frazer sat in the office, not as apprehensive as June had been, but wondering what the Super wanted.

"Morning Melanie, just a few minutes of your time to see how you are doing".

"Things are a bit quiet for me at the moment sir, since DI Dale left for the Met and sergeant Musgrove has moved over to work with DCI Webb I have been helping Constable Busion on research".

"What you do there with Compton is very necessary, but I feel you are able to do more for us. I see from your records that you have already applied to sit your sergeant's exam, this I will set in motion now. It is my intention to create another Criminal Investigation unit, I cannot say when but very soon, I hope you will be an integral part of that".

"Thank you, sir, I would like that very much".

"Good, good. You'll hear about the exam soon; if you need time to study take what you need, work permitting of course, just inform the desk sergeant of your whereabouts".

Munroe smiled and indicated that was the end of the meeting by looking down at a file on his desk.

"Sir, thank you".

Melanie rose and left with a big grin on her face thinking 'about time too'.

'So far so good' Walter Munroe thought, 'now for Sergeant Musgrove'

He decided to have a walk about the station, partly to stretch his legs and to see where everyone was. He was really looking for Musgrove but could not see him. There were several officers going about their business as usual when he spotted Compton Busion at her computer. This was one officer he needed to stay where she was, no one better at that machine than she. He was concerned that ambition might cause her to want to move on. He set a mental reminder to have a chat, find a project, which might motivate her. He approached her desk; she turned as he came near.

"Sir?"

He indicated for her to stay seated.

"Just passing through is everything okay Compton?"

"Yes sir, thank you".

"Good. We must have a chat soon, when you're not so busy, to see if there is anything we can do to help you with, some new equipment, a trainee assistant, maybe. Have you seen Detective Sergeant Musgrove around?"

"I believe he is informing the parents of Miss Pargiter's death at the moment sir".

"Ah, yes, thank you, don't forget when you're free come and see me".

"Sir".

He returned to his office and called the desk officer to ask Sergeant Musgrove to come to his office as soon as he comes in. He was wondering what else he could do to beef the force up a bit PC Keith Crane came to mind.

Crane had shown some initiative when working alongside Andrews, he might consider him for a move to plain clothes, but that would leave the station short of uniform officers, it was always a balancing act. If they solve this case quickly, perhaps he would have a good argument for a budget increase. He had started the process; all he had to do was persuade the ACC to find a suitable DI who would want to come to Basingstoke, easier said than done.

Chapter 12

Jonny Musgrove pulled up outside the house of the Pargiter family to see a patrol car with two officers waiting on the roadside. He parked behind them, left his car and moved over as a WPC exited hers, on seeing Jonny. She leaned through the window spoke to her driver who started the vehicle and pulled away.

"Sergeant I'm WPC Mandy Heavers family liaison officer".

"Hello Mandy, I'm Detective Sergeant Jonny Musgrove, are you familiar with what has gone down?"

"Yes, sir the Chief Inspector told me, shall we go in"?

Jonny nodded and led the way up the flower bordered drive he had not long ago left, leaving a mother with doubt and anguish behind him. Now he was bringing a terrible confirmation of that doubt. Before they arrived at the door Mrs Margaret Pargiter was opening it her husband behind her. This time there was no sign of the welcoming Labradors.

"Have you found Verity? Is she with you? You said you would get her to call".

The desperate look in her eyes was demanding an answer but was dreading what it might be. Mr Pargiter just stood said nothing holding his breath.

"Please can we come in we do have some news".

She stepped back almost stumbled her hands over her mouth stifling a cry still hoping it was not what had leapt into her mind when she saw the officer's approach.

Jonny moved into the living room behind her Husband. Mandy guided Mrs Pargiter to be seated on the couch and sat beside her. Henry Pargiter sat the other side and took his wife's hand away from her face and held it tightly. They knew what was coming Jonny could see it in their faces. He hated this, but it had to be done.

"I have to tell you that we found a young woman, whom we believe to be your daughter Verity, in a very serious condition and am sad to say that despite immediate medical help she died soon after. I am so, so sorry for your loss".

Mrs Pargiter burst into tears beating her hands against her legs wailing unintelligible words. Mr Pargiter sat with his hands raised to his ears, his eyes welled and streamed but in silence, as if he could undo hearing what he had just been told.

Several minutes passed to allow the reality to sink in a little. Jonny then spoke looking at the father.

"Is there anyone we could call for you sir?"

"Are you sure it is her?" he whispered,

"She was identified by her boss Mr William Grimm".

"Bill was there, oh my God he will be devastated Vera was his..." He cut off mid sentence choking back a deep shudder. "How did she die?"

"We can't be sure at this stage, but it may have been a heart attack".

Jonny did not want to add to the shock by giving details or mention the need for an autopsy.

"But she's too young for a heart attack are you sure?"

Jonny did not answer the question, as that would have led to the demand for details, but again asked.

"Is there someone we could call a relative, a neighbour or friend maybe?"

Mr Pargiter wiped his eyes took a deep breath and exhaled slowly before replying.

"Joan next door I think she'd help, Joan Flaxman she is my wife's good friend, but I don't want to worry her, I don't understand, why a heart attack?"

"A friend would be good for your wife at this time I'm sure she won't mind, I'll go and get her".

Jonny looked at Mandy who nodded her approval, so he left leaving the front door ajar. He did not know which next door to go to but guessed that the left and nearest would do for a start. The woman who answered the door was indeed Joan the friend, a tiny bit of luck in this luckless day. He explained the terrible circumstances and was more than pleased to find someone, who after the initial shock, put her own grief to one side and was ready to help her friend. On the way to the house he asked if she knew the family GP.

"Same as mine I'll call him from their phone".

Jonny left them all in the capable hands of Mandy Heavers and Joan Flaxman with the promise to keep them informed and said that his boss would be along some time later to explain what would happen next. He was glad to leave.

On his way back to Westfields Jonny Musgrove went over the day's events in his mind. How the family liaison officers do this every day he did not know, it got to him every time, there was no way to break news like that gently. He must let the boss know that in order to soften the blow he had left the true manner of her death in limbo, knowing that after the autopsy Toni would have to let them know the full story soon enough. At least when her parents asked to see the body of their daughter, they wouldn't be looking at a face mutilated or damaged by some maniac with a knife or club or some such instrument of death. A heart attack left no marks. But what awful event had triggered such an attack in one so young, he and Toni would find out what, why and who.

How had they known that she was not at home? Then he remembered her bag had been stolen. Maybe there was some information gained from that, a diary, a mobile text message. He would have to look into the theft of the bag but could not face going back in to the house today. He would tell the boss she would know what to do there. He decided to go back to the station; he needed to see if anyone else had turned up something.

He walked into the station the desk sergeant collard him.

"Super left a message, wants to see you Jonny when you come in, what you been up to then?"

"He wants to give me a pay rise I think, or maybe a month's holiday on Barbados".

"Not likely young man, he promised me the Barbados holiday, you'll have to settle for the extra pay".

Their banter was a way of relieving the tension that builds during a case and has always been a thing with desk sergeants and all those that passed by. They were the guys you went to when you wanted to know where anyone was or what was new. Gossip mongers some say, but not in the eyes of those who knew the score.

Jonny wondered what the Super wanted, for sure it wasn't a holiday, or a pay rise.

He had to find out the current situation from Toni before going to find out what the Super had in mind.

Chapter 13

'Ginger' Harold Martin was in the Moulton Arms toilet being violently sick. He'd only had one pint and hadn't even started his second when he was taken with a sudden stomach pain and nausea, he only just made it to the loo in time. He felt better after losing his pint and the cheese roll he had eaten earlier. He returned to the table where he and Tommy Green, his friend of many years, always sat. Tommy was well into his second pint he looked up.

"You all right now Ginge you look a bit off mate?"

"Better now ta, but I don't think I can finish that".

Pointing to his untouched bitter.

"I need to go and lie down, I must've eaten summint a bit off like".

Tommy downed the remainder of his ale and helped his friend to his feet.

"Come on let's get you home".

He said linking his arm under Ginger's and looking back as they left, reluctant to leave the full glass of beer on the table. The pair staggered as if drunk, not an unfamiliar sight, out of the pub into the almost empty street even though it was lunch time no one near enough to help.

"Not much chance of a cab here Ginge we'll go to the train station, bound to get one there".

Ginger did not reply at first as he was struggling to walk.

"I feel real bad Tom, I think I'm going to be sick again".

Tommy leant him against the wall.

"Look mate you hang on here I'll go and get the taxi won't be long".

Tommy ran to the corner and looked back to see Ginger had slumped to the floor. He was in two minds; go on to the station or go back. He went back to find that Ginger had been sick again and was out cold. He went to pull out his phone but remembered that the guy had taken them from him and Ginger after the job. He went back to the pub and asked them to call an ambulance.

Whilst waiting Tommy was wondering what else his mate had eaten, nothing different came to mind they both had a cheese roll first thing, they hadn't had lunch yet.

Yesterday was a great day with an even greater pay out. They had carried out the job as instructed without a hitch, in and out and didn't see a soul. The doors were open as they were told they would be. He went behind the reception into the office had emptied the safe into a bag. Ginger had gone upstairs to bring out the equipment from the laboratory. They put the stuff in the back of the van along with their phones, took away the envelope exactly as they had been ordered closed the van door and then went in the car that had been left at the station to get there. They were told to leave the car where they had picked it up, but couldn't as there were no late trains back to Victoria. Ginger decided they would drive back to London and leave it in a street around the corner from where they lived no harm in that.

The envelope contained four grand in unmarked notes. Two grand each, for a few minutes work and they didn't even have to break in. No contact with anyone, all done by phone.

Tom accompanied his friend in the ambulance and was now sitting in A & E waiting room wondering what the hell was wrong. Little did he know what a dangerous place the laboratory was, and that Ginger had been a little greedy and had pocketed a small lone 'diamond' that had been left in the lab next to the experimental apparatus. It still rested in his trouser pocket emitting its unseen poison, the cause of his current sickness.

The nurse had removed Ginger's clothes and place them on the chair beside the bed. He was unconscious but breathing.

"Mr Martin, doctor".

She said as Doctor Anwar moved in to examine Ginger. He was puzzled by the burnt looking hands and the very dark burn on his hip. He began by examining his eyes and in so doing moved the hair back out of the way. Some of Gingers red and curly locks came out in his hand he recognised the signs.

"Bloody Hell Radiation"!

He hit he emergency push button to trigger the contamination alarm and ordered everyone away from the area. He headed for the cupboard in the hall that contained the detector and protective clothing. It was the first time he had used it in more than six years and was grateful that the equipment he needed was here. He reminded himself to thank the person, whoever it was, that kept the cupboard in order. Before he approached again he removed his own clothes and instructed the nurse who had prepared Ginger to do the same and for her to put on a hospital gown. He called the A&E sister to move all patients and personnel out of the ward and to empty the isolation room.

"Anywhere will do just away from here".

He donned a protective suit, apron, gloves and facemask with built in breathing filters. He thanked the unknown cupboard-person again finding that the G.C. batteries were working, approached Ginger with the Geiger counter that clicked and crackled a little on switch-on. His approach caused an increase in the clicking till it was a continuous buzz at the site of the burn on Gingers hip. His hands also had a very measured effect on the noise level. Other parts of his body showed some degree but not at the same dangerous level. He passed the machine over the clothes and again had a huge reading. In one particular place. The clothes he put on the bed and covered it all in a protective lead blanket. He then moved the whole into the isolation side room that he was able to close off. This room was kept for isolating those with possible dangerous infections. He hoped it would help contain the unseen menace that had come into his hospital. On hearing the alarm Tommy wondered what was going on he moved from the waiting room and poked his head into the area where Ginger had been.

Doctor Denni Anwar turned dressed in his protective gear and looked at Tommy who had the fright of his life to see this almost alien form, he nervously asked.

"Where's me mate, is he okay?"

Dr Anwar removed his mask and spoke.

"I'm sorry your friend is seriously ill we have moved him to isolation. I will need to examine you for you may have been in contact with it too".

"Bloody 'ell what's he got?"

He approached with the G.C. that clicked a bit more than normal but was below the danger threshold.

"Your friend has been exposed to a high level of radiation, it seems that you have been in contact too but are probably clear now, but indications are you will almost certainly need treatment. Are you feeling unwell?"

"No, I'm fine what about Ginger is he going to be all right? What treatment?"

Tommy's mind was in a whirl thinking that in their visit to that lab they may have picked up some bloody infectious disease. 'The bastards knew it was dodgy why send us in there when they could have got the stuff out themselves for nothing; I should have known'.

"Too bloody easy shit, shit, shit!"

'What did you say err Mr....?"

"Sorry doc just upset for me mate like, I'm Tommy Green, will Ginger be okay"?

"It is very serious, we will do our best, but I think in Mr Martin's case you should be prepared, for he is in for a difficult time; now we must get you started on treatment immediately".

He called the nurse to find a bed nearby for Mr Green. A brief phone call from the doctor to his hospital manager set into motion a chain of events that were to lead Toni and her team one step closer.

Tommy lay in the bed, wanting to get up and run, but had no idea where he could go. What if Ginger died, that doctor didn't give him much chance, the police would be all over them. If he left and didn't have the treatment, he might get sick too. He'd wait a bit, get the medicine and then he would leave. If Ginger pulled through all would be okay, if not they couldn't question him if he was dead could they and he would be long gone. He would nip back to the digs get his money and Gingers too, he wouldn't be needing it, and be off up north somewhere.

Chapter 14

The autopsy area had three slabs, a sink; adjacent side tables laid with various tools and to the layman, some unfathomable pieces of equipment. A white sheet covered the body of Verity Pargiter laid out on the centre table.

The viewing gallery was a mezzanine floor set back about six feet from the front of the tables high enough, so they had a good view looking down on the subjects through a long plate glass window. Dr Taylor entered followed by another person. They were both dressed in green gowns with hats. They had facemasks and protective goggles hanging loose ready for use if needed. The two approached the body. Dr Taylor looked up at the window and spoke, her voice coming from a hidden speaker such that they could hear every word as if they were in the room.

"Good morning Detective Webb, this is Dr Hart you have met before I think, she will be assisting me in this procedure are you ready"?

Toni nodded a hello and waved her arm to proceed. Her and DC Andrews sat close to the glass partition knowing this would take some time.

Dr Hart removed the covering to reveal the body of Verity Pargiter.

So, it began.

"The subject is a white female of approximately twenty five years of age she is a little underweight but appears to have been in good health otherwise".

The autopsy proceeded as expected until Debbie halted and spent a longer than normal time in examining the heart.

"This heart appears enlarged and there is a bicuspid aortic valve forcing the heart to operate inefficiently. This defect seems to have been there since birth. Breathlessness is a common symptom, but her body muscle development is poor indicating that she did little exercise, which would have masked the defect. She was obviously unaware of the problem the tragedy being that if detected it could have been treated or the valve replaced. There is bruising to the arms and legs indicating a struggle to free herself from the tight bindings. The tape round her mouth would have left her breathing through her nostrils alone. The panic and restricted air due to the cloth bag over her head would have led to a massive increase in adrenalin, her heart was unable to deal with this leading to a major attack. This certainly happened before or in the first ten minutes of being locked in that cupboard, too late for anyone to have saved her. I don't know why she didn't die at once. Her brain would have been starved of oxygen leading to massive damage. I will need to do more tests to be sure of these findings, but her death was due to an existing heart defect and failure brought about by partial suffocation".

The autopsy continued for an hour where Verity had been photographed, finger printed, visually examined all over, now opened fully down her front from throat to waist, her organs removed and weighed, her heart sent for examination in detail. Blood extracted, stomach contents collected, nails scraped and all the usual processes of learning the way of demise. Fluids were sent to the laboratory for analysis.

The doctor had commentated on her actions and conclusions to the recorder as well as to the attending detectives. DCI Webb had seen many an autopsy before but felt so sad to have such a young life end in the way it had. They waited until Doctor Taylor had finished and was removing her gloves before they left to descend the stairs. Doctor Hart was left to close the body and return it to the cold storage drawer.

"Was this murder?"

Toni questioned herself and Doctor Taylor.

"Not for me to say, you have no idea of the intentions of the perpetrator, did he know of her heart condition, I doubt it, difficult to prove murder, I would say, maybe manslaughter"?

"Surely not. This was a callous act with no care for the life of this girl. They used her in order to carry robbery, threw her in a cupboard not knowing if she would be found, even without a weak heart there was a good chance she would have died, they didn't give a damn. Hunting her murderer is how I will proceed?"

"Good luck Toni, I'll send you my full report after all the analysis is complete".

"Thanks, Debbie, see you soon enough, no doubt".

She would have to leave the fatal decision to the C.P.S. when she delivered up the evil bastards who did this monstrous thing.

Her immediate action was to call everyone together gather the information gained from interviews and coordinate her officers into creating a murder file, for that is how she was going to treat this case, at least for the time being.

Toni did not believe in holding back anything from her team. Everyone should know about the investigation in detail. Ideas, wild theories and gut instincts were important and encouraged, but hard facts were the lifeblood of a case. Each snippet of conversation may have some relevance, the notebooks were the record of interviews that individually may mean nothing, but collectively could lead to the solution. The case file, or here, the murder file, was the Bible for all to study.

"It seems odd that she didn't know about her heart don't you think?"

Peter asked with a frown.

"Maybe she did, but would not say anything, she could have been afraid to admit it to herself, people do that sometimes. You can check with her GP Peter when we get back, oh and if they knew, which I suspect they did, why did her parents fail to mention it".

Toni and Peter returned to the police station and called everyone involved to gather for a midday conference.

Chapter 15

"Right listen up everyone".

The noise of chatter in the packed squad room ceased almost at once.

"Thanks for all your work so far and for those of you that have missed some sleep, I am sorry, but we have to press on, you can catch up later there's lots to do".

A murmur here and there and a shifting of feet that lasted only a second. Toni turned to the white board and drew a circle in which she wrote WESTFIELDS from that she drew some radiating lines like the spokes of a wheel.

"We have a dead girl Verity Pargiter".

The name was written and picture posted at the end of the top spoke of the wheel.

"Until I am told differently, she was murdered by person or persons unknown. Let me tell you what I do know and then you can add your ideas and information. This is the murder file".

She held up a green file high above her head, so all present could see it with the name of Verity Pargiter in bold letters on the cover.

"Not very thick at the moment but I want every one of you to read it, often, and add to it as you gain information. Constable Busion will be responsible for this document, make sure your notes are typed up as soon as you can and give them to Compton here, she will do the rest. This is our Bible everyone, get to know it please. Every scrap of info you get goes in here, this is where we will find peace for her and her family. It does not leave this room, you read it at your desk, you cannot make copies of it. You may make notes, if you wish, in your notebooks to enable you to make enquiries. If you need a photograph from the file WPC Compton Busion here will print one for you, which must be returned to her when you have finished with it. Remember this file and your notebooks may become part of evidence to secure a conviction, keep them in good order. I want no leaks to the press, so no casual chatter outside this building".

Toni paused to let that sink in and slowly lowered the file gathering her thoughts.

"Westfields was broken into Friday night, jewellery stolen, technical equipment taken, in the process the night watchman was injured, and a young employee Verity died. I believe that someone planned this well in advance. Verity Pargiter was taken from her friend Julie Wells' house the evening before the break in. I think she was chosen because she was the only person who had access to all areas of the company and was the most vulnerable.

Her handbag had been stolen some days before; it had not only her purse and phone but also her diary. This provided the thieves information on her habits and probable whereabouts at any time. Her pending visit to Julie was their opportune moment. Julie was bound and gagged and left in her house. Verity was taken to Westfields during the night and forced, by threats to the safety of her friend, to use her key card to gain entry to the building.

It was there that Mr Horace Peables the night watchman was attacked and lay unconscious. She then used her card and voiceprint to open the office door. I believe she was finally forced to open the safe. After that she was taken to the second floor, I suspect to use her card and voiceprint again to open the laboratories. At this point I think she collapsed and was unable to speak. They put tape round her face a bag over her head bound her arms and legs and threw her in a cupboard.

They wanted to get into that lab by any means so jemmied open the doors not worried about any alarms. The main alarms did not go off we don't know why yet. There was a small alarm on the door that did sound however but this was just a reminder for those that entered legitimately to close it after them.

This is where things are out of the ordinary, that laboratory contained radioactive material as a consequence the Environment Agency were called to secure and make safe the area and decontaminate anyone affected by the radiation. This process delayed our being able to enter the building and the discovery of Verity who by this time was close to death. Despite the best efforts of the paramedics she died at the scene".

There was some shuffling of feet and clearing of throats, but the room was almost silent.

"I thought we had let this girl down by not getting to her sooner, she lay there a whole day trussed up like a chicken, but the autopsy revealed she had a weak heart and that death was inevitable within minutes of the tape being placed over her mouth restricting her breathing and starving her brain of oxygen. She was killed by these thieves during a robbery and I want them found and put away for a long time".

She paused waiting for her officers to respond. Compton was the first to speak

"This is very strange, from the tapes and logs, given to us by the security man Dunbar, we have CCTV images of the normal comings and goings of the staff from the day before, but when the last person leaves at the end of the day at seven pm, the tapes are blank and remain so until two am, and I mean completely blank, no recording. At two am the tapes restart, to show images of the hallways on the first and second floor and the foyer, you can clearly see the office door is open behind the reception desk and the half open door to the lab on the second floor.

A few moments after the tape restarted two men enter the building, they are dressed in black. One goes behind the reception into the office and the other goes up the stairs. We pick him up moving into the lab through the open glass doors and coming out a few minutes later, he is carrying a package about three feet long. The coverage is restricted to the foyer and the hallways upstairs, so we can't see anything outside the building or in the rooms. They were only in there a few minutes no sign of anyone else.

I have the security logs with the timings of the entry and exits for several days but on the night in question Verity is recorded as entering the main door at just after midnight the office three minutes later and the safe five minutes after that. Then nothing. How come there was almost a two-hour gap from the original break in, to anyone going in again to remove the stolen items.

I questioned Mr Dunbar who told me that someone had set the CCT to switch off as soon as the last person left the building. It was done at the computer terminal in the security room. The fact that it switched on again at two am Saturday morning was triggered by the two men as they crossed the front door sensors. He doesn't know if it was intended or, just that the person who set the CCT to be off, was not aware of the possible triggered restart. He could not tell me who or when the system had been interfered with as the daytime log had been erased. The tech guys have the hard drive from the security computer and may be able to extract the deleted files and tell us more later".

She paused for breath and stopped to allow her information to sink in.

"Thank you, Compton, the whole thing stinks, it may be someone from the security firm but in my book it's inside Westfields we need to look. There is more"?

Compton had indicated to Toni that she had not quite finished.

"Yes Ma'am. Only one other company has CCTV on the estate this is from a car spare parts supplier that is quite a long way from Westfields, it sweeps across their forecourt but just catches a part of Westfields at one end of its travel, it is just a few seconds every minute. There is obvious activity outside and some vehicles, but it is too dark and far away to identify people or vehicle types. However the timing is significant, as vehicles pass this camera at just after midnight and leave twenty minutes later, a single vehicle arrives at five to two, then two vehicles leave separately at ten past and half past two. The system is a low-grade device with poor quality and slow refresh rate, the moving camera is just a deterrent really. The vehicles flash by in a second. I've tried everything but cannot get an ident of any kind, I couldn't even tell you if they were cars, vans or trucks. The only valuable information we get here is the timing of their actions".

"Thanks Compton I am almost sure about it being an inside job but let's keep an open mind. If you would continue and check out the current and recently dismissed staff, pay particular attention to Bob Chaney the accountant. The account books and back-ups were taken, so get bank statements and whatever can be found on the Company computers. See also if there are any oddities with the security people.

Jonny follow this up with more in-depth questioning at Westfields. The time gap is mystifying. One group breaks in and much later another takes the plunder. Right who's next?"

DS Jonny Musgrove rose slowly his notebook in his hand. He reported his visit to Verity's parents with a heavy heart, the sound of Margaret Pargiter's sobs still echoing in his ears. The room was silent for a long moment at the end of his report, everyone felt the grief.

Jonny went on to report that Julie Wells had recovered physically but was extremely traumatised and more so having learnt of her friend's death.

"I kept my questions brief. She remembers little except that Verity was in the sitting room watching TV, whilst she was in the kitchen preparing a meal, when there was knock at the door. She shouted to Verity that she would get it, but a soon as she had started to open the door she was forced back into her hallway and immediately had a bag placed over her head. She caught a brief glimpse of she thought two men but there could have been more. She was held so tight by one man that she could not move and was bound by another. No one spoke that she can recall but she did hear a short scream from Verity, then nothing but the sound of the TV that continued for a few minutes, then silence. She was carried she thought upstairs and then nothing till we arrived. There may be more, but she was in no condition to be pushed. I'll go back later if need be".

"Did forensics find anything"?

"No joy there, Ma'am, not a thing no prints other than those that should be there. The only items of use were the tape and bags used to bind Julie. As expected, these matched the same material used on Verity. Standard stuff you could buy anywhere. One piece of good news, there were partial thumb and index finger prints on the tape used to cover the face of Verity, not a good sample; no match in the system yet but have only just started the search. I think the tape was removed and replaced more than once, I suspect so they could use her voice print to open the doors, whoever did it was careless and wasn't wearing gloves, whereas the guys who abducted her were more professional and did. Maybe two teams, I'm thinking".

"That's good Sergeant. Your idea that there was a division of labour seem a real possibility. One team to abduct, one to break in, one to collect and another to take away. It explains the oddities on the CCTV. Follow up on the prints and set up second interviews with the employees, we need to winkle out the insider for there is sure to be one".

Detective Constable Peter Andrews rose next, his notebook in his hand.

"I have gathered all the interview information from the uniform officers, theirs and my reports will be in placed in the murder file today. Nothing stands out that I can see at this time. I interviewed Horace Peables who has thankfully recovered quite well. His head injury looked worse than it was, quite a lot of blood but only a minor concussion. The medics believe his unconscious state was induced more by the use of chloroform than the blow to the head. A cloth containing the chemical was found under a table in the canteen, there were traces of skin and blood on the cloth, we are waiting for DNA results but think it is from Horace. We are waiting for the final autopsy report but suspect that Verity was also subdued using chloroform.

Horace recalls quite a bit up to a point. He was surprised to see Verity at the front door so late at night, he doesn't remember the time, anyway he went over as she entered she said something about collecting a document that William Grimm needed for an early morning meeting. She looked distressed which he put down to having to come out so late. She said she felt feint and asked Horace to get her a drink. He sat her at his desk and went to the canteen to get some water. He remembers nothing after that".

Peter waited a moment to see if there were any questions; none came; he sat down.

"Apart from some forensic results and details which may be in the post mortem report, that's where we are.

Sergeant Musgrove, please follow up on the jewels, badger the usual fences and see if any of your snouts have heard what is going on. Also have Dunbar brought in for a formal interview we need to find out more from him.

Detective Andrews and PC Crane, you will re-interview all the staff someone inside has some secret to tell, liaise with Compton dig into their finances see who has difficulties or has suddenly become better off. Check on any employees that have been dismissed in the past year who may have been able to pass on security information.

I will have Mathew Walker brought in, I may be wrong, but he doesn't seem right to me.

Constable Busion please look into the finances of Westfields and their employees, see if they have any problems.

DC Frazer please check on the insurance see what they can claim.

Well that's it, thanks everyone and don't forget to read the murder file, and I mean everyone, come to me if anything strikes you as odd. This one is not going to be easy".

Toni stood back and looked at the white board with its information she had been updating as her team were making their reports, adding names times and relevant facts. She could see it was now covered in names and data but all with question marks, there were no real suspects yet. Sometimes studying, or even just glancing at the board, would, like reading the murder file, trigger some hidden germ of an idea, or confirm some gut feeling. Her looking now did nothing, day three already, we need a break soon.

The room began to empty leaving only the permanent staff behind. The day shift was about to change so many officers were heading home as the skeleton night crew arrived. She moved over to Jonny's desk.

"Been a long day Jonny fancy a drink on the way home"

"Wouldn't mind boss my heads full of crap a beer might help to clear it"

"The Four Horseshoes then, see you there in ten".

The pub was an old inn in the middle of the village of Sherfield, three miles, along the A33, from where she lived and close to Mattingly where Jonny lived with his family.

Jonny was sitting in the old public bar with two pints of Doombar ale already waiting when Toni walked in. There were two areas in this fourteenth century inn, the bar he was sitting in and the larger saloon which served as a restaurant. The food was plain home cooked fare, a necessary addition to the drinking, in order for it to survive the modern requirements of running a public house. Toni often ate here as her cooking alone was a bore and a chore if done on a regular basis. At this time there were a few regulars in, having a swift one before going home after work.

"You were quick off the mark".

"Only just got here, look I haven't even had a sip".

She sat down opposite him; they both reached for their glasses and had a long pull before putting them down on some new fancy brewery beer mats. It felt good doing something normal like the others here, like those who smiled and nodded their hellos at them, unaware of the horrendous hours that had been their day. They did not mention work. Toni asked about Jonny's family and he about her garden.

"You know what Toni, I don't want another day like today".

"I know sunshine, me neither, it beggars belief but some people are just plain nasty".

They both had another half and left for their respective homes more relaxed than when they arrived.

Chapter 16

Before he left for his enforced sojourn in South America, Toby Jones, under the name of Alan Mortimer, had established not only ownership of property but had invested as a silent partner in several new enterprises. Never taking on so much equity, for those that ran these companies, to feel that he was a threat, in fact, he always gave over proxy voting rights to whoever was the largest shareholder. He never interfered with the everyday running of these companies but kept an eye on their growth or decline. Many never progressed far beyond their original levels, often just about providing a living for those that operated them, giving Alan a small but acceptable return on his investment. Some failed to grow or regressed and became a liability, whereby Alan sold off his share even if at a loss. There were those that just failed. Alan just walked away if he could, but once he had to provide funds to avoid bankruptcy. He kept a close eye and usually got out before that happened. The total of these investments added up to provide a considerable return. There were two companies however that had grown into very successful enterprises. These were to become the basis and the stepping stones to his future empire.

Majority Travel Ltd. had offices in London, Manchester and Paris. From a two-man operation in Catford south London it had grown into a thriving operation, due to the expertise of Haley Clarke the wife of Dennis the managing director. She had seen that the internet would become their means of growth long before their competition, even beating some of the big boys like Thompson to the idea of a super website where you could book everything from taxis to airports, parking, car hire, flights and hotels. The personal package holiday that you pick what you want and not what is offered. Of course, other companies had followed suit but M.T. were the first and the best. Haley had visited every hotel offered to make sure they were going to provide the quality that was promised and achieved block bookings at competitive rates. It was at a time when many companies were selling package holidays where the hotels were either unfinished or were set in a building site; a trap that she was not going to fall into. Customer satisfaction and repeat business her prime aim. The best legitimate investment Alan had ever made.

Westfields Laboratories Ltd. were a completely different proposition. At the time he invested they were only a small medical research company, they were working for the larger pharmaceuticals, providing analysis and running trials for their products. Alan (then known as Toby Jones) had met the managing director James Grimm at an Association of Estate Agents dinner in the city many years before. They had sat next to each other just by chance where James was a guest of one of the members. They chatted where James revealed the nature of his business.

At that time, they operated out of Sydenham and employed four chemists one secretary and a part time book keeper. James's son William, a chemist, had returned to university to expand his knowledge and had recently graduated with a Masters-Degree in Physics. He re-joined the family business with a mind to develop the range of their services. James made it clear that he had faith in his son and was going to step back a little. They were going to expand and needed new premises away from London where the rental and rates were less expensive. They left the dinner and exchanged business cards as you do at these events. Alan decided to investigate and was more than pleased with the results.

The company was jointly owned by James and William holding forty five percent each; the remaining ten percent equally by the four chemists who were also employees. The company had grown steadily but had reached a point where they either expanded into new markets or stagnated and lost contracts to cheaper rivals, eventually to become an also ran.

Through his venture capital company, Conway Investments Ltd. where he was sole director, and without revealing his name, Alan offered to invest sufficient funds to allow Westfields to move out of London into purpose-built premises.

His share-holding was a modest sixteen percent, a good five percent less than the company valuation compared to his capital investment. James and William jumped at the chance whereby James had given up the sixteen percent from his holding; Alan redressed the balance giving James his proxy vote. He knew that they would need further capital if William's ideas took off. With his foot firmly established in the door and the trust brought about by his lack of interference, they would accept his added investment without question. It was then that he would be able to increase his percentage share and eventually take control.

The move to Basingstoke began soon after into a purpose-built laboratory where William could develop his ideas for ground-breaking medical procedures. Another long term and hopefully successful investment for Alan Mortimer. Westfields, named after their old family home, was about to take a big step forward.

Alan woke to find himself in a strange bed unable to see. At first, he panicked then remembered where he was and what was happening. This was the last stage of his transformation his nose, eyebrow position and finally his cheekbones had been reshaped. The bandages covered most of the top part of his head obscuring his vision and forcing him to breathe through his mouth.

"Hello, is anyone there" His voice was croaky and weak, he needed a drink. He called again but no response. He ran his right hand along the edge of the bed to find the safety rail in place. The cable to the patient call button fell to his probing hand, he tried to use his other hand to pull the cable but found his arm restricted by a cannula connected to a drip in his wrist. He ran his fingers along the cable eventually locating the plastic device. He pressed and waited. Within a minute he heard the gentle voice of his nurse Juanita.

"Ah, Meesta Alan you wake now you feel good yes?"

"I'm okay, I think, I need to drink please Juanita"

She brought him some water in a bottle with a tube feeder.

"Drink slow now, I come back soon press bell if you want me, yes".

He sucked the cool water through the tube and immediately felt better. 'Not long now' he was excited by the thought of his return to England. Sleep came easily.

Dr Ramos Estaban was sitting in his office when Juanita came and reported that Mr Alan was awake. He was pleased to have finally finished the surgery for this patient. Demanding but cooperative, Alan pressured for a rapid and often dangerous rate of progress in this major reconstruction. Estaban had carried out the same procedures several times but never all on the same person. With this final operation, where he had carried out three reconstructions at the same time, there had been some complications with the anaesthetic and very low blood pressure. He had almost stopped, but after a short break during which the anaesthetist had managed to stabilise his readings he continued to the end. Losing a patient through taking chances was not something he wanted but this Mr Mortimer was a determined man who did not always accept his advice. Payment was only forthcoming if he went ahead as demanded.

Nearly all reconstructions for younger men, were not for aesthetic reasons but in order to hide who they were. This was more than true for Alan Mortimer. He will be gone soon, and Dr. Ramos would be considerably better off.

Chapter 17

The phone call from Frank Jones to DCI Webb was a surprise as she felt they did not get on too well, but here he was being all excited, saying that he may have some information related to her case.

"I did not find out until this morning or I would have called Saturday night. I could not get you till now as I was told you were out. It may not have anything to do with your current investigation, but I think you ought to know".

"I'm sorry I was at an autopsy in Richmond, what have you found"?

The bombshell came as soon as he mentioned that a colleague had been called out to a serious case of radiation sickness at Lewisham hospital in South London on Saturday night. Although miles apart he thought they may be connected to the one in Basingstoke the day before.

"We don't get many incidents like this in years let alone two in the same couple of days".

"Thank you Frank I'm sure they are connected; do you have any names"?

"No, I'm sorry it did not come from the bulletin we sent out but was mentioned as part of a general conversation, I didn't think to ask".

"That's okay, we will look into it at once, I'll keep you informed".

"Good, I can do something though, Chris Fellows is our officer on site I'll let him know you are coming".

The only officer available was Melanie Frazer, Toni thought she was not experienced enough to investigate this possible, no, probable connection so decided to go to Lewisham herself. She looked in on the Super on her way out, but he wasn't in. She scribbled a note and left it on his desk. The squad-room was empty, just Compton at her computer as usual and Mel with her head buried in some files.

"Detective Constable Frazer are you busy"?

"No not really Ma'am, just catching up on some paperwork for Constable Busion and the Sarge".

"Good, leave that and come with me. Compton when Jonny comes back please tell him we've gone to Lewisham Hospital, I'll call him if it pans out".

She did not want to make this latest news public yet so did not want to tell Compton or Jonny until she was sure.

"We'll take my car Mel, you drive I want to make some calls".

Not familiar with south London Melanie set the satnav for the Hospital in Lewisham and headed off for the M3 junction.

On the way Toni sat in the rear. She phoned the local police station to find out what their involvement was if any. She didn't even know if they had been called in, and if they hadn't Toni wanted to make sure that an officer was to go there at once to secure anyone who may have been affected by the radiation. The only information she had from Jones was the name and mobile number of the Environment Agency Team Leader at the hospital incident, a Christopher Fellows. She rang his number and was pleased to find that he said they had the situation safeguarded and had informed the local police, but no officer was needed as they had it under control. He said he would be waiting for her when she arrived. "Thank you, Mr Fellows please make sure no one leaves before I get there".

The traffic on the M25 and A20 leading into London was bad as usual but kept moving. They arrived in under two hours. Jonny called her during the journey when she explained what was happening, she promised to call him back as soon as she confirmed that the two incidents were connected. The Super also called wondering why she had gone when she could have left it to one of her officers. She made excuses that no one was available and that it was urgent. He wasn't pleased but let it go without too much argument but insisted she see him as soon as she returned. He was right in some ways of course she should delegate more and act more like a Chief Inspector, but she had a need to be involved on the ground, for her it was the only way. Perhaps her promotion was too soon, it had come about by her being available and officers retiring leaving a vacuum, but it was a fact she had to deal with. She would have to be more careful in the future and create a balance that was acceptable to her bosses.

Chris Fellows took on board what the DCI had said, although, unlike the police, he didn't have the power to arrest anyone, he could use *'danger to the public'* as a reason to detain and isolate Tommy Green. There was no problem with the man Martin, he was severely ill, but Green was itching to leave. As soon as he had been examined he said he felt fine and was demanding his clothes, promising to come back later for the course of treatment. The doctor tried to explain that he should stay but he became more insistent almost abusive. Chris entered the room to find Tommy Green sitting on the bed with his finger on the call button.

"About bloody time where are my clothes?"

"Mr Green, I'm Chris Fellows from the Environment Agency, I know you are frustrated but we'll have you out of here as soon as we can. Your clothes are being decontaminated at the moment as there are still traces of contamination. Your exposure seems to have been minimal but for your and the public safety you will have to wait a couple of hours or so. We must test that you are clear before you can leave. You will certainly need to continue treatment for some time after".

"It's like this doctor I have something I need to do now, lend me some clothes and I'll come back later today".

Chris did not try to correct his thinking that he was a doctor but used it instead to re-enforce his argument.

"Take my advice young man, for if you fail to take further treatment you could develop serious infections leading to organ degeneration in the next few days or develop cancer very quickly later. Take it easy now I'll see if I can speed things up for you".

Chris was stretching the facts a little but wanted him to stay in his room until the police arrived.

Tommy thought a couple of hours won't make much difference and he didn't fancy no organ thingummy or to die of cancer. He'd wait a little longer.

The constable arrived from Lewisham police station having been told he needed to guard a patient. He didn't know what for exactly just that he was to make sure he didn't leave until a DCI from Hampshire arrived. He spoke to the E.A. man and the doctor who explained the situation. He was very happy to stay well clear so waited in the corridor, not quite outside, Tommy's room but near enough to stop him if he decided to go. Not that he wanted to grab someone who was covered in radiation, so prayed that he stayed put. He'd been told that radiation poisoning wasn't catching but didn't trust that too much, he'd keep his distance, it felt safer somehow. It was fortunate that he was out of sight as Tommy would have had kittens if he'd seen the police and would for sure have done a runner one way or another.

Lewisham Hospital lay back alongside a wide largely tree-lined avenue midway between Catford and Lewisham town centres. A mixture of old and new buildings, with services and car parks to the rear, the railway ran behind the carpark and parallel to the main road. Adjacent to Ladywell park and the river Ravensbourne there remained a feeling of the country in its surroundings, unlike what they would find inside. Toni left Mel to park the car and hurried into the hospital. The reception had been informed of their pending arrival and had a porter waiting to guide them. Toni waited for Melanie and all three proceeded to the isolation ward. She was glad they had the porter for there were two stairways and a maze of walkways to negotiate before they arrived.

She had visited their local hospital in Basingstoke but had never been in a London hospital before. She was aware of the problems of NHS funding shortfalls and long waiting lists but was taken aback to see several patients lined up on trolley beds in the hallways on route to their destination. The NHS was too successful, it created a demand that never would be satisfied.

No dignity, no privacy, parked by a toilet in a public corridor. A nurse was noting on a chart the blood pressure of the old man on his trolley come bed. Low, but then he was sleeping off a sedative she had given him half an hour before. He was part dressed his feet in black socks with blue toes stood out from the too short orange blanket covering his frail form.

The band of the BP machine encircled his left arm, the glowing pulse monitor on the end of his index finger rested on his chest moving up-and-down with the rhythm of his shallow breathing, his mouth was wide open a toothless cavity delivering a near silent snore. The family stood against the wall almost unseen, like shadows, waiting for the nurse to finish before returning to the side of this thin loved one.

The trio passed by with a just a sideways glance each with their own thoughts, none of them wishing to intrude but feeling guilty that they, of course, had done so by their very presence.

Toni thanked the porter as they arrived at the isolation ward, clearing her mind of the unhappy scene presented to her on her way here, she pressed the buzzer to gain entry. Chris Fellows was at the door in seconds, glad that at last someone with the power that could deal with this chap, one frustrated man who was becoming decidedly difficult. He updated Toni with the latest information. The facts were Mr Tommy Green was at risk of infections and could develop cancer later in life, his friend Ginger Martin was not so lucky and was almost certain to die quite soon. The crystal found in Ginger's trouser pocket was radiating at dangerous levels and had been isolated and sealed in a lead container by the E.A. team. The isotope and its half-life were unknown until test were carried out but was certainly the cause of both men's contamination. The stone had burned through the outer layers of Ginger's leg muscle, so severe was the exposure that already his major organs were shutting down, there was no treatment and little hope. The doctors and staff although exposed to the radiation from the stone, were at little risk through the swift actions of Doctor Anwar to isolate everything. They would all still need a course of antibiotics to prevent related infections.

Toni asked to borrow a white coat, she wanted to question Tommy Green, without arousing his suspicion in the first instant, posing as a doctor would do that. Dr. Anwar although somewhat larger than Toni handed over his coat, which fitted well enough for her deception.

"Do you have his clothes Mr Fellows?"

"No, they have been taken away by my guys, if they can be cleaned they will be returned, but if not, they will be burnt, and the ashes shielded until considered safe. His dose was so low I think they will be fine, but they won't be ready till tomorrow".

"That's a problem. Doctor are there any outside clothes in the Hospital that will fit Mr Green?"

"I'll send a nurse to the head porters office, they often have stuff there to help the homeless that come in here, they may have something".

"Thanks, if she finds some ask her to bring them to me in Green's room".

Toni turned to Mel.

"Look I'm going to try and find out Green's address, maybe persuade him to let me take him home or at least organise a taxi. I'll pretend to trust him to come back for treatment, but I'm sure he'll do a runner. If he bites well and good, if not I'm going to let him go. I want you to follow him. I won't be far behind".

"I'm sorry Detective Mr Green can't leave until he has had his antibiotics, he needs an injection now and follow up tablets for two weeks at least".

"That's good, send a nurse in to give him his injection and give me the tablets, it will cement his trust in me".

"That's all very well but why are you doing this, I can't just give you his tablets, what has Mr Green done apart from being exposed to a dangerous substance?"

"I'm sorry Doctor I can't tell you the details, but these men have been involved in a serious crime. I would arrest him here, but he is liable to keep silent and I need to find out where he lives as there may be more of this stuff about, so I need your cooperation now or you can call your superior, who I am sure will help".

Doctor Anwar handed over a box of pills.

"He is to take one four times a day for two weeks, no missing or stopping mind. I'll send in the nurse with the injection".

Toni took the pills and walked down the corridor, passing the police officer half way down, and entered Tommy's room.

"Bout bloody time, when can I get out of 'ere".

She could see Tommy was sitting on the edge of the bed in his hardly respectable hospital gown, his eyes flitting from left right, obviously frightened his mind buzzing with what to do.

"Hello Tommy, I'm Toni I've come to get you ready to leave. Your clothes will be here soon, and I have your medicine. You will need an injection too, before you go, the nurse will be here in a moment. How do you feel?"

"I'm okay, I just want to go home, I will come back honest. Any case I've got to visit Ginger when he's better ain't I. The other doc. says he may not make it but Ginger's a tuff old nut he'll pull through".

"As soon as you have had your injection and your clothes have arrived, I'll give you your pills and you can go home. By the way where do you live, I can organise transport for you if you like".

"Nah, that's all rite Doc Catford ain't far, I can get the bus".

"You have had a rough time you shouldn't be hanging around waiting for a bus, I'll get a hospital car, as it's not far the hospital has an arrangement with volunteer drivers and will pay for cases like this".

"If you think so, that would be great".

"What's the address so I can tell the driver to be ready when you are".

Tommy didn't want anyone to know where they lived, just in case. This black lady doc seemed okay, nicer than the Indian bloke, at least she's letting him go where the other one wanted him to stay. If she wanted to get him a free cab that was alright with him. He might even come back and visit Ginger, but probably not, after all if Ginger was to pop his clogs, he wouldn't be needing the money anyway.

"That's all right doc, it's a bit out of the way like, I'll show 'em where to go".

Toni did not want to push for the address and spook him into having doubts so let it be.

"That's fine I'll go and chase up your clothes and organise the cab. Won't be long".

Toni went to the Constable.

"Do you have a police car here Constable err?"

"Constable Rogers Ma'am, no it's my own, I left it in the car park".

"Good go now and park to the left side out front. Keep well down I don't want the suspect to see your uniform, I'll be along soon wait for me and I'll explain when I get there. Thank you, Constable Rogers".

She wasn't worried about leaving Martin unguarded, he wasn't going anywhere soon if at all.

He hurried out of the corridor and down the stairs glad to be leaving. Toni walked over to Sergeant Melanie Frazer.

"Mel. He has swallowed my story and accepted the offer of a lift home. You will act as a cabbie, use my car, I have told him you are a hospital volunteer driver. The address is somewhere in Catford I think, unless he was shooting me a line, but I don't think so, he let that bit of info drop in the conversation. Park by the exit we shouldn't be long. I will follow with the constable in his car. We will wait till he has gone in before we arrest. Got it, any questions?"

"Got it guv" Mel was amazed how DCI Webb manipulated people, she has a real knack. Her old DI Colin Dale would have had this guy up against the wall demanding his address and getting nowhere. She followed the PC down the stairs excited that something was happening at last.

Dr. Anwar, amazingly, in a new white coat, had collected the clothes from the nurse and gave them to Toni. "I will give the injection I don't want my nurses near him he could be dangerous".

Toni did not argue there was no time she just told him not to speak just give the shot and leave. They moved together into Tommy's room.

"Ganging up on me eh".

Said Tommy with a small chuckle at his own joke, happy to see the clothes in the hands of the black doctor, but not so the syringe in the hand of the other.

"Just want you on your way young man. Your own clothes are not ready, but I do have these from the Hospital store. Your wallet and keys have not been returned from being decontaminated yet, you can collect them tomorrow, is that a problem".

Tommy did not like the idea of someone else's clothes but did not want to delay his departure so agreed that it was fine.

"I don't think so I have money indoors and the landlady never goes out much, in any case she leaves a key under a pot in the back".

"Here are your tablets take one four times a day, the instruction are on the label, don't miss any or stop taking them, finish the course. Dr. Anwar will give you your injection now".

Anwar stepped forward and asked Tommy to lean over the bed, he injected the drug into his buttock, wiped the area with a swab, collected his paraphernalia and left.

"Rum one that don't say much does 'e"

"Right you are, get dressed and you can go, I'll take you down stairs, show you where the driver is parked".

Toni left the room to give him a chance to get dressed and waited outside. A few minutes later Tommy emerged in clothes that fitted him quite well considering.

"The togs are all right, shoes a bit big, but okay. Let's go doc".

Tommy followed Toni down the two flights of stairs and along the corridors past the ward-less patients on their trolleys following the signs towards the exit, thanking goodness that the signs were there as she would have had no idea where to go once she had reached the ground floor. The foyer and reception eventually appeared after several turns and through more than a few fire doors.

Mel was waiting outside as arranged.

"Here is your car Mr Green please come back next week for your check-up and prescription".

"Thanks doc see ya".

Tommy climbed into the car confident and unaware of the deception, Melanie turned and spoke to Tommy then pulled away slowly.

Toni moved along the drive searching for the PC and his car. She found him some fifty yards along slouched down in the driver's seat. She climbed in, he sat up.

"Where to Ma'am?"

"See that silver Vauxhall pulling out of the drive follow along behind, not too close mind".

Mel Turned right out of the hospital drive headed along the road towards Catford, Toni and the PC not too far behind. They reached the one-way system around the old school, now demolished, in its place a MacDonald's, and proceeded north. After several left and right turns they pulled up outside an Edwardian semi in Longhurst Road. Tommy got out and walked up the short path to the door, he rang the bell and waited; a few moments later the door opened, and he stepped in. Mel remained seated in the car, when a few second later Toni arrived.

On the ride Toni had put PC Rogers in the picture.

"Right constable you go around the back in case he tries to run out that way. Mel. you knock on the door he or his landlady will not be too surprised, say you forgot he has to sign, or you won't get paid. I'll stay to one side until the door is open and Tommy is in sight, then I'll secure him".

Mel knocked and waited just a moment. Tommy answered the door. "Oh, it's you, what's up?"

"Sorry sir I forgot, you have to sign this for me, or I don't get paid".

She stepped back holding out her pen and notebook. Tommy moved forward, so as to reach the pen, totally unaware of what was about to happen.

Chapter 18

Tommy had been sitting in the interview room for ages, a large uniformed policeman had been with him and stood to the side of the door saying nothing. A single caged fluorescent light illuminated the central large heavy table with a Formica type top. Ingrained reddish brown stains were visible in the surface, which Tommy hoped were from spilt coffee or tea. The table was fixed to the floor as were the chairs, two each side. There was a high wired glass window to one side well out of reach, it did not appear to open or let in much light. The mirror on the far wall opposite the door was there for them to be observed from another room. A camera was visible in the top left-hand corner. The room was cold and smelled of stale sweat. He was really pissed off if only Ginger hadn't been ill, he wouldn't be here. When Tommy stepped out of the house the cabby told him she was a police officer, he was shocked, it all happened so fast that black doctor was there too. He didn't know what to make of it and like an idiot he agreed to go with them for an interview. It was a very long drive to the police station he did not recognise where he was going but had a good idea, one he did not like.

He felt apprehensive and such a fool; that smooth talking black woman turned out to be a bloody copper too, she'd had him on a bit of string pretending to be a doctor saying he was sick and that, the bastard had no right. He'd make a complaint. They searched my room without a warrant, stupid landlady invited them in and said it was okay to look round. Now they had his money and Ginger's too. He hoped they didn't know about the job but if they did, he'd play ignorant and put the blame on Ginger.

Jonny Musgrove had been given the task of interviewing Thomas Green, Toni knew that he would not respond kindly to her being there. He had already expressed his opinion of DCI Webb in several unrepeatable phrases. Jonny was observing the growing and obvious frustration through the one-way glass whilst waiting for the results of the finger print searches.

Both Tommy and Ginger had their finger prints taken also a few partials were found on the envelope containing the four thousand pounds that was found in Tommy's room following a brief search carried out at the time of his arrest. They did not search Ginger's room at the time. Having obtained a search warrant, SOCO had carried out a more thorough search of the whole house later. They found a few watches, cameras and new boxed mobile phones which were obviously stolen, but nothing significant pertaining to the current case.

WPC June Owens entered the observation room.

"The results of the finger prints are here Sarge". She handed him three sheets of paper.

"Tommy here has two convictions for shoplifting way back when a youngster and one last year for breaking and entering. He pleaded guilty to all three. Bound over with community service for the shoplifting, and two years suspended for the break in, this is still active. Ginger, on account of his red hair, real name Harold Martin had shoplifting charges at the same time as Tommy, same punishment, but after that had two counts of disturbing the peace just police warnings, lastly one for burglary July two years ago for which he served six months of an eighteen-month sentence; this was in Wandsworth. Let out on parole. Finally, the partials appear to be from two different people one unknown, but one cross matches with prints found on a pistol, the murder weapon from an unsolved case in London, June 2011. WPC Busion is looking that up now, she is also looking up who Ginger's cell mates were when in Wandsworth, she let you know as soon as she finds anything useful".

"Thanks June that's great, I have a lot to work with here will you sit in with me observe and take notes. If you see or have an idea and want to ask him a question just give me a nudge and I'll let you in, you'll know when".

June was thrilled not even out of uniform, yet she was at last being allowed to do something other than run around after the detectives. Was this the Super's doing pushing her to accept the offer he'd made earlier. She didn't think she would want to butt in and question a suspect, however she would observe closely and talk to the Sarge after, if she thought of anything.

They entered the room the uniformed officer left. Jonny turned on the tape.

"This is an interview conducted at Basingstoke police station at seventeen ten on Sunday August 17th two thousand and fifteen. Present, Detective Sergeant John Musgrove, Constable June Owen, Mr Thomas Green. For the tape Mr Green, please state your name".

"Err. Tommy Green".

June did likewise.

"Constable June Owen".

Jonny continued.

"Mr Green do you understand that you are here voluntarily and that you can have a solicitor present if you so wish. I'm sure you want to help as we just want to ask you a few questions concerning your friend Mr Martin who is currently in isolation in hospital".

Tommy nodded.

"Mr Green please speak for the tape".

"Okay I understand".

He didn't feel like he was here as a volunteer, he'd much rather be anywhere else, but if he answered their questions' they may let him go. If he asked for a solicitor that would tell them he had something to hide.

"Would you like a solicitor present, if do not have one we can provide one for you"?

"No sir I don't, I ain't done nothing".

"It has been established that your friend Ginger has serious radiation burns and that you have also been exposed. Can you tell me where you were when you picked up this exposure"?

"I don't know it must have been Ginger who got it then he passed it on to me, he was the one taken sick I just took him to the hospital".

"From what I can gather you and your friend are never apart you even share accommodation, you must have been with him when he was exposed".

'We're not always together we're not gays you know just mates".

"I'm not saying you are homosexual but that you are very close friends. You must know where you have been. Tell me where you were Friday evening from eight onwards".

"We went to the pub as usual then we went home to bed".

"It's unlikely that you were infected in the pub are you sure you weren't somewhere else, maybe you've got the wrong day perhaps you were in the pub the day before. You see we have reason to believe you were here in Basingstoke that evening".

Tommy's mouth went dry he was back in Basingstoke, 'they bloody know don't they he must think what to say they're not giving him any time'.

"Mr Green please answer the question, where were you Friday evening".

"Well I may have got the day wrong. I did go with Ginger one of those days, I don't remember which. He said he had a job to pick something up for someone he asked me if I wanted to go for the ride".

"How did you get there".

"We went by train from London, then we had a car at the train station to a place I don't know where, Ginger drove us".

"What time was this?"

"Late maybe eleven".

"What next".

"Nothing, Ginger went into this factory and came out again he was only gone a few minutes then we went back to the station to come home".

"What happened to the car?"

"We left it in a street in London".

"Why?"

"Because there were no trains and he told us to".

"Who told you?"

"Some man; no, it was Ginger he said that's what we had to do".

"When you got out of the car did you go into the building with Ginger?"

"Who said I got out?"

"I thought maybe just to stretch your legs like".

"Perhaps, what if I did?"

"Nothing, this man who told you to leave the car, was it the same one who paid you four thousand pounds?"

"What! No, the money was Ginger's not mine he was the one who got paid I just happened to be there".

"The money was in your room, you were there alright we have CCTV and witnesses".

"I never did nothing, Ginger was the one who took the stuff I just wanted to see what was going on, he gave me something to carry I put it in the van I didn't know what was happening. I've told you everything, can I go now?"

"You picked up the money your fingerprints were on the envelope, yours and the man's who is he".

Tommy was panicking now they knew what had gone down, thinking he'd have to give them something or they would lock him up.

"I don't know it was arranged on the phone with Ginger, I never spoke to anyone, I just heard the name once something like Carrol no that's not right it sounded more like Worrel that's all I know. None of this was my idea I just followed Ginger to keep him company".

Jonny stood "Interview terminated eighteen hundred hours". He turned off the tape.

"Does that mean I can go now?"

"I'm afraid not. Thomas Green I'm arresting you for theft and receiving stolen goods, you do not have to say anything, but anything you fail to mention that you later rely on in court……"

Jonny continued to read him his rights and then took him from the interview room to the custody sergeant for processing. He spoke to the custody sergeant.

"Sergeant, after he is processed please put him back in the interview room and call the duty solicitor to come and see Mr Green".

Jonny knew the next interview would be much more fruitful. The solicitor would advise Tommy to come clean or he would be liable for the all the charges related to this break in, including the abduction and killing. He did not think Tommy or Ginger were responsible for the death of Verity but were only complicit after the fact. He would use that to apply pressure he was sure Tommy would crack. He also knew that Tommy thought his friend Ginger would recover. He still believed Toni's subterfuge was just a scam and there was nothing much wrong, where in fact Ginger was very close to death. If and when he died someone else was certainly to blame for that too. These two went into the building following instructions from someone named Carrol or Worrel who, as sure as eggs are eggs, was aware of the danger, but said nothing.

Jonny was seldom given the opportunity to conduct interviews when under the wing of DI Colin Dale. The DI, always, wanted to be in full control, not saying they were not a cohesive team, they were in fact an excellent pair, producing good results for several years. Now under DCI Webb he had freedoms he had not enjoyed before. His feelings towards her were changing, in fact had changed.

At first, he was prejudiced and more than a little uncooperative because she was new and foreign. He didn't think he was racist but now questioned his feelings. If he watched a multi race sporting event he always championed the white guy it just seemed natural, however, if it was an international, he would support the Brit. whatever his colour. In dealing with criminals he was always impartial he disliked them all and would work equally hard to put them away regardless of their colour or where they came from, a scumbag was a scumbag and his job was to put them away whenever he could. He didn't know what that told him about himself, but now after some time working with Toni Webb, he saw past her gender and colour, to find an excellent boss who was very straight, her origins no longer clouded his feelings and reactions. His ambitions for promotion had been stifled for some years under Colin, but now her attitude and encouragement had awoken desires he'd forgotten.

Chapter 19

Toni was sitting quietly in her office just thinking if she would find a few minutes to contact DCI Dale. She knew that she should be getting on with the case in hand, but the name of Jones kept popping up in her head, she had to do something about it or her concentration would keep drifting away from the main task. She picked up the phone and called his number.

"Hello Colin, Toni Webb here how are you"?

"I'm fine hope you're okay too, love to chat but I've got something on at the moment. I could get back to you later if is it important".

His reluctance worried her a little, maybe he was really snowed under, so she gave him the benefit of the doubt but pressed for some information before letting him go.

"No not really just thinking about our old friend Jones and wondered if anything had come your way recently"?

"I don't mean to rush you but Sunday evenings the wife and I go out to some friends for dinner and a game of cards".

"That's okay, Colin call me tomorrow, I was forgetting it was Sunday the days all roll into one sometimes".

"That's alright I've got five minutes, Mary's not quite ready yet. Jones does the same for me you know, I feel we let everyone down by not getting that guy when were so close. I've kept an eye on Joseph Mallard just in case he is contacted but nothing at the moment. I know I didn't tell you at the time but following our orders to lay off the case I waited till I'd moved to London before executing the old search warrant. I retrieved the files from the Mallards secretary about Toby Jones; she didn't notice the warrant was out of date but didn't seem worried either, any incriminating stuff may have been removed long ago. Mallard wasn't there".

"Pity that. There is something you could do for me though. We've had a big jewellery hoist here, not jewels exactly uncut stones, diamonds, rubies, emeralds and the like, see if your snouts have got wind of it, we think it's likely a London team, someone was killed, so there may be a whisper going around".

"Will do. There was nothing in the Jones files to show us where he might have gone. They just show details of investigations into various companies that he was trying to acquire. I couldn't find anything in there that stuck out as illegal. I'll send you copies of these, perhaps you will see something I couldn't, oh there's a photo of Jones and Mallard together at some function or other. Must go now, Mary's on my back you know how it is, let's meet up and have a proper go at this eh, give me a ring".

"Thanks Colin have a nice evening, I'll be in touch soon, bye".

She thought back to the old case and what they had found out already, the fingerprints on the files from the land registry office matched those found in Sandra's room. They were not on file, but she was sure they belonged to Jones. The only other prints found in Sandra's room were from Sandra herself and Gerry her boyfriend whom she had killed. Not much, but she hoped that when the files arrived from London she would see something there that would give her some new ideas. She couldn't know the coincidence one of them would reveal, one that could not be ignored.

She felt better after the call but had this feeling that something may happen soon, she didn't know which case, but the vibes were very strong.

She looked up surprised to see Johnny standing in front of her desk. She barked, "How long have you been there Johnny?"

"Just walked in this second guv, I wanted to put you in the picture on where we are with Tommy downstairs".

Toni was annoyed at herself as her sharp voice was unwittingly directed at her unexpected visitor.

"Oh… okay….get on with it then!"

Johnny was a little concerned as Toni didn't seem to be aware of his presence and it wasn't like her to be short with him.

"Are you alright Ma'am you seem a little preoccupied?"

She deflected his question away from her thoughts, for Jonny was unaware of the ongoing Jones enquiries being conducted by her and his former DI.

"Sorry, Johnny just thinking about the case I can't seem to get my head around these people and their callous ways, anyway what have you got?"

Johnny related how far they have come with the interview to date, the fact that he had left Tommy with his solicitor to discuss the situation he was in and the best way to deal with it.

"I'm letting him stew for a bit, Jessica Hardwick is duty solicitor, she is with him now. When she's finished I'll go back in, then we should get something from him. I'm sure she will advise him of the consequences of keeping quiet. He's beginning to realise that he is a very small fish in a big shark infested sea. He'll crack soon".

"You don't need me to come down do you, I know you are managing perfectly well without me breathing down your neck. Let me know when you're finished with him. If he gives up something useful, we may charge him with just minor offense, use that as a lever, I will talk to the CPS".

Jonny left her office, on his way out, Toni's phone rang, she listened a few moments then hung up. She rose quickly from her seat and moved smartly to the door, she called out to Johnny to come back.

"What's up guv?"

"It's the hospital Jonny, Harold Martin just died".

Chapter 20

An hour had passed since Tommy had been placed under arrest. He had been sitting in the interview room with the solicitor they had given him, she was telling him what to do but he didn't trust the woman, she must be one of them after all, but what could he do he didn't want to go inside.

Jessica Hardwick had been serving her time as duty solicitor for quite a few years. She volunteered for this not so lucrative and sometime soul-destroying task because every now and then there was someone who was a victim of the system, one she could truly help. This man Tommy Green, most likely, was not such a case, she'd find out in due course. He was surly and uncooperative, she would have to bring him to his senses with a few home truths.

"Mr Green you are in no position to hold out on the police. They have your prints on the envelope containing a large sum of money which is incriminating, they have CCTV footage of you on the premises in question and have found goods in your house that have been reported stolen. When the interview continues, I think the police will have more, and you will be in serious trouble so please tell me what you have done, and I will do my best to protect you from the worst charges".

"If I tell you anything, you will tell them; you are all in it together".

"I can assure you that whatever you say to me will stay with me. If you cannot accept that then I cannot help you. You can remain silent of course but a confession now will go a long way to reducing the charges. Tell me everything that has happened, and I will advise you what to say to keep you out of the worst trouble".

"I suppose. They have got me anyway".

Tommy then told Jessica what had transpired from Ginger getting the job and both their parts in it. The underhand police trickery during the hospital episode gave her some hope of negotiating. He also revealed the name he had overheard, even better.

"You obviously played a minor part in this; your trump card is the name so keep that back until I tell you. I can use that to negotiate a better deal. When they question you answer truthfully just as you have told me but before you answer anything you are not sure of look at me and I will give you the go ahead or not. Do you understand".

"Yes Misses".

"Mr Green, please call me Miss Hardwick not misses. They may ask questions about things you have forgotten to tell me, if they do that, I will speak to you and advise you what to do at the time. You have done a foolish thing here, but they are after bigger fish than you, so we may be able to salvage something if you stick with the truth. If they wind you up, as they will certainly try to do, just keep calm and say nothing. Okay, are you ready?"

Tommy wasn't ready but had no choice but to comply. This solicitor was nice, but so was that black doctor who turned out to be a copper. He'd go along with it for now and hoped that she was genuine but would clam up if things got sticky.

"Yes. Err, Miss Hardwick".

Jessica nodded at Tommy with a smile, left her chair to bang on the door indicating to the officer outside that she was finished. The constable opened the door at once having jumped out of his skin when she banged for his attention, feeling guilty for having had his ear to it hoping to catch what was being said, but no joy, as only muffled voices passed through the steel lining.

"Please get Mr Green some refreshment he has been here for too long without a drink. Call me before the interview is to start, I will need to have a brief word with my client then. Thankyou officer".

She left, and Tommy turned to the watching officer.

"Cup of Tea two sugars and a bacon sandwich would go down well Sarge".

"Don't push it Tommy, you may get a cuppa if you're lucky and I'm Constable to you my friend, not Sarge".

"Okay, Cons-table, keep your hair on, any chance of a biscuit"?

Tommy pretended to duck to avoid the Constable's non-existent but pretend back-hander, they both laughed. Tommy did get his cup of sweet tea, but no biscuit.

Chapter 21

Detective Sergeant Jonny Musgrove entered the interview room with a file under his arm, he was followed by WPC June Owen. Tommy Green was sitting next to the duty solicitor. A uniform police sergeant was stood by the door.

"Thank you, sergeant" Jonny indicated that he should leave. June turned on the tape.

"Interview commenced 1900 hours Sunday August 17th, 2015. Present Mr Thomas Green, please state your name for the tape".

"Tommy Green".

"Miss Jessica Hardwick, the solicitor for Mr Green".

"Jessica Hardwick".

"Myself, Detective Sergeant John Musgrove and WPC June Owens".

"June Owens".

Jonny again read Mr Green his rights which he affirmed were understood.

"My client understands the charges but considers them to be based largely on circumstantial evidence. He was unaware of the serious nature of the events into which he was coerced and wishes to cooperate in every way to resolve the situation".

"That is very good of him considering we have sufficient evidence to mount a strong prosecution on both counts, nevertheless we will consider his situation favourably after he has answered some questions. Please Mr Green would you again go over the events on the night of Friday last, this time stick to the facts and omit nothing; bear in mind that we have CCTV footage and forensic evidence surrounding this investigation".

Tommy looked at Jessica who nodded for him to go ahead.

"It started with Ginger asking me if I was free on Friday night, I don't know why he asked because I'm always free. I spend most of my time with him anyway. Still I said I was okay that night and he went on to say he had a job that needed two of us and I just assumed it was the usual pick up stuff and deliver it somewhere, man with a van sort of job".

"When did you discover that this was to be part of a robbery"?

"No, never, I thought it was just a pick up like I said. I thought it was strange when I had to empty the safe, but it was open already I didn't break in or nothing. I did as I was told 'it's all okay no questions asked' is what Ginger said".

"How did Ginger get the job"?

"He had a phone call".

"Who from"?

"I don't know who he was".

"Come now you overheard a name, or so you said in the earlier interview, do want me to play the tape to remind you or can you remember better now, I want the correct name not just a guess".

Tommy looked at Jessica.

"My client is unsure of his position. If he gives a name he may put himself in danger, he needs some assurance from you that by cooperating in this instance it will be taken into consideration. If he is prosecuted he doesn't want the fact that he gave a name to be made public, he fears retribution".

"All I can say is we will look favourably on assistance of this kind and will do everything to assure his safety".

Jessica indicated to Tommy to continue.

"Like I said I don't know who he is I just heard the name when Ginger was on the phone. He said something like 'yes Mr 'Cworrel', I only heard it once. When I asked him who it was he just said it was Jim with a job for us. I didn't say any more and neither did he, until he asked me the following day if I was free".

This was just what Jonny wanted a name to follow up on.

"Thanks for that Tommy continue how did you get there"?

"We took a bus to Victoria then by train to Basingstoke, when we got there about eleven o'clock, it was very dark. Ginger went to a car in the car park, he took the key from under the rear wheel arch, it was on top of the tyre, I thought that was a daft place to leave it anyone could have found it and took the car then where would we be".

"What type of car was it"?

"A red Golf, I don't know the number though, it was quite new or smelt clean like a new car does you know, I've always liked VWs reliable they say, if I learn to drive that's what I'd get. Anyway, he then drove five or six miles, it didn't take long, till we came to this industrial estate. We then waited a while. I asked Ginger what we're going to do, he told me to be patient and wait a bit. We sat there for ages".

"Did you get out or see anyone"

"Not then, no, it was dead quiet, I think I dozed off. Ginger then got a phone call, he didn't speak just listened and then rang off. He said we had to go into the building down the road a bit and pick up a delivery. We drove along to the end of this drive and stopped outside a big building".

Tommy paused and looked at Jessica again this is where he was committing himself to having entered and taken stuff. Jessica spoke to him.

"My client feels that what he may say next may be misconstrued and could incriminate him. He wants to make it clear that he was unaware that permission to remove certain good was not given and that he was only following orders in the belief that this was an above board, even if strange, task".

"I hope he will continue with what happened and his role in it as we wish to eliminate him from our enquiry. There was a serious assault which took place at this scene and a suspicious death. If your client can show that, what he and his friend did were outside the time frame of these more serious crimes, the pending charges would be considered more favourably".

"That is not good enough, the charges against my client being 'considered more favourably' means nothing. We would like some guarantee".

"The charges relating to this case will not proceed if the information given proves to be correct. At this point in time your client is not considered to be a suspect in the assault or suspicious death however those charges relating to stolen items found in his property will be forwarded to the C.P.S. for consideration, I can only say I will advise the C.P.S. that his cooperation has helped us and should be taken into account".

Jessica thought that this offer was the best that could be achieved and advised Tommy to continue.

"Does that mean they are going to let me off" he whispered in her ear. She responded likewise.

"Not exactly Tommy but you will be getting off very light, you must tell them everything now or you may get charged with the assault or suspicious death if they can't find anyone else".

"Bloody Hell! I didn't do no assault or kill no one". said in less than a whisper.

"I know you didn't, but you must convince them by telling the truth"

Tommy took a deep breath. 'In for a penny' he thought.

"Ginger went to the boot and took out a couple of bags. We did go in like I said, it was all open the doors and everything, I thought they had closed down and were having a clear out or something. Gerry told me to go to the room behind the reception desk and empty the safe. He gave me one of the bags to put the stuff in. He went upstairs. I collected the stuff and waited for him on the steps. He came out a few minutes later and we both went to the van which was parked to the side a bit. The van door was open we put the stuff inside, that's it".

"Not quite Tommy. What did you take from the safe"?

"I don't know really, there were some small bags of stuff, two books, a file and some of those memory stick things. I only took what he told me, I put them all in the big bag Ginger gave me".

"What stuff was in the small bags"?

"I don't know I didn't look, I just wanted to leave quick".

"Carry on"

"What do you mean, carry on, that's all there is"?

"Why did you only take one file"?

"I don't know, Ginger said take the one marked with a six, leave the rest, so I did".

"What about after you put the stuff in the van"?

"Oh, you mean the envelope, yes Ginger took that and made me put my phone in there too with his. I didn't want to I'd only just bought it, but he made me".

"Why do you think he did that"?

"He said Cwarrel told him, so we had to".

"So, he said the name Cwarrel again, you heard it more than once then".

"Yes, I suppose I did, I forgot didn't I".

"What next"?

"We went back to the car and to the station. When we got there it was too late, no trains till the morning.

Ginger said we would drive back to London it didn't matter, we could leave it in a side street near ours. He'd tell them where it was, so they could collect it later. When we got home we went to bed".

"Did Ginger tell them where the car was?"

"I don't think so we didn't have a phone, he didn't seem worried about it. We got up about eleven and went to the pub, I didn't see him use a phone there either, then he got sick".

"Who was the money for"?

Ginger said we would share it later. Err will I get it back, my half I mean"?

"I think not young man".

Jonny said with a laugh. 'Cheeky Bugger' He had everything he wanted at this time. Following up on finding out where this Jim Cworrel fitted in was his priority. He would pursue the stolen items found in Tommy's house later, just small fry. Mr Tommy Green was a fool but not a serious villain.

"Thank you Mr Green your frank explanation will help us I'm sure. You will remain in custody pending confirmation of what has been said here. Interview terminated 1600hours". June turned off the tape.

"I did not want to bring it up during the interview Tommy, but I am sorry to inform you that your friend Ginger died earlier this afternoon. We will obviously need to question you about this later but in the mean time we will ensure you receive adequate medication to counter the effects of your exposure".

Tommy said nothing but was led away by the custody officer with tears in his eyes, as soon as he was out of earshot Jessica demanded to know what was going on.

"What's all that about Jonny, you didn't tell me about the deaths and he didn't tell me about his friend being so ill, exposure to what"?

"Sorry Jessica, before your Tommy got involved, Westfields, a nuclear medical research facility, was broken into by others as yet unknown, they abducted and killed a girl who had an access card and codes to the safe. They also assaulted and disabled a night security guard. The reason they did not go further was because the place was radioactive and unsafe. I believe they duped Ginger and Tommy to go in and take what they wanted not giving a damn that they would be exposed to the radiation. Tommy is lucky his exposure was minor, but Ginger died from acute radiation poisoning, I only found that out five minutes before we came in or I would have told you. I can't go into details of the Westfields case. I know what Tommy has told us wasn't much, but it backs up our evidence and the name Jim Cworrel may help us trace the real villains. His story is close enough to the truth for me to pass it off to the CPS that he was unsure of what was going on. You and I know he really was aware he was doing wrong from when he entered the building. He was so under the influence of Ginger and didn't know what he was going into until it was too late. I'll keep my promise and do what I can for Tommy to keep him out of prison, he needs to be away from the likes of Ginger. Given the chance and with a good probation officer he could go straight, prison would only serve to pull him deeper into the mire. We have enough hard villains to deal with without spawning one more".

Jessica thanked him, surprised to find a long serving CID Sergeant who had not lost empathy for his fellow man. She would remember this officer with a kind heart. If it came to trial she would ensure Tommy had a good brief, not one of the tired, couldn't care less, court appointed lawyers. She would call in a favour or two if necessary, there were plenty that owed her. Tommy was worth saving.

Chapter 22

Compton Busion was strolling around the squad-room when Jonny and June Owen walked in, he handed her a copy of the interview tape. Pointing to her computer he said.

"What's up Compton you're normally attached to that thing like an old married couple"?

"Just giving everything a stretch Sarge. My arms were falling asleep, and my head is spinning. I've been here too long".

"Haven't we all, sorry about this".

Indicating the tape that needed transcribing for the murder file.

"That's okay so much data is coming in some of the uniform officers are helping out, it will all be done soon".

"Thanks. One more thing though can you look up the name of Jim Correl or Cworrel or something like that, probably not local, London maybe".

"Sure, give me half an hour, I'll see what we have".

He went to his desk, picked up the phone and called Traffic.

June had already moved over to the other side of the room to her desk, one she shared with two other constables and luckily empty at this time. She was typing up the notes made during the interview. Writing it down first and then transferring her observations onto the computer enabled June to think about what had been achieved from the interview. Jonny ambled across to her and stood in front waiting for her to finish. She stopped typing and looked up.

"I won't be long sir, or do you want me to do something now"?

"No, no carry on. I was just wondering what your impressions were of what went on in there, I can wait till you're finished".

"I'm a good multitasker you know, I can talk and type at the same time. It seems all we got from him was a single name, a name that didn't seem real either. You gave away an awful lot for that name. He put all the blame on his mate Ginger who could not confirm or deny what was being said about him. I don't believe he's as innocent as he makes out. I do believe however that he was totally unaware of the danger that they were going in to, if the name leads us to find out who did this I suppose it's worth it".

"Your dam right it's worth it, anything else"?

"No. I don't...think...so... Oh crikey yes the car! I forgot the VW is still probably there in the street, it may have prints or DNA, we'll find out who owns it from the registration, someone must have driven it there ready for them to collect, we should be looking for that car now, shall I call someone"?

"Don't fret, that's already in hand, I've called Traffic they are going to contact their colleagues in London to look for it. Ginger must have left the keys probably where he found them on the tyre, I told them where to look and warned them about the possible radiation. They'll find it soon enough and do what's necessary. Forensics will search out anything useful if it's there. I wouldn't hold out much hope with the registration though it's almost certain to be stolen. Think on June what else have you learnt"?

"If what he says is true then Ginger knew the man from whom he was getting instructions. He was, that is Ginger was a bit afraid of his boss, or bosses, as he followed instructions to the letter, he or both of them could have taken some of the precious stones but it seems they didn't".

"That's where you're wrong June, for Ginger had picked up a crystal from the experimental bench in the laboratory that wasn't among those in the safe. He put it in his pocket thinking no one would notice it was missing, but unbeknown to him it was irradiated from the source used in the experiment. It stayed in his pocket all night and into the next day and it was this crystal that killed him. The irony of this is that he must have thought it to be a diamond but in fact it was just a cheap piece of quartz".

June's mind was racing now going over the interview again trying to see if she had missed something more.

"It's certain that whoever sent them in there knew it was dangerous but didn't care about those two getting radiation poisoning. If it was only the jewellery that was valuable, why risk going upstairs to the laboratory for a piece of equipment that only had a couple of rubies attached, hardly seems worth it to me. Perhaps the true target of this break in was not the precious stones but the experiment itself, along with the data in the files. That must be what they were really after".

"You see, give yourself some time to examine the information June and you'll find yourself thinking like a detective. You must assume nothing, study everything, the smallest thing is often the key to a solution. For your first time you did well young lady, you'll make a good detective one day, but keep in mind that no respectable thief turns down the chance to nab a bag full of uncut precious stones, even if someone else wanted them to steal the equipment.

They are criminals, despite what is commonly thought there is little loyalty, just greed and fear. Everyone involved will have his own agenda and will lie to save their own skin. We have to seek out what is important, or the self-preserving stories could confuse us in determining what really went on and who is responsible. What I do know is these two guys have come out with nothing but grief and for Ginger he lost his life for a two-penny bit of glass".

Jonny moved back across the room to his desk to wait for Compton to come up with something and to plan his next move, before going to the boss with an update. Many possible lines of enquiry were opening up he just needed to prioritise.

June finished up typing her notes, then added a precis of her thoughts as a rider, printing them off to be added to the murder file. She was fascinated and surprised by her sudden interest, she would normally listen to what was being said, carrying out the tasks asked of her with care and diligence but not particularly interested or aware of where they fitted into the overall picture of a case. Perhaps, it was the Super's pep talk that had inspired her or the fact that the Sarge was taking notice, maybe a bit of both. Anyway, she was going to get more involved, being in the interview with Tommy Green had touched her, stirring emotions of disgust at the way he and Ginger had been duped to enter a place where death lurked. She felt sadness that

Tommy faced an uncertain future unlike his dead friend who had none. She walked over to Compton's desk to put her brief notes into the Murder File with the intention of borrowing it for a while.

Jonny knocked on the door of Toni's office; it was her old room which would normally be occupied by the current DI with Toni having moved to an office upstairs. There was no DI at the moment and she wanted to be closer to what was going on until the manning situation changed. Toni could see the outline of her Sergeant through the frosted glass.

"Come in Johnny".

Toni was sitting behind a desk as her D.S. entered she moved the computer screen to one side. Sit down Jonny how did it go did you get what you wanted"?

There were two chairs in front of the desk one with a cushion one without, he chose the one with.

"Yes, Ma'am we did, well sort of, I had to give away some of the charges that we might have made in order to free him up. He gave us the whole story or as much of it is makes no difference. I don't think he was the big villain here, he was duped into going there in the first place and achieved nothing but a lost friend and a good chance that he might end up sick and in prison. Three very useful things came out of the interview.

Firstly, the name of Cworrel which Constable Busion is searching for now, second the fact that they dumped the car in London when they were supposed to have left it at Basingstoke station, I have London Traffic looking for it as we speak. Finally, I'm certain the main target for this break in was the experimental equipment and the notes that went with it".

"Ma'am, Ma'am you should see this err... sorry I didn't know you were busy".

Compton had burst into the office without knocking, or thinking it would seem, her excitement having got the better of her normally reserved approach to everything.

"That's okay Compton what is it"?

"I've found him, or I think I have, the man's name is Jim Quarrel we were spelling it wrong. It must be him his fingerprints match the ones on the envelope from Tommy Green's house".

Chapter 23

Alan Mortimer arrived at Lisbon airport after his long haul from Rio full of confidence in his new skin. When he looked in the mirror he was still unable to believe what he was looking at. Dr Ramos Estaban had done a great job for he could now move among people he had met before and there was no chance he would be recognised, not that he intended to mix with old acquaintances he had other plans. The company, Conway Investments, he had created in his adopted name, before he had to escape, had invested in several businesses. These were to become the target for the next phase of his new life. He had employed a manager to deal with the everyday running of the business.

He checked into the Grand Hotel, he was going to enjoy this week; one week before he moved back to the old Country.

Kevin Blackman woke today to find an email that would motivate him like no other. The twenty seven year old bachelor, was five feet ten, thinly built with dark black hair and sallow complexion, he went swimming twice a week to keep fit, enjoyed listening to jazz and often went to the cinema rather than watching television. He obtained an HND in management whilst working for an advertising agency, this he accomplished by going to night school and attending seminars. His girlfriend, Amanda, of the last three years, lived with her parents and still worked at the agency where he used to work. He saw her once during the week and most weekends she came to London and stayed over. They talked of marriage but were waiting to see how secure his job would be.

He received a regular weekly e-mail from his employer Mr Alan Mortimer, to which he replied with his equally regular report on the progress of the Company and its share holdings. His instruction were simple, to watch the share prices daily of Conway's investments and providing the movements were small to report once a week, any significant changes should be reported at once. He collected the rent from the let apartments, found new tenants when they became vacant and organised maintenance of the portfolio of the properties under his management.

It had become an easy job once he had learnt what was required, his organisational skills were excellent and being computer literate, he soon had everything on digital files controlling everything from his small but very comfortable office.

He was interviewed in the very same office by a woman name of Sandra, whom he met only twice, once at the interview and again the first day of his employment, he never knew her full name; he had never seen or spoken to Mr Mortimer. When he received the letter offering him the job he couldn't believe his luck, accepted at once and started one week later.

The terms of his employment were generous well beyond his expectations. Sandra explained his duties in detail and left, he never saw her again and had no idea how to contact her, his sole personal contact was with Mortimer via e-mail. His salary, the five weeks leave, the company car and to top it all, his top floor apartment in a prestigious block in the heart of the City of London were beyond his wildest dreams. His total freedom to run the business was a responsibility he had never had before, being always under the scrutiny of bosses, afraid of losing their position, who stifled his ambition. He worked hard at making sure that all was in order, he knew every detail of the company investments and could recite current values and trends at the drop of a hat. Occasionally there were instructions to sell or buy shares. Once he had been asked to purchase a property and oversee its renovation. A block of six flats in Peckham. He was excited by that as he had never done anything like that before. He sourced an architect, a builder and had project managed the whole thing. He must have done a good job for he had let all the flats within a month of completion. An income yielding eleven percent, well above the norm. He even had an e-mail complimenting him.

Today's e-mail had him wondering how it was all going to go for the boss was coming home. He had been asked to go to the apartment on the Edgware Road and prepare it for his boss's arrival next week. This was one property that he was told would not be let, it was for the exclusive use of Mr Mortimer's on his return. Kevin's task was to check the four-bedroom luxury apartment was ready for occupation. He knew this day would come sometime, so he had prepared a check list of things to do. Employ a cleaner, make sure the larder and fridges were well stocked, the bed linen washed and aired, flowers bought and a host of other things. Kevin was in his element.

Chapter 24

Robert Chaney was seated in his living room, not listening to his wife but appearing to do so, he was good at that, he would nod occasionally and shake his head at times with an um! and an ah! Whatever she was saying his auto responses seemed to fill the gaps to her satisfaction. She hardly ever stopped talking and never listened to his replies anyway. His mind was elsewhere, thinking about poor Verity and Horace. He hated his weakness and wondered if the company would survive the loss of its experimental data, he knew the stolen precious stones were covered by insurance, but would they put any value on lost information. He did not know how the loss of data gained already might affect the progress. Would it put them years behind finding that medical miracle, the one he was told, they were so close to achieving? Thank goodness the analysis laboratories were still producing good income.

The clothes he wore at home belied his normal work suit and tie. The forty eight year old was wiry, five feet eight, streaky grey hair worn long like in the sixties with a full but trimmed beard, grey like his hair. Corduroy trousers a thin V neck jumper revealing the crew neck T shirt under, brown worn out slip-ons, without socks, completed the ensemble. Very long sighted he always wore his horn-rimmed glasses and gold leather strapped watch. He had worked for the Grimms ever since they moved to Basingstoke. Their expanding business had demanded a full time accountant, whereas before in London they had just used a part time bookkeeper.

His departure from the Basingstoke and Dean Council was a welcome change. His boss of many years there had given him a super reference, for he was a good accountant, which helped secured him the position at Westfields with more responsibility and money too.

His house, on the 'Bird Estate' at Kempshot, his wife's pride and joy, was bought soon after, her saying that with his improvement in status and his larger salary they should move. Her argument being that now the children had left home it was about time she had a bit of luxury in her life. He reluctantly acceded to her demand so enlarged his mortgage to make the move. His new salary although more than he was earning at the Council was on the margins of acceptance for the new mortgage, but he was easily able to circumvent the banks checks on his income by returning their reference enquiry document showing a higher salary than he in fact had. Mr James Grimm signed the document on faith for his eyes were not able to read the small print. With a little economy he thought they would manage and if he worked hard and the company did well he would get a pay rise.

The family who owned Westfields cared for their employees, or certainly Mr James did, with good conditions and benefits. He was very happy in the beginning, but it all started going wrong when his wife ignored his advice for prudence and purchased, without thought, the expensive trappings to go with their new home. Instead of waiting and being careful, credit cards were the answer to her desires.

His first slip into the trap was when a computer-generated invoice, from one regular supplier of chemicals used in the laboratories, had been issued twice, he didn't notice it at the time and it had been paid automatically as normal along with the correct one. On discovery later, he requested a refund and created a special account for this purpose. The supplier paid back the excess at once. Robert neglected to enter this account in the books at the time, meaning to do it later. It wasn't a large amount of money just under fifteen hundred pounds, it sat there forgotten. Some weeks later the same thing happened again, this time he phoned the supplier who was very apologetic explaining that there was a glitch in their computer programme and promised a refund at once. Keith was very understanding suggesting if it happened again they should set up an automatic refund as before until they could sort out their IT problem. It happened another three times before the error was fixed, by then the account held over seven thousand pounds. At the end of year audit this forgotten account had not been included and passed unnoticed by the auditors and Robert.

Mrs Chaney's card spending had grown reaching its limit and although this had stopped her indulgences for the time being the damage was done. The minimum standing order payments were more than he could afford where one such payment caused him to be overdrawn at the bank leading to a missed mortgage direct debit.

He used his work as a means of forgetting his problems the constant activity there helped to keep them out of his mind. He came across the forgotten account during his six monthly routine computer housekeeping task. There it was, seven thousand pounds that no one knew about. At first he was going to transfer it into the Company B Current Account which was used to cover employees travel and hotels expenses when working away but hesitated and thought about where else it could go. His thoughts drifted in a direction which would solve his problem. Thinking that no one would miss it, and that he would only borrow it until he had got his finances in order led him to his first of several acts of theft. He transferred the funds to his bank and deleted all details of the special account from the files. If he had left it at that one discretion, he would probably never have been found out. He paid off the card and the missed mortgage payment, but it did not arrest his sleepless nights, or his wife's constant tirade. The sums he embezzled at first were small. He overpaid invoices and obtained refunds to his special accounts which he emptied and deleted. A few hundred here and a few hundred there. He often paid back the refunds into the company account for the auditors to find, several legitimate corrections hiding the false transactions.

It worked well until this year when The Inland Revenue letter arrived stating they would be carrying out a review in about two months. It was pure chance that Westfields had been chosen, there was nothing wrong, as the company returns had always been accurate and well presented, they said it was purely a random check carried out from time to time and would not take long. They would receive a letter as to the exact date with the names of the officers who would be attending.

Unlike the usual auditors who took his immaculate accounts on face value, he knew the revenue would delve deeply into the books finding his subterfuge. He had to do something, he didn't know what. If only he had the money, he could put it into the system backdated, so that all accounts would balance. They might question his methods but there would be nothing missing so he would be okay.

He had occasion at times to borrow from a guy he had met through his local pub darts team. A hobby he'd had since his days at College. He'd borrow a couple of hundred here and there to tide him over until his salary was paid in at the end of the month. He always paid back on time with interest that made him wince, he was made to feel very afraid of the result if he did not. He would try and see if he could get the money from him. He called in at the pub on the way home but the man he only knew as Thomas wasn't there, he didn't have a phone number so all he could do was wait and try again the next day. He was getting desperate but on the third day he saw him standing at the bar, relieved in some ways but very fearful of what he was getting himself into.

"Well hello Robert old chap what are you drinking"?

"Just a half for me Thomas".

Thomas leaned over the bar and spoke to the barman.

"Large scotch no ice please Harry, and half of bitter is it Rob"?

"Yes, thanks".

He didn't know how to approach this, what he was about to ask for far exceeded anything else he had borrowed. Thomas solved that for him, he had a nose for when people were desperate and like the predator that he was he set upon his prey.

"You look like you've had a bad day Robert is there anything I can do to make it go away I'm always ready to help where I can you know that".

"It's like this Thomas I'm in a spot of bother I need a bit more than usual in fact a lot more than usual I don't know if you can help with that".

Harry came with their drinks placed them on the bar and stood to one side pretending to polish some glasses, all ears. Thomas paid for the drinks looked daggers at Harry and moved away.

"Let's go and sit in the snug over there we don't want nobody listening to our conversation do we".

Once settled in the corner well out of earshot, Robert sipped his beer summoning up the courage to ask for a way out of his predicament.

"How much are we talking about old man?"

"Twelve thousand I think".

"You think, that's a lot of dosh don't you bloody know"?

"Not exactly but twelve should be enough".

"What is it this time does the wife want a new car or and exotic holiday"?

Thomas was enjoying watching this little man squirm, he had a good idea that he had been up to no good and wanted to find out more.

"No, no, nothing like that it's just that I have to pay someone back soon".

"Not someone else lending you money is it, that's not very loyal"?

"It's the firm you see, I wouldn't go to anyone else would I"?

"The firm been lending you money then?"

"Well sort of, it's difficult to explain".

"No need, I understand your difficulty, I'm sure I can find a way to help you, but you must tell me what the problem is".

Robert foolishly explained about the IRS pending visit and his problem. Thomas was delighted this revelation gave him some real leverage with this fool he would now do anything he asked.

"Of course, I am sure I can help Robert, but first I need to be sure you will be able to pay me back. I don't see how you can find that sort of money this time, you won't be able to dip your fingers in company funds again, for a while at least so we must find another way for you, my loyal friend, to extract yourself from this nasty situation that you are in"?

Robert wasn't sure what he meant by that, hinting that he would get the loan and wouldn't have to pay it back. What other way could there be, what did he have that would be worth twelve thousand pounds plus interest? He was soon to find out.

Clinton Macaulay said goodbye to Robert telling him not to worry, that he would be in touch soon. He stayed in the snug sipping his whiskey thinking it was a good day. He was five feet ten, of medium build with a slim waist, he wore blue sneakers with grey socks, light tan slacks, and a salmon pink sweater over a blue check shirt. At close to sixty his hair was kept short going white and thinning but only slightly receded. An unlined face held dark eyes, a small narrow nose and thin lips above the signs of a double chin.

Clinton was not one to miss an opportunity; when the accountant had first come to him to borrow money he knew it was only a matter of time before he became really hooked. Loan sharking was only one of his many nefarious enterprises where his sometime casual customers only knew him by the singular name of Thomas.

This time it was different he saw a way to extract more than just *a pound of flesh* from Mr Robert Chaney. Investigations into Westfields revealed their use of precious stones in the laboratory experiments. These alone were not enough to justify the major expense needed to extract them, but when he discovered they were using radioactive materials and lasers in ground breaking medical medicine, that was where he thought he could make real money.

There is great rivalry and secrecy among the pharmaceutical laboratories, no gentlemanly conduct there. Overseas medical companies were much less controlled by the authorities than in Britain and certainly had less qualms about poaching other's ideas. Ones that were doing similar work to Westfields would give their eye teeth for information on their progress. What would they give for the whole shebang?

He was aware that handling radioactive material was dangerous which meant this would take a bit of unusual organising. He set about the task of finding out all about what would be needed to pull this off. He pumped Robert dry of information, but he was so medically ignorant, was of no help in that department however on the computers, cameras, and security set up he was the main man. He learnt about the staff, their functions and all areas of security. Not so secure as it might seem the weak link being that one person had access to all areas, the bosses P.A.

Clinton had many contacts not least a private investigator who could sus out anything he wanted, this time a suitable contact in the Industry that would do a deal was his brief.

Robert had been given twelve thousand in cash and had secreted it back into the system, it did not look too professional and might be picked up by the IRS however 'Thomas' agreed to remove the ledgers from the safe as well as the stones, and he would be in the clear or at least delay the revenue's visit. In exchange for the money he had passed on all the information about the company and its security; he knew they were going to empty the safe but had no idea of the real target, or how they meant to gain entry.

Two weeks later a plan was in place, soon Jim Quarrel and his team would be prepared, the modified vehicles would be ready, Robert had re-programmed the security computer ready to disarm the alarms and security cameras as instructed some time before, he had made a duplicate of William Grimm's key-card to log into the security computer, that way they wouldn't be able to trace the alterations back to him; all that was needed was the time and date to activate the programme.

Chapter 25

Jim Quarrel was really pissed off when he found the car was missing

"Bloody Ginger never did as he was asked".

Jim was in the van along with George, who was supposed to pick up and follow in the car that should have been at the station. He had no choice but to drive together to the prearranged isolated meeting point. They approached the deserted yard with its tumbledown barn which was six hundred yards at the end of a small track beside an abandoned farm, off the A33 five miles before it joined the Motorway by the Reading Town crossover. An ideal out of sight spot, surrounded by woods, that no one ever used. He paid Manny and Geoff their money and reinforced the instructions about staying out of sight. The brothers Manny and Geoff Carter left in one car leaving the other one for Jim and George. They checked the van inside and out to make sure nothing they wanted was left behind George then doused the van with petrol all over soaking the seats and rear floor and saturating the bag containing all the mobile phones. Standing well away he lit a small book of matches and threw it into the back of the van, the blaze was instant making them jump back as the vapours exploded. The flames lit the darkness of the yard reflecting light off trees for the first few moments; the flames quickly died down to burn more steadily destroying all trace of their activities. They waited half an hour to make sure the van was reduced to a smouldering unrecognisable wreck then drove away in the car.

"We must find that bloody vehicle, I bet the stupid buggers have parked it right outside their place".

It suddenly occurred to Jim the reason why they had taken the car.

"You know what George, they took the car because it was too late when they got to the station and there were no damn trains, I never thought to check".

"That's a bugger Jim I guess you can't think of everything, they didn't have any phones either, so they couldn't call anyone to tell them what was going on. The car is bound to be near where they live they wouldn't have parked a ringer right outside though would they"?

"You never know with them two, but I doubt it. It's no immediate problem it 'll be in a quiet spot safe enough this time of night I'm sure, we'll go and find it tomorrow and get rid of it like the van, let's go home now I'm bloody knackered".

The pair had stayed at Jim's intending to go to find the car in the morning. That never happened they slept through till early afternoon, eventually leaving to carry out their task much later than they intended.

"Drive by! Drive by! Don't stop" Quarrel shouted at George. He had spotted the police forensics van outside Ginger's flat and the uniform copper by the door.

"Fuck me, now how the hell did that happen what are the cops doing here, what did those silly buggers do to get caught so quick and where is that sodding car. Go around the block George we'll see if we can find it"

Find it they did, in the very next street, as they went by they saw it being loaded onto the back of a police trailer. There was no way Jim could go home or round his dad's now. Ginger and his mate would have left their prints all over the place. Jim had an old habit of clearing his prints when delivering a ringed car. Expecting to have had the car back and to have destroyed it by now, he wasn't sure how well he had wiped down this time. Was he wearing gloves? He couldn't remember, nothing he could do about it now. They waited until the police had gone before returning to Gingers house. George questioned the neighbour and found out that Ginger was ill in hospital and the police had Tommy in custody. Time to make themselves scarce.

"George take me to Victoria Station, loose the car go back home and stay in, I'll call you in a day or two".

"How you going to do that none of us has a phone now"?

"Oh yes, I forgot with all this going on. Look get a pay-as-you-go and call my Dad with your new number, I'll get it from him and call you, that'll work"

"Are we still on for the meet Friday, Manny and Geoff will be there for the rest of their money"?

"I see no reason to delay, I'll let you know if not, I'll have to get the cash from the boss before then, with this problem things might change. It's only Ginger that knows me and if questioned he knows better than to talk. I don't know about his mate though, I've never met or spoken to him and Ginger would have kept things to himself I'm sure, so we may be in the clear. I'll try and contact Clinton, he will know what to do".

"Alright Jim but remember Manny and Geoff will kick up alarming if they don't get paid, I don't want them coming after me and neither do you. They'll break your legs first and ask questions after, the Carter brothers don't take prisoners"

"Don't worry I'll get word to them somehow, we'll continue with the meet if all is quiet, stay low buddy, see you soon"

Chapter 26

Toni woke early long before her alarm which was set a six. She lay there for some time in the semi darkness, the dawn light pushing its way through the curtains where they didn't quite meet, urging her to get up when she did not want to. No doubt they were getting closer, today maybe would be the breakthrough day, she would see what her officers had gleaned from their interviews and computer searches. The legwork of the old days still needed to be done, but much had been replaced by trawling the internet and computer files.

Restriction of information from one force to another, officially, no longer existed except when it was a deliberate action by those in charge, usually to protect witnesses under threat or officers under cover; occasionally personal ambition by certain officers who guarded their territory would hinder another's endeavours. Police were human after all and over the years the force had attracted all types, from those who joined up to help his fellows live in peace, to bullies who relished using the power the badge gave them. Fortunately, through modern psychological testing of candidates, the latter were now mostly weeded out at an early stage of recruitment. Some of the older and more senior officers were from times past and still wielded their power unchallenged, things were changing slowly for the better as this breed of rough men retired or were occasionally forced out by internal investigation. Somehow one or two slipped through the net; these ambitious officers used cunning to advance their position, their intimidation was hidden, nasty and effective.

She left the warm bed to open her curtains revealing a mist hovering above the nearby stream, patches of which drifted across the narrow valley hiding the base of the trees floating magically unsupported. The sky above was clear, promising a sunny morning which would soon evaporate the mystical vapour from her view. These end of summer mornings often brought the resident family of deer out to graze by the stream and when spotted made her feel less lonely somehow. Not today though or perhaps they were hidden by the mist; that pleasant thought prepared her well to face the long day ahead. She showered singing a little song her mother used to hum, when preparing breakfast, dressed quickly in her usual slacks, blouse and jumper, snatched a slice of toast with the inevitable double strong coffee, almost bounced to her car raring to go.

Toni arrived well before most of her team however Compton Busion was at her desk beavering away at her machine. She looked up and smiled as her boss walked in.

"Morning Ma'am"

Compton looked tired and dishevelled she was either wearing the same clothes as yesterday or had been up all night, her initial smile quickly faded.

"Good morning Compton. Have you been home since yesterday"?

"Yes, Ma'am, but I have extracted so much information here it played on my mind, I couldn't sleep much so came back in early to sort it out and get it all down on paper. The murder file is up to date now with what I've found, plus some of the interview reports from DC Andrews and Constable Crane. I haven't seen Sergeant Musgrove or the others yet, I expect they will give me their stuff when they come in"

"You're a sucker for punishment you never rest do you. Please give me a quick rundown on what you have, I'll read the file after, whilst we wait for everyone to arrive"

"Yes, Ma'am, it's just the way I am, anyway here goes. The man James Quarrel is an old hand, as a young man he had a suspended sentence for shoplifting and served time, just one year, of a three-year spell, for breaking and entering, I don't know why he was released early I'm looking into that. Since then he has been formally questioned several times for extorsion and assault, but the charges had never stuck. The witnesses refused to testify, but without them the evidence was insufficient for CPS to proceed. He had a good brief who made him keep his mouth shut and has been careful since then. No activity for the last three years till now.

Known acquaintances of interest are our dead guy Ginger Martin, one Henry Meaker a known fence who had some minor offences as a juvenile but nothing since. Two brothers Manny and Geoff Carter who both have a record for violence, they usually work as a team, and finally a Clinton Macaulay, a known loan shark who has no record as yet but has been watched by London CID from time to time. Reports from some officers in the Met believe he has masterminded some of the larger jobs, but their snouts won't talk, you can guess why. There are others, but these are the most recent contacts"

"That's great, do we have photos"?

"Yes, some mugshots, a bit out of date but good enough, the Met sent us a file on Macaulay with some okay surveillance photos, no prints or DNA though".

"We are getting closer we will round these guys up and interview them, see what we can shake out. Anything else"?

"Lots. Prints inside the car matched those of Ginger and Tommy and a partial thumb print on the internal mirror matched Jim Quarrel's on several points not enough to stand up in court but good enough for us to assume he drove the car at some point a definite connection to the job. You remember the prints found on the tape round Verity's face they were too corrupted to be definitive but show a distinct similarity to those of our friend Mr Quarrel. Prints found on the outside of the car and under the bonnet were not known. The car itself was stolen two weeks ago fitted with false plates a genuine duplicated number matching the same make, colour and model. Brings back memories eh"?

"It certainly does, but that was another time, I doubt if there is any connection" They were both thinking of an earlier case where car theft had been part of the crime.

"Moving on, the next line of enquiry was with Westfield's accountant Robert Chaney. There are a number of things which don't add up, his official income does not match his life style, or should I say his wife's. She has run up credit card debt of several thousand pounds over a two year period all of which have been paid off from several accounts, a different one each time. These accounts no longer exist, I can find no other transactions on them, it seems they were used only once. All transactions were electronic no paper or trail except one, last week, when two lots of six thousand pounds cash were paid into his personal account and transferred out again the next day with the record of where it went having been deleted".

"Now that does need looking into, Mr Chaney has some explaining to do, I think our interview rooms are going to be very busy".

"One more thing, when I was updating the murder file, I was reading everything too, as you said and came across some files you left on your desk. I thought they were about this case but when I saw they were from that detective agency concerning our old friend Toby Jones I wasn't sure. I was going to put them back but had a sneaky read first and noticed that one enquiry was concerning the Grimm family, nothing much just a financial search and a breakdown of their company Westfields. The sort of enquiry done when considering investing. I didn't know whether it should be in the murder file or not, but seeing as how you must have noticed the connection, assumed it was, did I do right"?

Toni caught her breath, where did that come from. She had not read the files that DCI Colin Dale had given her, he told her he had studied them without anything significant. Thinking she would not find anything different she put off reading them till later. With a big smile and a wink, she looked directly at Compton.

"You clever girl, you certainly did, I actually hadn't got around to reading them yet, I'm glad that you are a nosey so and so, I may have never spotted the connection, it may mean nothing, but coincidences always need looking into. Were there any other similar company investigations in those files"?

"Yes, two others were for financial backgrounds and company valuations, the other files were mostly about the tenants of his properties. All these files are from a long time ago, well before he disappeared".

"Compton please if you can, get me a list of Directors of those companies including Westfields and of any share investments made over the past four years. Log anything else you and that marvellous invention have discovered in the murder file, I'll go through it all later today"?

Toni's mind was in a different place to Compton's who was only looking at the Westfields link to the current case, whereas she had suddenly switched onto the Jones angle again. She knew she should concentrate on the job in hand so put Toby Jones to one side in her head ready to come back to that later. He had been gone a long time, it could wait a few more days.

"I'm going to have a brainstorming this morning when everyone is here, you carry on for now young lady you have done well. When the meeting's over I want you to go home and have a good sleep for a few hours, come back refreshed later, by then I will have a lot more for you to do. June can carry on while you're gone, no arguments okay.

"Yes Ma'am".

A not too convincing response, for Compton did not want to leave her desk, as far as she was concerned she was *'Information Central'* and as the case was progressing faster, she was bound to miss the exciting bits if she went home now. She would hide herself away, so the boss wouldn't see her. There was a spare computer in Traffic that she could log onto, she would say she was having technical problems with her's no one down there would mind, they were out most of the time anyway.

Jonny was eager to get on and didn't fancy hanging around waiting. He walked over to where Toni and Compton appeared to have finished talking.

"There are still a lot of unanswered questions Ma'am what shall we do next"?

You are right Jonny, there are four directly connected people to interview in more depth. Dunbar, Chaney, William Grimm, and Walker. Bernard Dumbar has submitted a report, but it is full of waffle and very protective of his company and doesn't tell us the who's and whys. He's upstairs at the moment with the techies trying to recover the deleted files from the Westfield security computer. Jonny you get him down here and find out who changed the security profile and disabled the cameras. He may have been got at so put the pressure on, however I think it is more likely an insider. The main person of interest is the accountant Robert Chaney, he appears to have been a naughty boy with money in his hands he may not be able to account for. Mel you go and find Dunbar and back up Jonny at interview. Keith you likewise go and bring in Chaney, you'll be with me at interview with this one. We'll get to the other two later. Keith take a uniform officer with you, if Chaney has anything to hide he may try and run or worse become aggressive so don't take chances".

She went back to her office to wait for Constable Keith Crane to return with Mr Robert Chaney. This man was going to be the key that unlocked this case, she could feel it so strong she could almost touch it.

Chapter 27

Clinton received the text message at six am. The double ping to say it had arrived did not disturb him for he had been lying awake for some time. A mobile phone number and a please call me urgent from Jim. He did not respond immediately wanting to distance himself from any problems. He couldn't think of anything that might have gone wrong. He expected that the stupid accountant would be caught fairly quickly, but there was nothing Robert Chaney knew that would lead back to him. The two employed by Quarrel may well have been contaminated by radiation, but not so much that any sickness would be serious enough at this early stage to cause a problem. They did not know much either and he had never met them anyway. The brothers were very unlikely to have left anything to chance and knew better that to talk. He decided to wait and see if he could find out what was going on.

He trawled the internet and newspaper stories. Nothing in the Nationals. The Basingstoke Gazette had a report about the break in but very few facts, the police were obviously keeping it under wraps. A public scare about radiation leaking was not in their best interest. Not much to go on there; he'd make a call to one of his Met contacts before he phoned Jim. His contact had heard a rumour of a scare at some hospital in south London where someone had died of some strange infection, he didn't know what, nothing else. Clinton decided to make the call.

"What's up Jim I thought we were going to lay quiet for a while and here you are texting me after only a day".

"We have a problem Clint, Ginger has gone missing and his side kick Tommy has been arrested. The police have the car too".

"Bloody hell what went wrong, what about the van?"

"I got rid of that like you said, but the dam car was gone when we went to the station. There were no fucking late trains at Basingstoke station, so Ginger and his mate Tom drove the car back to their gaff. When me and George went to try and find the car the police were all over their place. We waited till the police had gone then asked around and found that some black woman copper had taken Tommy into custody, no one had seen Ginger, they said he had been taken ill and that Tommy took him to hospital".

"Where do these guys live"?

"Catford south London why"?

"Go to the nearest hospital now and discreetly ask about anyone sick of some rare infection, pretend you're a reporter or something let me know what you find out".

"I can't do that Clint I'm way out of it I have gone to stay at the pub in Salisbury and I'm bloody well not coming back till Friday when all this has settled".

"Okay, okay, calm down It doesn't matter. I don't blame you for disappearing. I think Ginger may be seriously ill if he is still in that hospital, I just wanted confirmation. Ginger is the only one who knows who you are and neither of them knows me. Where's George and the brothers"?

"Ginger's really that bad eh? George has made himself scarce someplace, I presume the brothers are at home. What about the meeting to make the payoff will you bring the money"?

"I'm not positive about Ginger, there's nothing we can do about him anyway, if he is still okay he won't say anything. We'll keep to the meeting schedule for now, it's only a couple of days away, everything may be alright by then. If not, I'll let you know. I'll contact the brothers if need be. George will have to fend for himself".

"I wouldn't worry about George he has gone to ground and will stay quiet till the meeting, he is going to leave his new mobile number with my Dad, I will call him if I need to otherwise he will go to the meeting Friday. He'll find a way to contact me if he has a problem".

"Look, Jim I'm sorry but I had to get you to use Ginger and his mate as that place was so dangerous, I did not want us or the brothers exposed any more than necessary. I expected them to get caught some time but not quite so soon, there is no evidence that links them to us, so just stay calm and quiet it will be okay".

" Fine by me I'll wait for your call or see you at the meeting in two days. Bye Clint".

Chapter 28

Jonny sat immediately opposite Bernard Dumbar with Melanie to one side her notebook in hand.

"Thanks for coming in Mr Dumbar this is just an informal interview to clear up a few points that arise from your report on the security at Westfields. My officer will take notes if you don't mind some of the things are technical and are easily forgotten, we would also like to record this if that's okay".

"No problem for me, I've been with your technicians to recover the deleted logs, anything I can do to help, it's a real nasty business that young lady dying like that".

"Yes indeed, what you tell us may help to apprehend those responsible. I see your report that shows William Grimm used his card to disable the alarms, the locking of their lifts and to turn the CCT cameras off but when you examined his card there was no record of the action. You don't say how that came about can you explain for us please"?

"Well as an added security measure the cards we use have inbuilt memory they record the time and date of every action on the card as well as in the computer log in this case there was no match. The log says he did, the card says he didn't".

"Was there a fault or is there some other way that could happen"?

"I did look for that, but no fault occurred that I could find. To start with this is a facility used by us to check the logging system is accurate and is not generally known by our customers. Customers do have the ability to make or amend cards, for example to give to new employees or if a card is accidentally lost or damaged".

"Who can do this"?

"Usually only senior management. Let me see, in the case of Westlands..."

Bernard opened a file and turned a few pages.

"Both the Grimms of course, Verity Pargiter, the personnel officer Marion Forbes and the accountant Robert Chaney, that's all".

"You did not put that in your report, is that logged too"?

"Yes of course, If I were to put every action in the report it would be huge you understand. I didn't think the day on day actions of staff would be important and, in any case, these took place long before the break in. I concentrated on reporting the log actions around the time of the robbery".

"That's fine I understand please go on".

Bernard shuffled through his file looking for the relevant section.

"Ah yes here it is. Only three cards issued in the last month. Two to Marion Forbes, one for a new employee and another replacement for one of the technicians who lost his card. I have details here the names and all that if you want. There was one other card made around that time, a new card for Mr William Grimm it says here a replacement for a damaged card".

He paused and looked again at the file.

"Now that is strange I never noticed before, that statement can't be true, his card was perfectly okay and I can tell he was still using his original card by the serial number. The new card however was the one used to disable the cameras and lift control".

"So, it looks like William Grimm was responsible for all this".

"Oh no, no, it was the accountant Robert Chaney who made the duplicate, it's in the log and will be recorded on his card".

Jonny and Mel exchanged glances, so there it was Chaney was the insider, he never did trust accountants he should have guessed.

"Just to be sure we know all the facts, who was the technician who lost his card"?

Again, Bernard looked through his files.

"Mathew Walker, yes, issued one week ago".

"Do you have a record for the use of that card"?

"Yes, it was used every day to go in and out and up to the laboratory, quite normal usage I believe".

"What happens to his lost card data"?

"When a new card is issued the old card is disabled, we still keep a record of its past use though".

He went on for another ten minutes going through the rest of the report, particularly Verity's actions but they learnt nothing new. He thanked him and asked if he would check the card of Mr Chaney which no doubt Toni would acquire very soon. Bernard gladly complied, relieved that his company had not been held to blame for any of this, well not yet anyway.

Chapter 29

Armed with Dunbar's interview report from Jonny, the file with Chaney's bank statements and account documents retrieved from the Westlands computer backup system, Toni moved into the interview room with a broad smile on her face. PC Keith Crane followed her and went to the table switching on the tape recorder and moving to sit by the door.

"Good day Mr Chaney, thank you for coming in today to help us sort out what happened at Westfields. For the tape Mr Chaney please state your full name".

"Err Robert Chaney"

"Thank you, also present" Toni nodded to Keith.

"Police Constable Keith Crane"

"And I am Detective Chief Inspector Toni Webb. The time is eleven thirty five Tuesday day August 19th".

She sat back and smiled again at Robert who was decidedly twitchy, his hands between his knees clasped together, his eyes flitting between the lady detective and the other officer. She spoke in a soft mellow voice

"We are interviewing everyone concerned and your input as a senior employee will be most valuable. This is an informal interview where my officer PC Keith Crane will take notes and record this interview if you don't mind. I'm Detective Chief Inspector Webb. You are not under arrest and may consult with a legal representative, before we start or, at any time if you wish".

Robert had relaxed a bit, her smile, soft voice and the fact that they were interviewing others made him feel more secure. They couldn't know about his involvement he had covered everything up. There was no money missing and anyone could have doctored the security, besides he was home in bed at the time. The sweat, that had started to form under his arms, subsided and his racing heartrate slowed, he would be all right, just answer their questions and he would be home and dry.

"I don't need a solicitor I haven't done anything, I will be pleased to help but I don't see how I can, I was home in bed asleep when all that happened".

"I'm sure you were at the time, it is what you may have said or done before the break in that interests us. Is it possible that when you were out somewhere, or in a pub, maybe you let something slip out in conversation, it's easily done when you've had a drink and chatting to your mates"?

"Well I don't go into pubs that often and I never talk about work so no".

"That's good, but someone has been talking, I'm glad it's not you".

Robert was on edge again, asking about him and the pub, they can't know about Thomas can they.

"Now let's look at this money we have found going into your account, twelve thousand pounds just last week how do you explain that"?

The shock was instant. Roberts face drained to a grey white and the sweat again oozed from his armpits, making his shirt wet and sticky. He had no answer he wasn't prepared for this.

"Please answer the question Mr Chaney".

"How do you know about that, it was a loan I borrowed it"?

"Who from and how were you going to pay it back?"

"Just some man, I've borrowed from him before, my wife you understand and her credit cards it's difficult, I pay him off every month".

"Is this the man you met in the pub"?

"Yes, but I didn't tell him anything".

"I didn't say you did. The money was only in your account for a day what did you do with it"?

"I paid off the cards".

"Now that not true, we have checked them and could find no payment anything like that amount to your credit card company, that's still a lot of money unaccounted for, where did you put it Robert?"

Robert did not know what to say, he couldn't tell them about the money he'd manipulated at Westfields he just sat their silent and bemused. Toni could see she had him on the ropes now for the knockout.

"We will leave that for now. Do you have your company security card with you"?

"Yes, I always carry it, it's never out of my sight".

"Please show me".

He removed the card from his wallet and held it out for her to see, she deftly took the card as if to look more closely.

"Do you mind if I take this for a short time, I'd like to check that it has not been tampered with, you can have it back before you leave".

He had little choice, if he objected it would seem suspicious, it was his card and had only used it to go in and out. He had used the Grimm copy to open security.

"Sure, as long as I get it back".

"Robert, do you know how the security system at Westfields functions"?

"Err yes, a little".

"Good, why is it that the alarm of the laboratory was sounding when all the other alarms were silent"?

"That's easy, it's just a door alarm to warn people to close it after they leave or enter, a bit like when you don't shut your fridge properly. It's not part of the main alarm you see".

"Thank you, you know enough to explain that little problem. Now can you tell me why you logged on to the Westfields security programme last week, surely that is not part of your normal duties"?

Another shock, his pulse was running at full pitch his mind racing now he felt sick, how did they find out about that, he thought he had deleted everything, they've got my bloody card now, why did I let them have it, the shit was piling up, what could he do to dig himself out. Please let me be. He wanted to tell her everything but hadn't the courage. He must stop talking but just couldn't.

"I didn't it was Mr Grimm".

"How do you know it was Mr Grimm"?

"He's the only one who has a card to do that".

"Yes, that is true, but the card used on this occasion was a copy and not Williams Grimm's original. Did you make a copy of that card"?

"No. No, why would I do that"?

"You tell me Robert. We will leave that for now and get back to the money. Can you explain why several accounts of Westfields were opened and closed on the same day over several months, accounts into which money from suppliers was refunded but appeared to go nowhere".

Robert slumped into his seat wishing a hole would appear and swallow him up. He was going to die in prison.

"I want a solicitor".

Toni let out a deep sigh thinking 'about time you foolish man'.

"Robert Chaney you are under arrest on suspicion of embezzlement and conspiracy to commit burglary. You do not have to say anything, but it may harm your defence if you do not mention when questioned something which you later rely on in court. Anything you do say may be given in evidence".

When Toni had finished reading him his rights and explained about the provision of a solicitor, she turned off the tape and handed him over to Keith.

"Constable Crane please take Mr Chaney to the custody sergeant for processing we will continue this interview when his solicitor is present".

Chapter 30

The squad-room was the usual noisy bustling place of business like any office, keyboards tapping, phones ringing, paper shuffling, and constant conversation between colleagues. but unlike a business where everyone was working to make their customers happy, the people here were endeavouring to do the opposite.

Toni opened her office door to hear this familiar and pleasing hive of activity, she stepped out to a din which diminished in a few seconds to a silence only disturbed by the occasional cough and squeaking chair.

"Good morning everyone, I believe we are very close to catching those that have kept us awake nights over the last few days".

A few murmurs of agreement and a shuffling of feet and chairs as everyone concentrated on what was being said.

"We now have a list of suspects that are at this moment being brought in. One, or more likely two have gone to ground but we will find them soon enough. I am sure most of you are aware that one of our suspects has died, him being almost as much a victim of the real perpetrators as Verity and Horace.

I know you all have been keeping data flowing to the Murder file, thanks for that, keep it coming, however many of you will not have had time to read it as you would have liked. Things have progressed so fast that even that document is not up to date. The purpose of this meeting is to put you all in the picture and to take on board any observations. So, don't hold anything back, no matter how trivial you may think it is. We may pull your leg if you ask a stupid question, but you are all big boys now so let's crack this today".

Toni waited a few moments for everyone to relax and get comfortable. Toni turned and referred to the now packed white board, names dates and photographs splattered its surface so that not much white was left.

"Here is what we have so far. Robert Chaney the accountant at Westfields is now in custody, charges in place. He was got at, we at first thought, by either Jim Quarrel or more likely Clinton Macaulay. Since then he has admitted to taking bribes from a man he knew only as Thomas. He identified Macaulay as this man from photos we got from the Met. A nasty piece of work according to his file, never been charged but a known loan shark and a bit more besides. He ordered Chaney to disable the alarms and camera system. He was not able to do all that he was asked, namely to gain entry to the safe and the labs. He did however provide information about the only ones who had that authority these being James and William Grimm and his personal assistant Verity Pargiter.

Verity being the weaker and more obvious target, was abducted from her friend's house the evening, before the break in, by two unknown men. Her key card and voice print enabled them to gain access to the main door and through fear for her friend, to lure the night watchman away to be assaulted and drugged. She then opened the office and safe. They endeavoured to get her to open the doors to the laboratory, but I believe at about that time she suffered a heart attack and was unable to do so. They physically broke down the double airlock doors instead, exposing the building to radiation. She was bound and locked in a cupboard with a tape over her face and a hood over her head. We found her several hours later, but she died at the scene. I won't go into details of the autopsy you can read that in the file if you wish later, but I believe this should be treated as a murder.

Once the safe was undone and the lab opened everyone left. We are not sure why they didn't take what they wanted then, but we believe they were afraid of the levels of radiation, so wanted to be clear of danger as quickly as possible. Much later Harold Martin known as Ginger and Tommy Green arrived by car at the site and entered the open building. We know this because at that point the closed circuit cameras began to work. Ginger went upstairs to the lab and took some laboratory equipment and a clear white crystal. Meanwhile Tommy emptied the safe. They then put their spoils into the back of a van or car and left. We are sure that these two were unaware of the danger and were used callously by their employer. Sometime later that vehicle was driven away by persons unknown. That sets the scene of the break in most of which information has come from Robert Chaney and Tommy Green. The precious stones were an obvious target but, when sold on, would fetch only a fraction of their value, hardly sufficient reward for such an elaborate plan. Why take the highly dangerous laboratory equipment? We think that must have been the real target and where the true value lies".

Constable Crane interrupted raising his hand.

"Yes Keith"?

"It seems a strong inside connection here Ma'am, perhaps it extends to others in the company we don't know about yet. What about insurance could it be a motive if the company was in trouble financially?" Constable Keith Crane had studied the murder file and had a feeling there was more to this that just a robbery.

"A good point Keith, I'm glad you brought that up, an insurance fraud had not escaped us entirely, but other events have pushed us into trying to apprehend the villains and not to dwell on the motive as yet. You are right it should be looked into, the detectives are at full stretch on other lines of enquiry, if you are free that is a task you could undertake for us"

"Glad to, Ma'am"

"Right to continue. I'm sure you are all aware that Ginger Martin died as a consequence of his exposure, certainly because he went outside his instructions and took a crystal from the lab, as well as the equipment he had been ordered to remove. This crystal was highly radio-active, and he kept it in his pocket for several hours with the inevitable result. He must have thought it was valuable, like a diamond, poor bastard didn't know that it was just a piece of cheap quartz.

Macaulay and Quarrel are being sought for questioning as well as their known associates. One Henry Meaker, a George Brown and two brothers Manny and Geoff Carter who all have records".

Compton Busion butted in.

"Result just in Ma'am, Meaker is currently doing two years in Wandsworth so he's out of the frame".

"One less to worry about, thanks Constable Busion. I don't think the others are aware we are on to them yet; Macaulay, Quarrel and Brown are not at their usual addresses so may have gone to ground as a precaution anyway. An APB has been issued with notices to ports and airports just in case they try and make a run for it. The Carters are being brought in now. We've managed to keep this out of the press for the moment, but it won't be long before it breaks".

Another pause, as there was a lot of information for everyone to take in; many were making notes so Toni gave them time to catch up.

"Next, William Grimm is still of interest, but we must wait for more information on the insurance and the results of the interview with Dunbar. I'm still not happy with the third possible inside man namely the technician Mathew Walker. He may have been got at too. Detective Andrews and Constable Crane please bring him in and see what you can get. I want to know why they took the equipment, grill him about that and how come he needed a new security card".

"Yes Ma'am".

Peter replied and Keith nodded.

"Rival companies may have resorted to using criminals to gain information or to knock back Westfields research programme we are looking into who would benefit most.

One more point, we have matched the prints of our suspects to those found at the scene, on the car and the envelope containing the money paid to Ginger and Tommy all except one. We don't have Macaulay's prints on file, so maybe his is the one unmatched partial found on the envelope and on a gun used in a murder from 2011. We'll find out for sure when we catch up with him. If he is our man and it seems most likely, then be careful, if he has killed once he may do so again".

As she moved on to the end of her update, Toni lost the formal addressing of officers by their rank and name, slipping into the more natural, for her, first name terms.

"Compton remember what I said and June you still have masses to do, once we bring this lot in it will be chaos unless we get ahead on the paperwork. I know it is a chore, but we don't want it to collapse with the CPS, or smart arsed lawyers pulling holes in our case because we have not documented everything fully. That's all, unless anyone has questions go to it and good luck".

The room again became a bustle of noise as detectives spoke to their uniform colleagues, grabbed their gear and left for their various destinations. Toni glanced over at Compton and mouthed a 'go home'.

Chapter 31

Two Carter brothers were sitting in separate rooms, apparently unmoved by their situation, Toni wanted to let them stew a bit before they went in. She would take on Manny and Johnny would tackle his brother Geoff. Their approach would take on the same pattern they just wanted to rattle them. They had no direct evidence of any connection to the crime other than they were known associates of the two suspects Clinton McCauley and James Quarrel. Their history made them likely to have been used by Quarrel, the interviews would maybe shake something loose

"I'm Detective Sergeant Musgrove and this is detective constable Frazer".

Geoff stood and looked Jonny straight in the eye.

"Am I under arrest"?

"No Mr Carter you and your brother are here to help us with our enquiries it is purely informal, and you can leave any time".

"What enquiries"?

"We'll come to that in a minute what I'd like to know is concerning your relationship with James Quarrel"

"What about him"?

"When was the last time you spoke to him"?

"I don't know haven't seen him for months, why what's he done"?

"What makes you think he's done anything I never said he had"?

"Well there's no way you would bring us in here to and ask questions about him if he done nothing, no point in that is there"?

"No point at all. What about George Brown have you seen him"?

"No"

"Clinton Macaulay is a friend of yours too I understand, when did you last see him"?

"Don't know the man".

"I find that hard to believe McCauley and Quarrel are best mates if you knew one you're bound to know the other".

"I said I don't know him and that's it".

"Okay now where were you last Friday evening"?

"I don't remember. I'm done answering your stupid questions, are you going to charge me, if not, I'm bloody leaving now"?

"As I said you're free to go at any time, we'll continue our enquiries elsewhere for now".

Geoff Carter stood up and walked towards the door which magically opened to let him pass through. He was expecting the coppers to make him stay and ply him with endless questions. They obviously had nothing and were just on a fishing trip. He wondered how they had cottoned on to Jim and Clint though, maybe they had picked up George or perhaps that bloke Ginger had spoken out of turn. He didn't think so, it would be more than their lives were worth to dob in either of them, besides that Ginger had no idea me and Manny were involved. He met his brother in the police station car park.

"What they want Geoff"? Manny asked.

"Trying to ask us about Clint and Jim"

"Me too. I said no comment though, I just asked to leave and they let us go".

"They knew I had met Jim before, it's on my record, said I hadn't seen him for months, but said nothing about Clint or George when they asked. They were just fishing, no sweat. Well find out more when we meet up for the pay-out Friday. The bastards brought us here, now how do we get home"?

"I'm going back in and ask the bloody desk Sargent for a lift".

"You can't do that, he'd laugh in your face"!

"I was only joking, I wouldn't give them the satisfaction, we'll call a taxi, have you got your mobile"?

Jonny and Toni were observing the two men climbing into a cab outside the station.

"How did Manny respond"?

"Mono syllable answers and lots of 'no comments' he then asked to leave".

"Same here, Geoff was rattled though, he had a sweat on, we have got them thinking".

"That's for sure. I want a twenty four hour watch put on those brothers they may try to skip or make contact with the other three, we don't have enough to charge them with anything and bringing them in again won't work, they will be all lawyered up and won't get a word out of them. We need some leverage and will just have to be patient and see what they do. Our main targets are Clinton, Jim Quarrel and George Brown, let's hope we find one or all of them soon. I'm going up stairs to see what the others have come up with and I want to see the result of Dunbar's look at Chaney's card, he's been working with our technical guys to recover the deleted logs, if it's what I hope we'll have him sewn up tight. I also want to have another go at Tommy Green I'm certain he has more to tell".

Chapter 32

Alan Mortimer walked down the stairway of the Airbus slowly relishing his first moments back home. He had been away too long. The small leather bag in his hands the only item he had brought with him. He hadn't bothered with a suitcase as there was nothing from the past years away that he wished to bring back excepting that he had traded his diamonds in Brazil through a respected company, paid the taxes and transferred the money in euros legitimately to a bank in Lisbon. He was actually looking forward to walking down the streets of London replenishing his wardrobe as the fancy took him. The old days of wearing the mandatory business suit and pretending to be what his customer expected were over. His new identity would be matched by a new presence, one more relaxed. He would no longer deal with people he did not like or trust. He would no more use fear as the means to an end, that only created enemies. He had learnt that playing the game openly and within the rules earned respect from those with whom he was dealing. He couldn't truly change his character but was now able to control the process of achieving his ambitions.

He had never had the normal desires of man, he wasn't sexually active and had never been the least bit interested in women or men. He was aware he was different but did not feel uncomfortable about his lack of libido. The only time he had an erection was when his bladder pressed on his prostate which he lost as soon as he peed, this was normal for him, he had never known anything different. He enjoyed the company of women more than men, probably because they paid him more attention but never had feelings of affection. He loved only one person and that was Alan.

He passed through passport control without incident and exited through the 'nothing to declare' customs hall, emerging into the bustling arrivals hall full of anticipation. A liveried chauffeur complete with cap held a notice aloft with his name in bold letters. He indicated his presence, the man stepped forward.

"Good morning sir, I hope you had a pleasant flight, may I take your bag"?

Alan handed him his bag and thanked him.

"Please follow me sir the car is close by in the short-term car park".

The man turned, Alan followed aware of the multinational nature of the crowd milling about in all directions, manoeuvring wheeled suitcases through small gaps apologising to each other in different languages when collisions occurred. He was loving this bustle he had spent too long alone in his Brazilian retreat.

He had chosen well in his manager, Kevin Blackman had his apartment set up as if he had never been away. Although he had never lived there and had visited it only once, it had been bought under his new name ready for just this day. Now newly decorated and furnished it was better than he remembered, the fridge freezer stocked with everything imaginable, he would have fun cooking again, something he had not done in Busios. The wine rack was full of a selection of his favourites, this man had certainly done his homework. He went into his bedroom and threw the bag on his bed. He opened the wardrobe and was amazed to find all his old suits had been cleaned and pressed, his shirts and jeans likewise in the drawers. When he left he had put all his belongings in to store and up until now had forgotten all about them. Kevin had done a good job here too, but he hadn't known Alan had lost considerable weight. He had swum daily and had been working out regularly, a six pack where he previously had been flabby. Everything would have to go, except his shoes maybe and one or two of his favourite T-shirts. He would have the rest taken to a charity shop.

There was a note and a new mobile phone on the dressing table. It was from Kevin a welcome home plus information about the phones, TV, and computer which had been set up in the study. He'd also written he would be waiting in his flat should Alan wish to speak with or text him about anything.

He would call Kevin later and arrange to meet him at the company office, for the moment he just wanted to relax, he fell back on his bed and was asleep in minutes.

Chapter 33

"Oh, it's you, you're no bloody doctor where's the other guy"

Tommy Green was sitting next to Jessica Hardwick his solicitor. He looked daggers at Toni as she walked into the interview room.

Toni went through the routine with the tape, reminding him that he was still under caution.

"Hello again Tommy, yes it's me, I'm Detective Chief Inspector Toni Webb and I am sorry about the deception at the Hospital earlier, but it was necessary to get you here with as little fuss possible".

"You should've just asked me I would've come".

"Maybe, maybe not, anyway you're here now and have been quite cooperative which will be considered by us and the C.P.S. but what you tell me next could further improve your chances of avoiding prison".

Jessica whispered a keep calm and tell the truth instruction in Tommy's ear.

"I've told the other guy everything, I don't know anything more. What about Ginger why did he die, will I catch it too"?

"I'm sorry about your friend, he was poisoned by the stuff he collected from the lab, and no it's not catching, but as you were exposed a little you will need to continue with treatment for a while. The hospital doctor prescribed some antibiotics which I gave to you there, if you need more we will get them for you".

"What was in that thing he got from the lab, is that what done for him, it looked like a bit of old junk to me, some tubes and wires and things"?

"We don't know, did Ginger say why he was asked to take that particular item and who told him"?

"No, I don't think so he said he had his orders over the phone and he told me what to take from the safe. I never met anyone".

"That's fine Tommy, have you ever met a James Quarrel"?

"So that's the name. I was nearly right, knew it was something like that. No, I never met him just heard his name spoke by Ginger over the phone".

Toni realised she was wasting her time here, he had no real idea what had happened.

"Think carefully through that day, you may remember something, if so call your solicitor it could help us and you too. You may go back to your cell now".

Tommy remarked with a grin as he left the room.

"You know what misses, you make a better doctor than you do a copper".

Toni and Jessica both laughed.

"Cheeky sod bugger off".

Chapter 34

Jonny poked his head round Toni's door.

"Dunbar has confirmed Robert Chaney's card was used to make a duplicate of William Grimm's".

"That's one thing out of the way thanks, Jonny, come in, come in. We can make the charges against Chaney stick for sure but that is only small piece of the puzzle we need the others, any luck in tracing them yet"?

Jonny stepped in but did not sit, he was keen to prepare the plan for the forthcoming interview with Brown.

"We have located George Brown, he wasn't at his flat in London, so we looked elsewhere. The local boys found him staying with his mother in Newbury. If he'd gone home to mum to hide it shows no imagination, did he think we wouldn't look there. He even answered the door and readily agreed to come for interview, maybe he has nothing to do with this business or is a fool, but just maybe he is very clever, we'll find out when he gets here. Macaulay and Quarrel have not been located yet".

"Good, let me know when he is here I will observe. You know that Chaney identified Macaulay from the photos as the man he knew as Thomas. So, we are really close now. All we need is to find him and Quarrel and we can set them all against each other, something will give. We now know enough to have another crack at the Carter brothers and with a looming murder charge they may want to find a way out. We could also use the fact that radioactive material was taken makes us to suspect them as assisting terrorists. I know it's not true but they don't know that. Worth a shot eh"?

Jonny wasn't sure these two would open up but had an idea that may work.

"They are very loyal to each other but I'm not sure the same could be said for their partners. They are unlikely to talk but if they think we have the others in custody and they are putting all the blame on them, they may want to save themselves. They are not stupid they will almost certainly suspect we are trying it on but we could instil some doubt. Might be an idea to put them together for a short while after we feed them the story, make it like a mix up by the custody officer then they may come to an agreement to open up about the others but protect each other. We'll give it a try. They are still under surveillance so I'll have them brought in with a caution this time that will make them think we have more".

Chapter 35

"Hello Toni, over here"

She spotted DCI Colin Dale sitting snuggly in the corner of the *Four Horseshoes* his former watering hole when he was a DI in Basingstoke. He'd introduced Toni to its good beer and even better home-cooked food soon after she arrived at the Hampshire station only a short drive for her and walkable for Colin from his old house.

"Ah Colin, you look good, London suits you".

"That's true but it's nice to come back to see you and I have missed the local beer. I see you are still using this nice old pub".

"Can't keep away. I try to come here sometimes, if I can, for a beer and something I haven't had to cook myself, usually with my neighbour, she drives, and I have a few or the other way around, sometimes we forget who's driving and go home in a cab".

"Good on you, work needs a break now and then, how is everyone and my old mucker Jonny M."?

"Jonny is fine, he has decided to go for promotion, he's been studying his backside off for the exams next month. He and young Andrews have been a great help to me on this current case. Everyone else is okay, busy of course we are a bit shorthanded so I'm having to do more of the ground work than the Super would like. I don't mind really, to tell the truth I kind of quite like it. How is the family"?

"Great the kids see their grandparents almost every day and Mary is much happier being back near her mum and sister she never liked it down here much, a town girl at heart you know. How's your little house, are you still there"?

"Oh yes I love it, I've even approached my landlord to see if he would sell, said he'd think it over".

"Buying eh? So, you are definitely staying no reconciliation with Larry then"?

The memory of the solicitor's letter came flooding back, she had put it out of her mind but now the question from her old colleague had given her the opportunity to share her problem without it becoming a topic of station gossip. She decided, no point in pretending and to tell Colin.

"It doesn't look like it, he wants a divorce".

"I am sorry Toni, I didn't see that coming I thought you two would get back together somehow".

"So did I, but my moving here changed him, he has moved on and I can't blame him, I was too selfish. I've accepted there is no going back now and I'm happy with that, I can move on too".

She had gone as far as she could in opening her heart to him and found herself saying one thing and feeling another, inside her outward shell of self confidence she was more than sad, but openly admitting it to Colin was not possible at the moment, subconsciously however she was resigned to moving on and that she was doing every day.

"That's enough about me and my domestic problems let's see how we are doing with our friend Jones; do you have anything significant or shall I go first"?

Chapter 36

George Brown had been sitting in the interview room for only a few minutes when a man and lady copper came in. He may not have had much of an education but had learnt from an early age to keep his mouth shut when questioned by officials. The police were as official as it gets so he resolved to say just enough to get out of here as fast as possible.

"Thanks for coming in Mr Brown, just a few questions to help us with trying to find a missing person. I'm Detective Sergeant Musgrove and this is Constable Owen. This is purely informal, we are trying to find the whereabouts of a Jim Quarrel and are questioning everyone who knows him to try and find where he is".

Jonny waited for a response but George just sat there, arms on the table looking around the room. He knew it would be difficult but was hoping for him to volunteer information. That obviously wasn't going to happen so realised he must resort to asking direct questions. He wanted to keep a gentle approach at first so a few white lies might help loosen this fellow's tongue.

"When was the last time you saw Mr Quarrel"?

"Don't remember, ages ago I suppose, why do you want him what's he done"?

"I didn't say he had done anything, it's just that he has gone missing and his family is concerned, if only we knew where he had gone it would put everyone's mind at rest".

"I couldn't say, he doesn't tell me his business".

"Have you any suggestions where he may go if he wanted to get away from his family for a bit of peace and quiet say".

"He may go to his Dad, he likes it there, can't think of anywhere else though".

Jonny was remembering the visit to Jim Quarrel's father who said he had no idea of the whereabouts of his son and was told to 'sod off' in no uncertain terms.

"When I spoke to his Dad yesterday he told me he doesn't know where he is, he was expecting him but is worried because he hasn't called to explain why he didn't turn up".

"It's cause he didn't have a phone see, otherwise he would've".

Jonny was puzzled by that answer; how did he know that Quarrel had no phone. He'd play along and see where it goes.

"That must be it I never thought of that, but he must have got a new one by now don't you think"?

243

George was stuck for something to say straight away, he needed time to think, he should have just said nothing, like he'd planned, why did he blurt that out, that bloody coppers too quick didn't give me time to think. He's fishing, he doesn't know anything about the job. Just keep telling them you don't know.

"Probably but I don't know the number".

"That's all right we can find that out later a phone is not important. How was he going to contact you"?

"I don't know".

"So, he was going to contact you later but you don't know how, now he hasn't got a phone".

"No, I didn't say that, you're confusing me".

"I'm the confused one George, he can't call his dad because he hasn't got a phone, and he's going to contact you but you don't know how. If you know all this you must have spoken to him just the other day, his dad said to ask you where Jim was as you were always together".

"His dad wouldn't say that you're lying".

Jonny knew he had to tread carefully here he was losing him; he'd seen George eyeing up June, attracted maybe, so he'd try a different tack.

"Look Jim I'm really concerned we only want to know where he is that's all. We won't talk about him anymore; would you like a cup of tea or something before we go on".

"What do you mean go on, I thought you were finished".

"Almost George, just a bit longer and you can go home, milk and sugar is it"?

"Err.. yes ta, two spoons"

Jonny asked June to go and fetch the tea, "...and a biscuit if you can".

"She's a good girl that one, young nice looking don't you think, but learning fast, make a nice wife for someone one day. Are you married Jim"?

"Not me, I don't meet many girls much, I'm a bit scruffy you know, they don't like that".

"You could tidy up a bit you're not that bad looking. What do you do for work"?

"This and that, labouring on the building sometimes, a bit of driving you know anything that comes along".

June came in with the cup of tea and a plate of biscuits and smiled directly at Jim and moved close as she placed his cup and the plate in from of him. So, close he could smell her perfume left behind as she retreated to her corner seat.

"There what did I tell you a real treasure".

"Thanks, miss".

George blushed a little and tried to hide his embarrassment by dunking his biscuit in the cup and swallowing it whole, followed by a big swig of the, lucky for him, not too hot tea. He relaxed and self consciously returned June's smile.

"Now you do a bit of driving you say, is that what you were doing last Friday, did Jim ask you to help him out"?

"Now you said you wouldn't ask about Jim again".

"Sorry George perhaps it was Macaulay who wanted you to do the driving".

"I don't know what you mean".

"Well that's what's been said".

"Who said"?

"He was telling us as how it was all Quarrel's idea and you were doing the driving".

"I don't know nothing about nothing, it was Macaulay who does the planning not Jim, and I wasn't in there".

"Where's that George"?

"The factory you bloody well know don't you, that bastard Clinton is trying to blame it on me and Jim".

"Look George I'm not sure what you are saying so I'm going to call a halt there, I need to caution you". Jonny read the caution to George and arranged for a duty solicitor to be called in.

"I hope you're not going to keep me here all night I've not done nothing wrong, anyway I have to be somewhere later, you can't keep me here".

George was worried he would miss the meeting with Quarrel tomorrow and wouldn't get paid.

"Speak to your solicitor he will advise you. All I can say is if you cooperate you might be able to go home tonight".

He left George in the interview room with a uniform PC. He needed to speak to Toni before he continued. It was obvious that George Brown was easily led. At this point everything he had said was not admissible, but it meant everything to the detective.

He now needed to get it down on tape with George under caution and a solicitor present. It would not be so easy second time as the ruse concerning Jim's dad and Clinton having given them up could not be used again. However, he was easier to deal with than the Carters. He would approach it in a different way. He would make sure that George saw the two brothers being led to the cells, adding to the lie that Macaulay was in custody.

How did Macaulay hope to get away with using such easily led men? He'd not been caught in years maybe he had become complacent, had an ace up his sleeve, or just didn't care and was gone for good just like Toby Jones. Who knows? He turned to June.

"Did you take notes"?

"Yes sir".

"Good, very good June. Sorry about the tea and stuff I just wanted him to stay loose. We now need to obtain the same result under official interview, your presence will be essential he likes you".

"If I ever need a pimp Meester Musgrove I'll know where to come. Only joking guv, it worked well I don't mind".

"Yes, thanks to you, wait here a while I'm just going to speak to the boss, won't be long".

Jonny walked slowly to the stairs and climbed even more slowly taking the time to gather his thoughts before he put his idea to his DCI. He looked through the half open door.

"Come in, come in Jonny".

"Can I have a minute Ma'am, just want to put you in the picture with George Brown before I go further".

"Sure, I was about to have the brothers brought in again for a second stab".

Jonny gave Toni a summary of the interview and his idea concerning the brothers.

"If he sees them he may think we have everyone in custody and tell us the whole story. I'm still not sure if

I have his measure but he seems a bit slow and has let things slip out, but maybe he is acting simpler than he really is. Just as I was leaving he said something that may change how we handle this. He has an urgent meeting somewhere, he was very agitated that we may keep him here and he would miss it".

"I see your point on the one hand if we let him see the brothers in cuffs and let him think we have Macaulay and Quarrel in custody too he may tell all, but will it be enough. If we just let him go he could go to meet with one or more of the others for some reason. He won't go to a meeting if he thinks no one will be there. What do you think"?

"He is hot now and I think we could get a result by continuing to question him today, but that won't get us nearer to catching the other two. He was probably only the driver and may know very little more than we have already extracted. If we let him go and follow him to this so called meeting we may end up with nothing, but we could also have all our culprits in custody. Is it worth the chance? If the meeting turns out to be a nothing we could pull him in again and hope he is still vulnerable to our tactic".

"Both arguments hold good. I'll risk it, I want you to let him go, make sure you don't lose him. I'll cancel bringing in the brothers for now, if there is to be a meeting of some kind I don't want to spook them, at the moment they think they are in the clear. There is a danger they may all scarper, but it's worth a go, this chance to bag them all may not come again. If we are wrong, I'm a big girl, I can take the flak from upstairs".

"Yes, Ma'am I'm with you there, err...not with you getting flack I mean, but doing something.... you know".

"I know what you meant, now off you go and set up the surveillance teams on both the Carters and Brown, you will be officer in charge for this. Make sure they are linked to you by radio as well as phones, good communication will be vital if we are to nab this lot in one go. Use Andrews and Crane, one on days, one on nights, we will have to use uniform officers too as we don't have enough detectives to cover everything. I want Mel here with me, we still have Grimm to interview, that leaves June working with Compton".

Toni was not happy with her female officers being involved with arresting possibly armed and dangerous men, so invented good reasons to keep them at the station. She knew they would be keen to get involved and that she should not have this protective bias, but she was boss now, so there you go. She didn't know it but Jonny saw through her ruse and was relieved the girls were not to be put in the firing line too.

"We don't have any idea when this could happen, if at all. You said George seemed agitated, afraid he may miss his appointment if we kept him in, so it may be sooner than later, let's hope so. If there is any movement I want them followed very discreetly and I need to be told at once".

Jonny left the room with a feeling that at last there was some progress forward and not just collecting small bits of information here and there. This DCI had a slice of the old school in her, like Colin but more subtle.

Jonny went back to the interview room, found June had left George with a brief he hadn't met before. He spoke before either George or his lawyer had time to say anything.

"Thank you, Mr Brown you have been most helpful, we have more important problems now than looking for missing persons who are quite capable of looking after themselves".

"Does that mean I can go"?

"Yes, George it does".

The young solicitor had no idea what was going on and tried to stop George from leaving, by holding his arm and attempting to say something, but no words came out. George just shrugged him off and left him sitting in the chair with his mouth open and was gone.

Jonny looked at the bemused, obviously newly qualified, lawyer wondering how they all seem so young lately, hardly able to deal with the likes of George Brown or the Carters. Still they had to learn somewhere and this nick was as good as any.

"Don't worry young man he'll be back you will get your day in court yet".

"I had not even managed to get his full name and address. He wouldn't answer any of my questions. What is going on"?

"I'm Detective Sergeant Musgrove, George Brown, your client was given a caution and you were called in as duty solicitor, but since then new information has come in regarding our enquiries concerning this man so he has been released. As you saw he did not want to stay here any longer than he had to. I suspect we may need to interview him again, if we do you will be informed beforehand. If you speak to the desk sergeant on the way out he will give you Georges details. Your name is"?

"I'm Cyril Maxwell, of Patterson and Jakes, I was a bit surprised he would not speak to me".

"No surprise for me, he has an inbred fear of officials, he thinks we are all against him, a common trait among criminals, you will find out soon enough now you are on our duty brief's list. It will take time for you to gain his trust but he will come around when he sees there is no other choice. This your first time here"?

"Yes, I didn't know what to expect".

"No one ever does; good luck Cyril, let's hope you have an easier client next time, we will meet again soon I'm sure".

With that Jonny left him still sitting in the chair gathering his papers into his shiny new briefcase. 'Poor sod', he thought, 'Paterson and Jakes had thrown him in at the deep end, he has a long way to go before he can swim in these murky waters'.

Jonny went to the squad room to see which uniforms were available, he needed to set up the surveillance on George and the Carters. After a half an hour with their supervising sergeant he had two teams working in shifts on both houses. Keith Crane would be with the early shift and Peter the late, both at the Carters. The uniforms would cover George. He had also asked for a radio so he could keep abreast of any action if and when it came, there was no way he wanted to arrive after the event. If there were to be arrests he wanted it to be by the detectives and not have the uniforms front of queue.

He now had his report to write and give it to Compton for the murder file, he also wanted to read it just in case new information had come in or he had missed something. He needed June's notes too so went looking for her. Compton had gone from her desk, and June couldn't be found anywhere on their floor, so he went to the desk sergeant to see if he knew where they were.

"Officer Busion has not checked out Jonny, neither has Owens they must be somewhere around"

He thanked him and called June on her mobile.

"I'll be up in a minute sir".

Jonny went back to his desk. Five minutes later June appeared.

"I need your notes June, for the interview report".

"I was already doing that sir, I thought it would help".

"Well that's good I don't mind one bit, but you don't have to it's not your job you know".

"I don't mind it helps me to learn about interview techniques".

"Have you seen Compton I need to look at the murder file"?

"The Chief sent her home".

"Well she hasn't left yet and is normally glued to her computer, she must be somewhere".

"Sorry sir, she's trying to keep her whereabouts secret, she didn't want to go home so has hidden herself down in traffic in case the Chief saw her. She is still going through the finances and tracking down the investors plus updating everything that has come in. No one is there at the moment so she's using the traffic department computer and has the murder file with her. I tried to tell her to go and have a break but she won't hear of it, says there is too much to do".

"Don't worry I won't tell, by the way we have let George go and are going to put him under surveillance so the official interview under caution will take place later. Did you meet Georges solicitor"?

"Yes, that's when I left, a bit wet wouldn't you say"?

"That's for sure. June be an angel and bring me the murder file as it stands, that way I can deny having ever seen Compton if anyone asks. I'll get it back to her soon".

"No problem 'Meester Musgrove' sah".

They both laughed. This enthusiasm must be infectious, Jonny didn't want to go home either, not until this case was closed.

Chapter 37

Clinton was waiting in his car on the nearly deserted top floor of Croydon's main shopping centre multi-story carpark. He was early not just keen but cautious, he felt trapped up here with no quick way out. He parked right opposite the down exit ramp as the best option to appease his paranoia. He had never met the man from Morgan Banks Medical, he was told to wait in the car park and he would be contacted. The equipment was in the back of the car still in its special case. The radiation check he made earlier hardly registered. The lead box was doing its job. He hoped they came with some strong guys as it weighed a ton he wouldn't be able to lift it out. The agreed meeting time came and went. Ten minutes had gone, no sign of anyone Clinton was feeling very uncomfortable. Had they changed their minds, what was he going to do with the bloody thing if they had. Just then his mobile binged making him jump and sweat even more.

He had a text from a withheld number, in it he was told to go down one level and park between a red Ford Transit van and a white Mercedes. Was it a trap, he had no choice but to comply, if he wanted his money it was now or never. He started his car and wound down the ramp to the next floor. There were a few more vehicles here but the van and Merc. were easily spotted as he drove round the opposite side near to the exit ramp. He backed in leaving a good margin at the rear. He saw no one in the Mercedes as he looked through the driver's side window. His passenger door opened and a tall thin, quite elderly man was in the seat next to him with the door shut in seconds.

"Mr Macaulay glad you could make it. You have something for us I believe".

Clinton's heart was racing he had never been in this position before he had always been the one calling the shots.

"Yes, I have the file you asked for, the memory sticks are here. The equipment is in the boot".

He gave the man the file and the USB SanDisks.

"Unlock the boot please".

Clinton pressed the boot release button on the dash, the click told him it was free. He could not see because the raised boot lid blocked the view from his interior mirror but knew the box had been removed by the car rising a good three inches. The boot lid shut with a small thump. No one was visible but the van moved off straight away. The man removed a package from his inside pocket and handed it to Clinton.

"Thank you Mr Macaulay, please make sure you destroy this car and everything that was anywhere near the source, we will not meet again, ever".

With that the man climbed out of his car and left on foot down the ramp to the next level. Clinton waited a few minutes opened the package fearing it might be full of paper but found the bundle of fifty-pound notes as agreed, one thousand of them. A broad grin spread across his face. 'Now to offload the stones and I'll be laughing'.

He drove out of the car park and headed back towards the M25 he turned west and left the motorway at the Sutton turn off. He had set up a meeting with an old fence who was interested in taking the uncut stones. His little second hand shop was just off Sutton high street. He managed to park at a meter fed it with some pound coins and walked the hundred yards to the so called 'antique emporium'.

"Hello Clint, not seen you in a while have you brought the stuff"?

A scruffy short balding man of sixty odd was perched on a three legged stool by the glass counter. The shop was full of mostly old second hand tat with a few bits of nice china and glass, some old pictures too gave it a feeling of being antique in style. A glass fronted cabinet with some silver bits helped to support the impression.

"Well Jock I see you have not moved much since I was here last, still sitting on that old stool with the same stock as last year".

"It's what you don't see that counts my friend".

"True, very true. Shall we".

Clinton pointed to the rear of the shop where there was a tiny office and a place to make tea. The toilet was still outside in the yard. No improvements had been made to this old building since the war.

Jock put the lock on the front door and reversed the open sign to closed, moved to his office with Clinton one step behind. Jock sat in the only chair and Clinton perched on the edge of the desk. He opened his coat and pulled out the bag containing the stones. He had never really looked at them closely before but spread out on the table Jock ran his hands over them like they were delicate and would shatter if he was not careful. He selected one and took an eyeglass from his waistcoat pocket snapped it between his cheek and brow perusing his selection. He turned it this way and that, picked another at random and did the same. After a few more he removed the glass and turned to Clinton.

"Look my friend I can't handle these".

"Why not they are uncut diamonds, rubies and lots of others, are you saying they are not real"?

"Oh yes they are real enough but are not uncut as they would seem to be at first glance".

He picked up a stone and offered the eyeglass to Clinton.

"Hold the stone in your fingers lengthwise, right now look at the end. What do you see"?

"It's all shiny, polished like".

"Right now, look at the other end"

"It's the same. What does that mean, why can't you take them"?

"They have been specially prepared, at great expense I suspect, by probably only one company that I can think of in this Country. If I tried to feed them in to the open market, alarm bells would ring and the police would be all over them and me".

"Couldn't you just cut off the ends so they looked different or something"?

"Any attempt to cut these stones would mean that most if not all of them would shatter and be worthless. They are all of a good size I know but could never be cut for the jewellery trade they have one purpose in life and that is laser technology, not my field I'm afraid".

"They must have some value just give me a price".

"Look I have no way of getting rid of them they are too unique, perhaps you could try someone who deals in technology, overseas would be safest, I'm sorry old friend but you have to find another way I'm not your man this time".

He scooped the not so precious stones back into the bag and turned to leave.

"I tell you what, if you can't offload them elsewhere come back I'll give you two grand and hope that some of them will cut without breaking".

"You are joking, that doesn't even pay the expenses, I'll find somewhere they are worth twenty or thirty at least".

"I hope you are right I wish you luck".

Jock closed the shop door as Clinton left and put the open sign back before returning to his favourite stool.

Clinton was a bit pissed off, a wasted journey. He had an idea though, perhaps the man from Morgan Banks Medical would be interested in the laser stones. He would look into that later plenty of time. Anyway, he now had the money to pay the guys off, he would contact Jim and give him the cash. He didn't want to go to the meet, just get back to the cottage in Surrey.

Chapter 38

Toni wanted to talk to William Grimm but not by bringing him into the station. She wasn't sure if he was part of this or not, her gut feeling was in the negative but needed to find out more.

She drove, along with Melanie, to Westfields having telephoned first and was happy to see a young girl through the glass who rose from the front desk to meet and open the doors just as she arrived.

"Mr Grimm is expecting you madam and miss, follow me please".

The girl used her card to open and operate the lift, then escorted us along the short corridor to an office at the end. It was not large and had no window but a wonderful large backlit picture on glass of fields and trees occupied the wall behind Williams desk.

He stood as they came in after the young girl knocked and opened the door for them.

"Thank you, Fiona I'll call when they need to leave. Please Chief Inspector have a seat and you too, young miss".

"Thank you Mr Grimm this is Detective Constable Frazer".

"Would you like tea or coffee"?

"No thank you sir we are fine, I don't want to keep you too long just a few questions and we have some news too. Do you mind if Constable Frazer takes notes it helps my poor memory, don't want to forget anything important do we"?

"Not at all, how can I help"?

"First to let you know we have some suspects. Not all in custody yet but we are sure we know who did this, however the true motive is unclear. As you must know we have your accountant under arrest at this time".

"I know, I know, but can't believe Bob would have done this, he has been so loyal and done sterling work for us, are you sure he is involved"?

"No doubt about it he has confessed to certain crimes indicating he played a part in the robbery, I'm sorry but cannot give you details but needless to say the information he has given us has helped to identify the suspects".

"You have suspects in custody you say"?

"Just one at the moment, apart from Robert Chaney, the others are being watched and will be arrested shortly. It seems like the stones were the target, but we are more inclined to believe that the equipment and data were the true reason for the robbery. What are your thoughts"?

"I don't know really it could be either, are we likely to get back our stones"?

"I don't know, why do you ask that, I would have thought your equipment and technical data would be more important to you after all the stones are insured aren't they"?

"Yes, we are insured for their value as precious stones, but they are of no use in the raw state the insurance does not cover the very considerable cost of having them re-worked, cut and polished or the time it takes to do that. It took us two years to acquire our collection, we don't have the time or funding to do that again easily. We have all our research information backed up so no loss there and the data on the memory sticks is heavily encrypted so will be of little use to a competitor. Even if they break the code on one stick it is different for each of the others a thankless task. The file loss is more important it does show where we have gone wrong and wasted precious time, that is unprotected as it is mostly hand written, technicians notes and the like. That could be useful to someone save them a lot of time if they wanted to follow our line of research".

"There were several files in the safe why do you think they only took that one"?

"None of the other files had anything to do with the experiments, they were day to day copies of memos and e-mails. The loss of the stones is the real problem. A competitor may not realise that at first, but if the stones on the stolen apparatus are examined they will at least have a good idea what we are doing and could replicate our experiments".

"It seems both the stones and your experimental data were what they were after. I wonder if they realise the significance of the combination. I believe they had a customer for your data and equipment, but the stones were a bonus they couldn't resist. Who are your competitors and are they likely to resort to criminal activity to gain an advantage"?

"Several come to mind, overseas mostly, I doubt if the UK companies would, there is not the funding for experimental science in this field for most of them. Morgan Banks are doing similar research, they have money too I can't see them needing to resort to this though".

"Let's get back to the stones what do you mean by re-worked"?

"The outside of the stones are coated with reflective plastic then they are polished on each end so that the faces are almost parallel small fractions of a degree offset, each stone slightly different, a very specialist and expensive job, it can take days just to do one stone".

"I see so what about cutting them again to make jewellery"

"Almost impossible the natural facets of the stones have been lost so cutting would not work they would just shatter unless you were lucky enough to strike in the right place. Our stones were selected to suit our specific technology requirements those used in the jewellery business are very different. Anyone in the trade would spot the difference".

"I don't know how that helps but it may make it difficult for our guys to off-load them so you never know they may be found. How does that leave your programme"?

"No two crystals produce the same results we have narrowed it down to the best types and are close to achieving the angles of cut that are the most stable. We cannot continue without some new prepared crystals, we were recently getting the best results using emeralds so have some new samples in the process of preparation, they are not ready yet, but could be up and running in a week or two, but that is only part of the problem all the lost stones and their matching data provides   information to move to the next level. Our bread and butter business of sample testing pays the bills, so we can carry on, but our investors are banking on a breakthrough from the experimental work to bring home the big rewards. If they pull out, we will have to reduce our experimental projects considerably".

"Thank you Mr Grimm, most informative, at least I have some ideas as to motive now, I can assure you we will try and trace your missing stones and equipment, once we have apprehended all our suspects there is a good chance we may salvage something. One last thing sir who knew which file was the one with the notes"?

"Oh, almost everyone it had a large yellow six on the front"

"Why was that, the six I mean was the number significant"?

"The number, no. Matt Walker put it on, he was always complaining of having to rummage through all the other files to find it so wacked on that yellow sticker to make it stand out".

"Good idea. That's all, if I need more information I will contact you again".

Fiona appeared as if by magic and escorted them back the way they came in.

"What do you make of that"? Toni asked Mel once they were seated in their car.

"A bit technical but I got it all down, That Matt Walker is ringing my alarm bell, a big yellow six marks the spot. The competitor company er...." She flicked through her notes. "...Morgan Banks could do with some investigating too, I shouldn't wonder".

"My thoughts exactly, what about Grimm"?

"I don't know, I didn't get any tells from his voice or body language to make me think he was anything but straight. He has nothing to gain as far as I can see, so I think he is okay".

"Too eager to tell us all about his experiments don't you think".

"Nah, just a scientist proud of his pet project wanting to show off a bit".

"Perhaps you're right, back to the station Mel let's see if there is some action about to liven this case up a bit".

Chapter 39

Jim Quarrel had been staying in a pub called The Bishops Mitre in Salisbury. He had seen no news since finding that Ginger had been taken to hospital and Tommy had been arrested. Tommy knew nothing and Ginger would clam up for certain. He phoned his dad on his new phone.

"Hello Pops, everything alright?"

"Don't know son a couple of young rozzers were here looking for you I sent them packing, don't think they knew much the uniform copper was working from a list lots of names on it, he crossed yours off, I saw. Don't know what that means though. I've got George's mobile number here do you want it"?

"Yea, text it to me. I wonder what they wanted coming to you. They must've gone to my gaff first and when they couldn't find me came to yours".

"Is everything okay lad, where are you staying, can I do anything"?

"I'm fine Pop, best you don't know, I'll call you later stay well, love you".

"Love you too son, look after yourself".

Jim was not sure what to make of the fact they were looking for him. Was it to do with the Basingstoke job or was there something else that had gone down locally where the police were trawling up the usual suspects? The bing on his phone gave him Georges number he would call him.

"Hi George, everything okay, all set for tomorrow are we"?

"I'm good Jim, I'll be there tomorrow alright".

"Have you seen or heard from Manny or Geoff"?

"No, I've stayed in mostly, the police had me in I didn't say nothing and they let me go".

"Did they ask about the job"?

"No, never mentioned it, said they were looking for a missing person, asked if I knew where you were, that's all, I said nothing , I didn't know where you were anyway".

"All seems quiet my end, see you Friday, how you getting down there"?

"My sister is lending me her car".

"That's good see you there, you can give me a lift back to London then".

"No trouble mate, bye".

George was scared to tell Jim about them asking about Clinton, he knew he had said too much but couldn't remember what, anyway they had let him go so it was alright he was in the clear.

Jim wondered where the police were coming from, had the Carters been picked up too, he had no way of contacting them from where he was, and for sure he wasn't going to go back to the Smoke and knock on their door. He would call Clint and see what he should do.

As soon as he had finished talking to George he phoned Clinton to explain what had occurred. Clint did not seem worried and arranged to meet his friend in a Dorchester café they had used before, it was an easy train ride for both of them.

When Jim arrived, Clinton was sitting in the second table along, he had a mug of tea and a full English breakfast half eaten in front of him. He stopped eating and waived Jim to sit opposite him.

"You hungry Jim"? he nodded to the waitress to come over to the table.

"Yea a little, can I have a black coffee and two eggs on toast pleas luv. I see you still have a good appetite, all okay with you, how's the cottage"?

"Very nice, I must come down more often, you haven't been there in a long while have you"?

"No, I sort of let time slip me by. I remember the old days we spent there as kids, it was great, no worries just good fun".

"Well we can have fun again once this all blows over. You may not know but Ginger is dead that's bad for him, he won't be talking that's good for us. His mate Tommy knows nothing. The cops went calling after

Ginger died, silly sod, he has been done for knocked off stuff they found in his flat, no mention of the Basingstoke job though. I think the police have been fishing around Ginger's known mates because of the way he died. They must have made a connection but can't have learnt much.

The accountant is buggered, whatever he tells them is irrelevant he doesn't know who you are and only knows me as Thomas. You go ahead with the pay out as arranged, I had a problem offloading the stones so I can't go tonight as I need to meet up with a new buyer. After the payoff go back to Salisbury stay away from London for a while tell the others to do the same when you see them tonight. I will call you later".

Clinton went on to explain about the stones and how he was going to sell them to the same people who bought the equipment and that they were worth much more than first thought. He had not even been able to contact the man from Morgan Banks yet but did not want to tell Jim or he might get suspicious as to why he wasn't going to the meeting. He wasn't so sure the police were out of the picture so the less contact with the others the better. He handed over a bag with the money, finished his breakfast and left Jim to his eggs on toast which arrived as he walked out the door.

Jim ate his breakfast drank his coffee and considered running off to anywhere with the bag he had been given. The thought only lasted a few seconds, as he would never be able to sleep safe with the leg breaking Carter brothers on his trail, let alone the wrath of Macaulay. He would go back to the Bishops Mitre this morning and to the meeting tonight at eight as planned.

Chapter 40

Alan set off for Basingstoke in the hired Mercedes, this time he decide to be chauffeured. He was going over the information he had been given by Kevin Blackman. He had been very thorough, a breakdown of the accounts for the past two years, reports supplied by Westfields on the progress made by the experimental division. A brief report made up partly from new cuttings and some transcripts of recorded phone conversations Kevin had made to Westfields and one to the Basingstoke police. He did not like being ripped off and as a shareholder, villains putting their hand in his pocket were not to be tolerated. This new person Alan Mortimer was not a Toby Jones to look at but he certainly was when it came to someone stealing his money, whoever they were they would regret it in a big way.

Kevin had phoned to announce the impending arrival of the managing director of Conway Investments and would they please have the senior personnel available when he arrives.

The chauffeur opened the door to the Mercedes at the front steps of Westfields. Alan was quite impressed, the building he had funded looked good, smarter than expected he had chosen well. He walked up the steps to be greeted by a young man who was standing in the open glass entrance doorway. Welcome Mr, Mortimer to Westfields, I am William Grimm please follow me. They walked over to the lift which opened when William offered his card to the reader and spoke his name. They both stepped in, it closed and ascended without any further action.

"We will go to the conference room sir, there is more room, my father is waiting for us".

"Please call me Alan and I'll call you William if that is okay".

"Of course Alan, William is fine, father likes to be known as James".

A short walk to the end room which opened to reveal itself as able to seat a dozen or so around a long oval table. A smaller table holding refreshments and cabinet with an antique clock stood to one side. There were no windows but drapes hung with backlighting on the rear wall giving the impression of there being some. The man Alan remembered meeting a lifetime ago when he was Toby sat at one end drinking what appeared to be black coffee.

"Dad this is Alan Mortimer, Alan my father James Grimm".

Alan took the hand that was offered.

"Hello James, please call me Alan".

"Ah yes we met before at that dinner a long time ago I never forget. Alan Mortimer that was not the name I recall though let me think".

"No sir I don't think we have ever met. I invested in your company some time ago on recommendation from a broker friend. This is the first time I have been here or met anyone in your company".

"Well your voice is very familiar, since my sight has gone I rely much more on sound and touch you know".

Alan was surprised that the old man remembered him, he hadn't known that he had gradually lost his sight, he wondered if Kevin knew, it would have been nice to have had a warning. If James had been able to see he would not have even thought about the voice, it did not matter he felt safe I his new skin.

"All us Londoners sound the same an easy mistake".

William stepped forward pulling back a chair for Alan next to James.

"Please sit down Alan would you like a coffee, tea or something else"?

"Coffee is fine black one sugar please".

A young girl appeared from behind Alan with the Coffee and a small plate of what looked like handmade biscuits which she place beside him. She disappeared through a panelled side door adjacent to the cabinet. William in the meantime had walked around the long table to sit opposite Alan. He laid a paper folder beside him, closed. Alan opened the conversation.

"I heard about your troubles from my office manager Kevin Blackman, they seem to be serious, so have come down to see if I can help in any way. I normally avoid getting involved with companies in which I invest. I choose to let those that know what they are doing get on with it. Incompetent interference is not my way. Saying that, I have worked with a variety of businesses and have come across some villains in my time so feel you may be out of your depth dealing with this. What have the police told you"?

It was William who spoke.

"Well they said they have one suspect in custody and expect an arrest of others any day now. Our accountant is also under arrest, I couldn't believe it but he has been stealing from us for a while now and apparently compromised our security to allow these people to break in undetected. Vera my assistant and good friend has been killed. They used her security card and voice print to open the safe and get up to the second floor laboratories".

"Why did they pick your friend"

"It was my fault she had security clearance to go anywhere, the only one apart from me and dad to have it. She did everything for me here it's so sad. I don't think they meant to actually kill her, she had a bad heart you see. Being threatened and tied up was too much, her heart just stopped. They took her from her friend Julies house and threatened to hurt her. They kept Julie as a hostage to force Vera to open the safe, they bashed Horace our security man on the head and then drugged him, they want locking up for life".

"That is terrible you must not blame yourself just because you gave her security clearance, it is the criminals who are responsible. How come none of this is in the papers and what about Julie is she okay and Horace too. Exactly what did they take"?

"Julies alright now they did not harm her, left her tied up gagged with a black bag over her head, she was petrified and still in shock over Vera. Horace is still in hospital but he will recover I'm told. They took all the precious stones, the computer memory sticks a file of notes from the safe, and a radioactive experimental apparatus from the laboratory. I think it is because it is classed as a nuclear incident that the police have kept it quiet; there is no danger now but they did not want to panic the public. The police don't tell us everything but think the robbers took the apparatus and data to sell to a competitor but they have kept the stones to sell elsewhere".

William went on to explain about the police suspicions concerning Morgan Banks Medical, how the stones structure was manipulated and why they were of no use as jewellery.

"Who is in charge for the police".

"She is a coloured policewoman Detective Chief Inspector Toni Webb, she seems most competent and has hinted they may recover the stones. She has a sergeant too named Musgrove, John I think".

Alan thought back to Sandra's incident, it was the then DI Webb who was in charge, seems she's been promoted; he may need to revive an old contact to get some inside info.

"That's good William, let me see what I can find out, I have contacts that can access information the police don't have. If you need a cash injection to get things started again we can discuss that later".

"Toby Jones, that's who you remind me of, tall fellow with stick out ears and black hair, I remember".

James Grimm had said nothing until then, he'd obviously been thinking and puzzling over their past encounter.

The old man's memory was good, Alan was somewhat taken aback but said nothing.

"Well it can't be him Dad his ears are as flat as a pancake and he's fair headed".

"It must be my accent we Londoners all sound alike".

Alan let his tongue slip back to his natural south London drawl instead of the more cultured tone he'd slowly adopted over the years.

"Concerning the offer of financial help I am sure we are fine, our cash flow from the analysis work is excellent and the insurance will enable us to replace some of the stolen items, our biggest problem is the time it takes to prepare them".

"Thank you James, William. If you need anything please call Kevin he will find me. I'm very sorry about the loss of your friend; I hope the police will catch those bastards soon".

"Thanks for your visit and concern Alan please come down any time we will be glad to see you, perhaps a visit of our facilities, see where your money is spent".

"Maybe when I have more time. My investments are in people like yourself, what they do with it I leave to them, a tour would be nice but I doubt I'd understand it anyway. I'll call you if I find anything".

"Till next time then, I'll show you to your car".

This little incident where old man Grimm knew who he was, without being able to see, told him to be more careful around people he had met before. His physical appearance he was sure would fool even the closest of acquaintances masking any other recognisable traits except the need for perhaps disguising his voice a little. He had for years adopted a way of covering the rough London accent perhaps he should just let his voice go back to its natural tone, easier said than done he thought. He'd been putting on his posh voice for years, no one had heard him speak the old natural way since his early twenties.

The car took him to his City of London office, he had never met his manager Kevin Blackman and wanted to surprise him. He was more than pleased with his work. His reputation and presence, in the company of Conway Investments, lent an air of legitimacy that Alan craved.

He told the driver he would not be needed again that evening and to pick him up from home at ten tomorrow morning. He would take the tube to Edgeware and walk the short distance to his flat after his visit to see Kevin.

The office accommodation Kevin had selected was smaller than Alan expected, but then Kevin had always been thrifty in spending the company money. It was adequate for one and a secretary but would not be big enough if Alan wanted to move in as well. He would think about that. He owned the building anyway and could take what he wanted. Kevin had the rest of the building occupied with various leases so would let things stand as they were for the time being. He would work from home for now, perhaps that would be better anyway, he did not want to become too familiar with Kevin an outcome that day to day contact might encourage.

Kevin was sitting behind his desk updating the figures for his next report as Alan knocked and walked in. Having never met before, Kevin assumed it was a potential customer, he rose from his chair and extended his hand.

"Good afternoon sir, I'm Kevin Blackman, manager here, can I help you"?

Alan ignored the hand.

"You certainly can young man I'm Alan Mortimer, weren't you expecting me"?

Kevin was obviously taken by surprise, Alan's intention. He sat down with a thump his hand still held out in front.

"Oh.....I am sorry sir I didn't know you were coming in today please have a seat".

Alan lowered his hand and stood again just as Alan sat in the one chair available.

"Can I get you anything, I only have coffee or perhaps a juice I think".

"No lad don't worry yourself I don't need anything and you can sit down".

Alan sat yet again feeling embarrassed by his reaction.

"I was preparing next week's returns things are looking better every week do you want to see sir".

"I'm only here to pick up my note books from the safe the ones I sent you last year".

Kevin made to stand.

"Leave it for now you can get it when I go. Enough of the sir, call me Alan when we are alone together and Mr Mortimer if we are in company, okay".

"Yes sir, Mr...errr, Alan. It doesn't seem right somehow you being the boss like".

"Don't fret you'll get used to it. If you do your job well you will hardly see me, if you fuck up, I'll let you know for sure. So far you have been better than I could have hoped. Is there anything you need or want that might need my approval"?

"Not that I can think of everything runs smoothly and I enjoy following the market like you requested. I don't like to ask is everything ok with Westfields, it is a considerable investment are we at risk"?

"I've been down there today it's all fine nothing to affect our shareholding and income".

"Good, I was worried about it when Mr Grimm told me of the break in".

"I'll work from home for now, I may ask you to do some extra work, out of hours or weekends sometimes over and above what you do now. Perhaps a secretary or personal assistant would help".

"I've managed fine I do have a girl come in two or three days to do the printing and mailing at the end of each month, perhaps if I ask she would do more".

"Do that, I'll leave it to you, I don't want your excellent work to slide because I make extra demands on your time, see if she will do full time, is she competent"?

"Oh yes she can use the computer and understands accounts".

"Get her on board you will need her later. How is the flat and the car"?

"Great, both are super".

"Fine and you are managing on your salary"

"Oh yes, my girlfriend and I are saving to get married this job enables me to put some by every month".

"Well you have earned it; good results and loyalty are what I like and are difficult to come by. Give yourself a two grand bonus, I'll send you a memo to that effect, and a two grand per year raise as well. I reward hard work. Now get me my note books".

"Yes sir, damn! I mean Alan thank you sir".

Kevin was on a cloud, rooted to the spot dithering which was far from normal for him.

"Go on don't keep me hanging about I might change my mind".

Kevin recovered at once, shot into the outer office and came back with a small package. He handed it to Alan who this time was the one to hold out his hand.

Kevin took the hand offered which Alan closed tightly pulling him very close

"Remember Kevin, loyalty and obedience, you will go far with me. I'll be in touch carry on".

Kevin was slightly shocked by the intimate exchange but, was excited by the outcome of his first contact.

Alan left with his book of names and information from days gone by. There will be some surprised faces when he calls in some favours owed that they thought were long forgotten. He walked out of the office strolled towards St Pauls tube en route for his apartment in Edgeware Road.

He stripped to his underwear put on his old dressing gown neatly hanging in the wardrobe, poured a large glass of lemonade, grabbed a packet of chocolate biscuits he found in the well stocked cupboards, and finally moved to the large armchair facing the window. His first call was to and old friend the private detective Joseph Mallard.

"Hello, could I speak to Mr Mallard please".

Alan recognised the voice of Jenny Franks Joseph's secretary come girlfriend introducing the *Mallard Detective Agency,* he put on an exaggerated accent to disguise his voice.

"Can I say who's calling"?

"An old friend, name of Alan".

"Just one moment sir".

"Mallard here who is this"?

"Hello Joe, wondered if you are busy, have a little job for you".

"Bloody hell, Toby Jones I thought you were long gone, how the devil are you and more to the point where are you"?

"It's Alan Mortimer here and now, back in town me old mate, the other guy is long gone like you said dead and buried".

"Same old, same old devious as ever, what can I do you for *Mr Mortimer* sir"?

"I need a bit of your expertise in finding someone, I don't have a name yet, but I see you are still in business from what the delightful miss Jenny said, so are you up for it".

"It's what I do, of course I am, what's with the Alan Mortimer tag"?

"You'll see, I'll text you the names later, then meet you tomorrow morning, to see what you've found, at ten Henrys Café if it's still there".

"It is, some things never change".

"Bye Joe till tomorrow".

Chapter 41

The ringing phone woke Fred Mann from his nap, he glanced at the mantle clock not really taking in the time, no one ever rang much he was not expecting a call and hoped the kids were alright.

"Hello, Mann here".

"Well if it isn't my old friend Manny, I bet you didn't expect to hear from me again".

Fred's heart skipped a beat and then made up for it by jumping from a resting sixty to ninety in an instant, beads of sweat appeared as if by magic on his forehead.

"Bloody hell! Toby......what do you want.....I thought you was a million miles away".

Fred and Toby came to be acquaintances as young men when drinking in the same pub in Camberwell. They were mates if not real friends. Drinking, playing snooker, darts and the odd card school were what they did together.

Fred trusted Toby even though he knew he sailed close to the wind when it came to his earning a living. He was more than generous, always had plenty of cash and did not seem to go to work much.

As a young policeman Fred followed his seniors and was encouraged by them in their dubious ways of operating. Many officers mixed socially with the criminal element who were often informants. Fred thought this was normal and approved; he naively slipped into their nefarious ways.

Toby had his ear to the ground of the criminal fraternity and often helped Constable Fred Mann with information which he in turn passed on to his DI.

The relationship slowed then stopped altogether when Fred moved to Basingstoke and became a sergeant. Toby Jones contacted Fred some years later for information concerning a case at his station, which for various reasons, he was obliged to hand over. Fred retired soon after to avoid being detected in his disloyalty and possible prosecution for corruption. Toby had left the Country at the same time, Fred thought that was the last of him, till today.

"Have no fear Fred nothing much, just some names".

"I've retired so don't think I can help any more".

"I know, I know, I'm sure you still speak to your old colleagues now and then. I just want to know who are the prime suspects in the Westfields break in, on your old beat isn't it . Make a couple of calls will you, I'll ring you in an hour".

Alan (Toby as was in Fred's mind) hung up leaving Fred a little shaken. This man from his past will never give him peace. IIe will have to comply he had too much on him to risk his wrath, he knew what he had done to others and could do to him or his family if he was crossed. He picked up the handset and dialled.

An hour later to the minute the phone rang again.

"Yes, what do you have"?

"Two names Clinton Macaulay and Jim Quarrel, both London lads, they are on the run or hiding out somewhere, the others are in custody or under surveillance, that's all I know".

"Thanks, Manny, check your post later this week".

He was gone, but for how long? Fred Mann did not want to go through all that again, being afraid that his friends and colleagues finding out he was not what they thought. What could he do, what would he do? Nothing.

Alan called Joseph straight away and gave him the names. If anyone could find them Joseph Mallard could.

At ten precisely Joseph arrived at the Café Henry, he looked for Toby but he was nowhere to be seen, he moved to a table near the rear, took a seat that faced the door and waited. The waitress came over he ordered a coffee no milk, and a double fried egg sandwich. He always ate when he could, you never knew when you would get the chance with his line of work. A few minutes later a tall man came through the doorway the light from outside around his silhouette obscured his vision preventing Joseph from seeing his features. It looked like Toby at first glance but as he moved towards the back of the café the ceiling lights showed him not to be his old friend. The man moved to Josephs table and indicated the chair opposite.

"Do you mind if I sit here"?

Joseph was not sure what to make of this fellow, had he been sent by Toby or was it something else.

"Actually, I'm expecting someone if you don't mind".

"Yes, I know you are".

It dawned the voice, the swagger.

"Fucking Holy Moses, is that you under there"?

"Yes, what do you think"?

"Alan Mortimer wow. It is brilliant, bet that cost an arm and a leg".

"Don't be funny, it took some doing".

"I'll bet, so when did you get here, where are you staying, are you back in business"?

"One question at a time please, a few days ago, a new London flat and yes I am. Questions from me now just two though who are they, and where are they"?

"Clinton Macaulay a loan shark and general no good villain, Jim Quarrel his side kick and number two".

"I sort of remember their names but never came across them, go on".

"Both have gone to ground, one of their team has died from radiation burns, the others are being followed by the London C.I.D. They will be taken in soon. Don't know where Quarrel has gone I'm waiting on mobile phone cell data, he is always calling his dad, when he makes the call I'll be able to track him but nothing yet. I've had better luck with Macaulay though, he has the use of a cottage, owned by his aunt, in Surrey, he and Quarrel used to play there as kids, he is not in any of his usual haunts and the police are watching his flat. They can't know about the cottage though or they would have been all over him".

Joseph gave Alan a piece of folded paper.

"It's all in here, with directions to the cottage, it's a bit out of the way".

" Just the job Joe, just one more thing, I want you to take a trip to Manchester using my name, put yourself about a bit. Here is the train ticket, my credit card and pin. The details of hotel and what you have to do are in here too, and little something for your trouble. Just be me for a day or so".

"I can do that, you look more like me now than you did before it should be fun".

Joseph spotted the waitress coming with his coffee and egg sandwich.

"Do you want something....err Alan"

"No thanks mate, I'll be off. Ta for this".

Alan said waving the precious piece of paper.

"I don't know how you get all this stuff, enjoy your breakfast, I'll call you".

Joseph had a peek in his envelope, a broad smile crossed his face as he tucked into his breakfast.

Chapter 42

He sat in his car two hundred yards from the cottage at the far end of the village. He'd pulled off the road into a quiet layby waiting for the final remnants of daylight to fade into shadow. The constant drizzle and cold wind had kept everyone indoors, even ardent dog walkers had hurried their mutts along at full speed, without objection, back to the warmth and sanctuary of their homes.

Alan moved slowly towards his target, eyes alert for any who had braved the cold and damp , he saw none. All was silent except for the trees moaning at the wind and the wind whistling back. A feint glow from the cottage windows grew brighter as he approached broadcasting the presence of his quarry.

Clinton Macaulay lazed in his armchair half way to sleep pleased with his day. The man from the medical company had certainly expressed an interest in the stones when he had finally got hold of him. He was annoyed at first for being called at all but softened when he heard what Clinton had for him. He was peeved that the stones had not been part of the original offer but accepted the lie that Clinton had only just acquired them. He wanted to see and evaluate them before agreeing a price. Clinton agreed to meet him tomorrow where he expected to get twenty or thirty thousand maybe even more, he would play hard, he was sure they were worth a lot more but just wanted rid so in the end he knew he would accept whatever he could get. With the thought of an extra twenty grand in his pocket he drifted off dreaming how he would spend it.

Alan could see his man, through the half drawn curtains covering the small paned windows, apparently asleep. He moved away from the window around to the side creeping passed the door to the kitchen along the edge of the extension conservatory to the rear of the property. The double glazed patio doors were shut tight but the small window to the side was an older style single glazed pane left slightly open. Alan squeezed his gloved hand into the small gap lifted the restraining bar opening the window fully. He cleared the windowsill of some cardboard packets and a glass jar to one side, eased his legs over one at a time being careful not to catch the rope, draped over his shoulder, on the window handle. He stood for a few moments letting his eyes become accustomed to the low light. He saw he was in in a small utility room. No light showed from under the door so he slowly opened it to reveal the hall where the front door and two others, one closed and one open, presented themselves. He moved silently into the hall and saw the opened door led to an empty kitchen. The closed door was obviously the one to the lounge where Clinton Macaulay lay resting. Alan moved to the wall adjacent to the door listening intently for signs of movement. No sound reached his alert ears except the rustling of the wind in the trees outside. He stood close to the door now hand poised ready, remembering the position of the chair from his earlier brief view through the window, his hand closed round the door knob slowly turning; a feint click as the latch disengaged, he froze, a long silence followed. He gently opened the door and moved swiftly and silently into the room. The glow from a table lamp in the corner barely illuminated the room. The log burner contained the remnants of a fire which had almost died through lack of attention, its residual heat having warmed the room inducing the relaxed slumber that had overtaken Clinton.

Alan stood behind the chair the thin chord wrapped around both hands the loop created hung poised above the sleeping man's head. Alan struck like a snake, the twine bit into the neck pulling the head tight to the back of the chair cutting off the air in an instant.

Clinton woke clutching at his throat instinctively, for a second unaware of his dire situation, his hands grabbed in vain at the restraining collar. Unable to get his fingers behind the tight chord, he panicked screaming silently his sight fading as the oxygen starved brain lost the fight to stay aware. Alan released his grip just enough for him to gulp in life giving breaths but not enough to move. Again he tried to get his fingers behind the rope restraint but Alan tightened once more, lent forward his lips an inch from Clinton's ear.

"Keep still and listen. I want a straight answer to two questions or next time I won't let go. You have one chance do you understand"?

He relaxed the chord enough for him to answer through the gasps for air.

"Who the ...hell ....are you...what.... do you want"?

"Do you understand, last chance"?

The chord began to press ...

"Yes. Yes, what do you want to know"?

"That's better. Where are the stones and who did you sell the lab equipment to"?

Clinton did not want to tell this guy anything but the ever present noose made him think twice. He'd give up the name but would try and negotiate for the stones.

"Morgan Banks they took the kit I don't know any names though".

"And the stones"?

"Look we can do a deal, you don't realise what...".

The noose tightened yet again.

"It's now or never speak up".

"Fuck…..in the …kitchen….in…..the….oven…."The words erupted between coughing fits.

Securing the noose behind the chair tight enough to hold the head in place with just enough slack for Clinton to breathe, Alan used his rope to bind the arms and body to the chair and wrapped his legs with the left over end of the rope. He was going nowhere.

Alan went to the kitchen and came back with the bag containing the stones. He moved round in front of Macaulay held out the bag.

"You did good there, now where is the money you got from Morgan Banks"?

"I don't have any money".

"I know you bloody don't, I have it here".

Alan held up the packet of notes he had found.

"In the freezer I ask you, you've no imagination".

"You, you bastard wait till I get out of here I'll….."

Alan applied the noose this time tight and permanent. He leaned close to his ear and spat the last words Clinton would ever hear.

"Yes mate I am a bastard, no one steals from me or mine. No one".

Ten minutes later Alan removed the rope and noose, returned to the utility room closed the window, replaced the items on the ledge cleaned the floor of footprints and left by the back double doors.

Chapter 43

Alan called Westfields and arranged to meet William Grimm at a coffee shop in Basingstoke town centre. He was sitting in the furthest corner table with his favourites, a large mocha and a chocolate muffin when William walked through the swing door.

He waved to attract his attention and stood as he arrived by the table his hand extended in greeting.

"Hello, William good of you to meet me here, I like to indulge now and again".

Pointing at his as yet un-eaten cake and signalling to the waitress for attention.

"What would you like"?

William released his hand from the overtight grip.

"Hello Alan".

He turned to the waitress.

"Black coffee, no cake thank you. Why here Alan instead of my office"?

"Sometimes a bit of informality is best and I do like a good muffin. Besides I have something for you that you may not want seen at the factory".

Alan passed the bag of stones across the table a few inches from Williams resting hands. William reached forward and peered into the bag.

"Are these what I think they are"?

"I suppose".

"Where the hell did you get them. No, no I don't want to know, you must take them to the police".

"I can't do that they will want to know where they came from. Needless to say, they took some finding and I don't want to reveal how I came by them. All I know is if you feed them gradually into your experimental system programme you will save a lot of time and money and no one will be the wiser. After all they were yours in the first place".

He could see the look of disbelief William was giving him but pressed him anyway.

"Look, take them and think about it. If you must take them to the police yourself, be very prepared for a lot of questions though. I of course will deny ever having seen them so be careful".

"I thought I knew you, but I don't. I have no idea what you are about or who you really are Alan, but I do know you make me feel uncomfortable".

"I may not have had the upbringing you enjoyed William, for my school was the streets of south London, I may be a bit rough round the edges because of that but I do have all our interests at heart. I am your friend, I care about your company and its future, just remember that. If you really don't want to use them just walk away and forget about it. I will support you to get back up to speed any way you want.

William Grimm had little choice, this situation presented to him was a lifesaver he would never have expected. This man was far from honest and he couldn't imagine how he had recovered the stones but knew Alan obviously moved in circles far removed from those of the Grimm family. His father had cut corners here and there in building their company but nothing in this league. He rationalised; the deed was already done, if he accepted or desisted, he could say nothing to anyone about this meeting making him complicit in approving Alan's actions. He picked up the bag and left without touching his coffee. He turned at the door and mouthed a '*thankyou*' to his nefarious benefactor.

Alan sat back and hummed to himself as he bit into his chocolate muffin and washed it down with a swig of his creamy mocha.

One part of William was shocked, the other pleased to have back the very thing that would put things back on track. For the company to progress to where he had dreamed it would go he needed the things in the bag, the bag that at the moment felt like a lead weight. Vera had died because of these bloody things he should inform the police, but they would keep them as evidence that would delay the project. He was torn, Dad would have no doubts what should be done but Dad had long since lost the desire that still burned in William's mind. He wanted to be the first to make a definitive treatment for as yet uncontrolled cancers. He decided to sleep on it but in his heart he already knew what he was going to do.

The following morning William Grimm began the process of reasserting his program of trials. The first step was to call in all the technicians involved and laid out his plans. The normal supplier and treatment company were unable to fill their immediate requirement but they would continue to use them in the long term. He explained how he had secured a source of some diamonds and emeralds reworked to their original specifications from an alternative company that would be available very soon. The new program of trials would begin almost at once.

No one doubted the boss or questioned his source. For sure all were pleased to be carrying on working as they had feared for their jobs.

He had lab two set up ready for the first batch which he said he would have in a couple of days. Lab one's door was still under repair but he wanted that made ready also, to be operational as soon as the door was fixed.

Mathew Walker was in charge of lab one but in order to speed up the preparation was instructed to help with the setting to work of lab two.

Matt was concerned; where the hell had the boss found another supplier, he knew that the skills demanded to make these stones were in very short supply. In fact, he had been tasked some years ago to see if the process could be carried out by any company other than the one they already used without success. So where had the boss gone, maybe overseas.

A few days went by and Matt had been so busy he had not given it a second thought until Mr Grimm handed him a package with six crystal stones. Two diamonds, two emeralds, one quartz and one amethyst. The deviation figures for the angle the cuts were hand written on a single sheet, not the full specification that normally came with each stone. Where had these come from?

He reassembled the experiment as per the test program of two weeks before. He noticed the coating on one of the emeralds had a mark which exactly matched the clamp used to secure it in position. It was then he knew the crystals he had been given were not new, he had seen them before. How in heavens name had Mr Grimm been able to retrieve them. Glad to have the means to carry on the work he did not want to dig too deep but his natural curiosity caused him to speculate.

He exhausted every possibility in his mind and came up with only one logical explanation; William must have paid a ransom to the thieves for the return of the stones. What was he going to do about it? Nothing.

James Grimm was walking up the steps of Westfields with the help of his driver. William had kept him informed of the troubles but yesterday he was very evasive concerning the return to work of the experimental team. He wanted to judge for himself what was going on.

"Hey Dad, nice to see you up and about",

He took his father's arm and thanked the driver.

"Shall we go to the office or would you like to have a coffee in the canteen"?

"Morning William, a coffee would be good".

He led him through the doors through the kitchen area to the small canteen area. He sat him at a table and proceeded to collect two coffees from the ever-ready machine against the far wall. There were a few employees having a break, who voiced their greeting to 'Mr James' as they came and went. James knew nearly everyone by their first names and was enjoying this part of his visit but wasn't sure that he would feel the same when he questioned his son later.

"Here we go Dad".

Putting his hand to the cup.

"Is there some reason for the visit or are you just on an outing"?

"Thanks. No special reason really, but I would like to know how everyone here is dealing with the aftermath of the break in and the tragic death of young Vera. I still don't know how her family are coping, is there anything more we can do for them"?

"Everyone is knuckling down just fine, we should be back on track soon. Vera's parents are obviously devastated, we have offered financial and other support, but they have declined to accept. They are still angry and just need time to grieve. Unfortunately, her body has not been released yet for the funeral, the police cannot promise a date but say they will not delay any longer than necessary".

"I'll go around, if you think that will be okay".

"Not now Dad, they are still in shock and have not accepted their loss yet".

"How is Horace bearing up"?

"He is out of hospital now, says he wants to come back to work. We'll see him alright".

"That's good, let him come back when he's ready, he'd be bored stiff staying at home. Any chance I can go to the labs, are we up and running "?

"Sure, no problem, the guys are setting up at the moment, the radiation source is still secured so you won't have to dress up in protective gear".

"What are you going to do about the lasers without the crystals"?

A direct question which William had avoided answering during earlier discussions.

"I have probably been able to find an alternative supplier, I will know later, you don't need to worry about that Dad, I'll get it sorted".

Another evasion, James let it go for now.

"Good, shall we go up"?

William guided his father to the lift and went to the upper floor laboratories. They went into the first laboratory, it was empty of personnel; they had already completed preparation.

"Looks like we are ready to go here, shall we move on next door".

Although James could not navigate well in strange places, he was familiar enough with the layout of the laboratories to form a picture of where he was. His peripheral vision was still working, to a certain extent, in his right eye and by squinting and leaning his head to one side he had an outline view of the equipment set up he and his son had designed some years before. He took his son's arm and followed him to the next lab. It was a busy place with several technicians beavering away setting up the laser bed and connecting the computer monitoring sensors as well as a number of safety guards. When the two entered, work stopped for a moment, all saying their good mornings before returning to their current task. James spoke first.

"Good morning everyone don't let us stop you please carry on".

At that moment Williams mobile beeped, he looked at the incoming message.

"Look Dad I have to go down I have a meeting and my visitor has arrived".

He went to take his father's arm to guide him to the door. James shrugged him off gently.

"You go son, I'll stay here for a bit, one of the lads will help me down later. I'll come by your office before I leave".

William was reluctant to leave him but did not want to cause a stir in front of everyone.

"Fine. I'll see you in a while".

William left for his meeting, one of the technicians brought James a chair".

"Please sit here sir".

"Thanks".

James sat and listened to the noise of a laboratory being prepared for work, a sound he was familiar with and one he liked.

Mathew Walker watched his bosses arrive at his workplace, he was hidden behind the computer screen and stayed that way until William left. He sat up on his departure knowing that the elder Grimm would not be able to see him. He wondered how much Mr James knew of the situation. He had it in his mind that the former company leader would not allow doubtful actions to occur but wanted to know for sure. He rose and moved over to where James was sitting.

"Hello Mr James, is there anything I can do for you"?

"Oh, hello is that you Matt"?

"Yes sir".

"Good. Good, how close are you to being set up here, next door seems ready to go"?

"We are almost there a couple of hours should see it done. We will be ready to fit the crystals then and start the run tomorrow morning".

James was surprised.

"How come you have some crystals I thought they were all stolen"?

"Maybe there were some left the robbers missed I don't know he didn't say but these are the ones that Mr William gave me. I'm not sure how though he says he will have a full set soon maybe from abroad. I know there will be none available from our normal source here in the UK, well not for some time anyway".

James remained quiet his normal smile had faded it was obvious to Matt that William had not kept his father in the picture.

"William is quite resourceful, I'm surprised he could go abroad and achieve replacements in such a short time. The quality is so important I hope they are up to spec".

"Oh, these stones are excellent sir, exact replicas of the originals identical in every way".

Matt knew he was sowing the seeds of doubt in James Grimm's mind he would say no more but wait and see what develops.

"Well good luck with the next runs Matt I'll be going now".

"Thank you, sir nice of you to visit".

rMatt asked one of his colleagues to assist James to the lift and down to the first floor office of his son. He then went down to the canteen he wanted to make a call out of earshot of his colleagues.

Chapter 44

Unit one. "Suspect is on the move" The uniformed officer reporting that George was leaving his house had only been on duty half an hour of his expected all-nighter, when George Brown set off for his meeting.

Unit two. "Understood, no movement here".

D C Peter Andrews responded. He also had only recently taken over from Keith Crane from his watch on the Carter brothers.

Unit one. "I Will follow at a distance subject on foot".

George was going to see his sister Megan, he wanted to borrow her car. She only lived a ten minute walk away, he needed the car to get to the meet, he knew she wouldn't mind, he always gave her petrol money or filled up before he returned it. He was oblivious of the pair of officers following; the payment he was going to collect was uppermost on his mind.

Unit one. "Subject has entered number twenty, Grove Road, his sister's house. Stand by".

Unit two. "Standing by no change here yet".

Peter turned to his driver.

"I thought something was going to happen there, we are probably in for a long night. Wait a minute someone's coming out".

The two Carter brothers left the house and climbed into their car unaware of their watchers.

Unit two. "We have suspects Carter on the move in car grey Vauxhall, Lima Tango six two Delta Lima Foxtrot, heading south on Forest road. Will follow".

Unit one. "Understood standing by".

Jonny Musgrove heard the calls, he'd been waiting for the suspects to mobilise all day it sounded like this could be the time. George came out of his sister's house and climbed into the driver's seat her car.

Unit one. "Suspect Brown on the move in red Ford fiesta Beta Alfa five six King Juliet November heading east on Downs Road. Am following".

Unit two. "Understood".

Jonny had been listening to the exchanges between the two cars he hit the press to talk button.

"Unit *five.* "Well it looks like this is it lads, be careful these men are dangerous and will not want to be caught. As soon as we have an idea where they are going I will dispatch units three and four. Happy hunting and wear your vests before you go anywhere near this lot. Out".

Both units followed their respective suspect vehicles, their radio reports indicating they were heading south and west. Twenty minutes later all four cars were on the M25 South section heading west towards the M4. Jonny dispatched units three and four from Basingstoke up the A33 ready to intercept. He followed close behind. Before leaving he called Toni on her mobile and told her what was going down.

"Don't fret Jonny I'm tuned in, bring them home and stay safe".

Unit one. "Suspects have left M25 heading along M4 west".

Unit two. "Still on M25 we are a few minutes behind you. Suspect indicating to follow the same route".

Unit five. "Units three and four head along A33 towards M4 Reading junction halt eight miles south of M4 Junction wait for further instructions".

Unit three. "Understood".

Unit four. "Understood".

Unit One. "Suspect turned off M4 heading south on A33. Now passing through village of Spencer's Wood. Wait. Suspect slowing indicating right turn and has entered narrow lane. We are passing by the turn off now and have lost sight of suspect car. Sat Nav. indicates track is a no through route to a farm. Will turn and park out of sight".

Unit two. "Approaching Spencer's Wood subject five hundred yards ahead. Now turning up same lane will stop and wait this side of lane".

Unit five. "Units three and four rendezvous with unit one south of lane, I'll be with you in two minutes, everyone hang fire".

The four police cars were parked in a side street away from the main A33 about five hundred yards short of the lane leading to the farm. The car of unit 2 was parked outside a general store on A33 north side of the turn off. DC Peter Andrews left the uniformed driver in the car and walked towards the lane.

"This is DC Andrews. Have left vehicle and approaching turn off on foot".

Jonny climbed out of his car and approached the other vehicles.

"Wait here be ready to move. On my signal, Unit one will move and park just short of the lane, Unit three to drive down the lane, unit four will reverse into the lane blocking the exit. Unit two stay as you are. Driver officers will remain in their cars all others will attend outside their vehicles ready to apprehend suspects should they try to resist, which they probably will, so take extra care. One or all could be armed so I don't want any heroics. DC Andrews and I are going down the lane on foot, will report progress. Radio silence till my call. Out".

Jim Quarrel had been sitting on a log in a small uncluttered space outside the old barn. This farm had been deserted for years. Most of the land had been acquired by developers and had been built on. The original farmhouse was a ruin and the barn was the only place left standing. The village of Spencer's Wood had encroached far enough when the local council had called a halt to further development. What was left of the farm had lain like this for nearly ten years. No one ever came here much just a few kids and the odd courting couple. The van they had set fire to a few days ago lay a black shell in the far corner looking like it had been there for years and would soon be overgrown by the ever invasive brambles which surrounded the circular clearing. He arrived early forgetting the journey would be much quicker on his motor bike than by car. His helmet and leather jacket lay over the seat of the Yamaha parked out of sight inside the barn. The three packets of cash in his backpack. He was looking forward to getting away. His attention was drawn to the sound of a car coming up the narrow lane, he stood and backed out of sight into the barn. He watched the car pull in and turn ready to leave. He did not recognise the red Fiesta so waited a few moments before revealing himself. He saw George illuminated by the lights of the car as he got out and stretched his arms above his head. Jim stepped into view.

"George over here".

"Oh, there you are, thought I was the first, where's your car"?

"I came on the bike too much traffic otherwise and I like to give it a ride now and then. Who's car you in"?

"My sisters".

The both turned together as the lights of another car approaching up the lane took their attention.

"That'll be the Carters".

George walked towards the grey Vauxhall as is came to a halt next to the Ford.

Jim stayed back until he was sure it was the brothers. They emerged together and closed in on George. Manny shook his hand and Geoff slapped him on the back. They looked round and saw Jim walking towards them. Geoff demanded.

"We all here then, where's Macaulay"?

Jim shook both their hands,

"He can't make it, he's doing a deal with the Jewels today. Sent me with the money though. Said there would be a bonus later depending on what he gets for them".

Jim slipped the back pack from his shoulders to the ground between his feet. He reached in and drew out the packs of cash he gave one to George and threw the other two to the brothers. George just put it in his pocket as did Geoff. Manny however opened the packet and started counting out the notes.

"It's all there Manny, Clinton wouldn't let you down".

"I know. I know, it's that I just like to feel it".

Jonny and Peter were moving up the lane on opposite sides, the lights of the cars were visible a few yards ahead. They stopped just short hidden by the overhanging foliage. They could see four figures standing close together, one of the cars was facing down the lane and the other lighting up a large old barn. If they moved any closer the car lights would reveal their presence. Jonny decided it was now or never. He clicked the radio.

"Go. Go. Go".

The unit three car was upon them in a few seconds light ablaze. The officers on foot were a fraction behind.

Jonny stepped out and shouted.

"This is the police stay where you are, you are under arrest, keep your hands where we can see them".

The four men all turned towards the approaching police car lights and were rooted to the spot for a just a moment. They either didn't hear or decided to ignore

Jonny's order. Peter and Jonny were now running towards the four men.

George immediately made for his car, he was in and had the engine started before either Peter or Jonny could reach him. He put the car in gear and drove towards the incoming police vehicle. His exit was blocked but he failed to stop in time. The two cars crashed head on, by then Peter was at the car door he reached in and dragged the disorientated George out rolled him on his front and had the cuffs on him before he realised what had happened.

The two brothers were a little more canny and realised that their car was useless so decided to run down the lane. Manny was first and side-stepped Jonny as they were about to meet head on. Jonny reached out to grab his sleeve but was quickly shrugged off. Manny was quickly followed by Geoff who tried the same manoeuvre as his brother but Jonny was ready for him and rugby tackled him around the knees bring his large frame down with a crash. The falling bodies were both winded, Geoff tried to wriggle free but was pounced upon by two uniformed officers. He heard Manny yell as he ran headlong into three uniformed policemen. Jonny left them to deal with the struggling villains. He got up looking for the fourth man. Jim had acted quickly glad that he had come on his bike for the chances of escape by car were zero. He was out of sight of the coppers in the shadows of the barn. He toyed with the idea of using his bike to drive down the lane but dismissed it at once as he was unsure if there was enough room down the side of the cars. He envisaged that there would also be back-up cars and police in the road. His only chance of escape was to try and use the overgrown path at the back of the barn and circle round the old farmhouse. He had been there before so knew the route well enough but it was bound to be overgrown. No choice, it was do or die. His decision was made within a second of the sight of the police presence. And was soon clambering over the wood pile at the back of the barn to a hidden gap in the wall. He was through and dropped down to the old path his clothes catching on the brambles which seemed to be everywhere. He wished for the protection of his biker's gear resting on the back of his machine as he pushed his way forward in the near dark. His gloveless hands were being torn by the sharp spikes but he was oblivious to the pain in his attempt to escape.

Jonny ran into the barn, it was empty, not knowing which way his quarry had gone, he stood listening intently, the shouting from outside overpowering his ability to detect any hidden presence in the barn. Then he heard it, the single word.

"Shit"!

It came from outside the back of the barn, Peter ran out of the building round the left side. It was a mass of impassable shrubbery and brambles; the right side revealed the same obstruction behind a burnt out blackened van. Back inside he could see no way out but knew there must be one, he worked his way along the back wall with no sign of an exit. The mound of logs looked impassable but as he climbed up on the pile he saw the broken section. He quickly clambered to the top and dropped through without thinking. He met the same deadly thorns which had caused Jim Quarrels expletive. Jonny pulled the standard issue protective gloves from his side pocket, glad too of the vest he was wearing. He made his way forward using the gloves to protect his face. Now further away from the commotion on the other side of the barn he could hear the rustle of movement up ahead. There was little natural light to guide him, but the path ahead was being partially cleared for him, his route was flanked on either side by an impenetrable dark green mass.

Jim did not know if he was being followed or not but pressed on almost at the old farm building now just a few more yards. He stumbled over a pile of fallen bricks that had not been there before, he swore picked himself up and was standing in what would have been one of the farmhouse rooms, he'd forgotten which. Clear of the overgrown pathway, there was enough light for him to see where he was. He paused to catch his breath and listen. He wiped his sweating brow with the back of his hand not realising he was covering his face with blood. The stinging sensation in his hands and face began to filter passed the adrenalin fed fright and flight instinct his brain had been operating on for the last few minutes. He swore as the pain registered, and the fact that he had no idea where to go next made him sag at the knees.

His mind was made up for him as Jonny emerged from the path running at full tilt flooring Jim with his shoulder. Jonny turned him onto his side put the hand cuffs on one wrist but Jim pushed round releasing the other hand, slippery with blood, free from Jonny's grasp. To no avail Jonny pushed him back down onto his bloody face, knelt in the middle of his back grabbed the flailing arm and snapped the second half of the cuffs closed.

"You are under arrest". Was all he could get out having been winded for the second time. He would read him his rights later when he found out who he was.

Jonny made Jim stand and pushed him back the way they had come, two officers helped him back through the hole in the wall he didn't know which of the villains he had captured as it was too dark but four had all been apprehended. He hadn't seen anyone else so wondered who was missing. In the light of the cars Jonny saw that he had Jim Quarrel, so it was Clinton Macaulay who was missing, still four out of five not a bad day's work.

Each of the captives were transported back to Basingstoke in separate cars. Jonny arranged for a forensic team to visit the site, he was especially interested in the cars, motorbike and the burnt out van.

Toni was sitting in her office with a big smile on her face, her team had done well. Her turn next. She would let Jonny tackle George Brown again as he was familiar with him and was the obvious weak member of this team. She would have at Quarrel with Melanie. The two Carters would come later. She did not know what forensics would find at the meeting site but did not want to delay the initial interviews. Compton would keep the interviewers up to speed if anything was discovered.

"You and June take on Brown again, caution him and see what you can get have a word with his lawyer before. Mel and I will tackle Quarrel this time".

"Thanks guv, I presume finding Macaulay is our prime objective"?

"Not only that Jonny, I want to know who abducted Verity and threw her in that cupboard to die".

"Right you are, meet here in thirty or so Ma'am"?

"Fine, that should be long enough to see where we are heading".

Chapter 45

George Brown was sitting in the interview room again, not quite the same circumstances as before. His solicitor Cyril Maxwell had no idea how out of depth he was. He had spoken to his boss who told him to play it by ear, no help at all from him. He decided to advise George to answer their questions as he thought this would give him the best chance. Not bad advice even if it came about through ignorance. He had listened to the officers and their offer to be lenient if he came clean. He would make to intervene when he felt George was being overwhelmed or might incriminate himself, after all George was guilty of some of the charges, he had admitted as much to Cyril, but not necessarily the more serious ones. George wasn't completely naive but was easily led and a little bit simple at times.

Jonny entered the room with June. George had already been charged and had been read his rights, he introduced everyone present and repeated them for the tape. When the preliminaries had been completed June started the questioning along the lines that her and Jonny had agreed.

"Now George the charges against you are very serious and may see you spend many years in prison after your trial. Telling us the truth now can only make things go better for you. Please run through what happened on that Friday when you broke into Westfields".

Cyril decided that he would do his best for his client but considering the circumstances of his arrest and the pending charges he didn't hold out much hope. A full confession at this stage would not be good as he may need to bargain a little to illicit some leniency later. The officers offer needed to be on record so decided to open the proceedings.

"My client is prepared to cooperate but wishes to point out that he was only asked to drive the vehicles and was not involved in the criminal activities that took place before or during the said break in".

"I have listened to what your solicitor has just stated and if that is true perhaps some of the more serious charges may be reconsidered, but you must tell us all you know before we can offer that as an option".

George looked at his young solicitor who nodded for him to go ahead. He turned reluctantly looked at the nice lady copper who smiled at him, maybe she could get him off with doing less prison time if he told her everything, but what about Macaulay and the Carters, they would break his legs if he did. He needed to be sure he would go to a different prison or he was a dead man.

"Look I will tell you what I can but I want to know that if I go to prison it must be in a different one to the others, they will kill me if they knew I'd said anything".

"What you say here will not be made known to them from me. If necessary we will ensure your safety by placing you in a secure unit well away from anyone who may be a threat. These people did a terrible thing that you tell me you were not aware of. If true we will put them away for a long time, you could be out long before them and make a new life for yourself. Let us start with Clinton Macaulay, do you know where he is"?

"No idea he didn't come to the meeting place as expected, Jim said he was trying to sell the jewels so couldn't come".

June was now about to put doubt into Georges mind by stretching the facts a little.

"I think he knew you would be caught that is why he didn't turn up, how did we know where you would be meeting. Maybe he was the one who tipped us off and dropped you in it".

"Why would he do that it must be someone else".

"There isn't anyone else think about it; saves him sharing the proceeds from the sale of the stones with you".

"Bloody bastard do you think he would do that, even to his mate Quarrel, what a shithead".

"I'm sure he is looking after himself and doesn't give a toss about you. Now George tell us about what happened on that night".

He looked at his solicitor who nodded for him to go ahead. The police lady was smiling waiting for him to speak, he knew he was in a hole and had no other way. If he wanted to reduce his time in prison he had to give it up now.

"I suppose I don't have much choice do I. It started when Jim and me came down from London by car, it was my job to drive that's all. Clinton was there with the Carters, they had the girl in the back of their car. They sent her up the steps to the door. She opened it and the old guy came to meet her. They talked a bit then went out of my sight. Jim got out and he and Clinton went into the building along with Manny and Geoff. I could not see what happened after that. About ten or fifteen minutes later they all came out. Clinton got in his car, Manny and Geoff got in their car then Jim told me to drive. We went to a layby up the A33 and waited with the others. We were there a long time I don't know how long I fell asleep. Jim and me went back later and collected the van. Clinton took something out of the van and put it in his car, I didn't see what it was I was too far away. Manny took our car and Geoff left in theirs for the meeting place, Clinton drove off. Jim and me went in the van to the train station to collect another car, it was gone, Jim was really mad about that at first but later he said that there were no trains so it was alright. We went to the meeting place. The brothers were there waiting for us. Jim gave them some money and they left together in their car. We stayed a while to burn the van and left for home in our car. That's everything I can remember".

Jonny had been listening quietly letting June's soft approach deal with George. He had learnt a little more about that night but now decided to step in to gain some more solid information concerning Verity".

"That is good George but I'd like you to tell us a little about who brought the girl to the site and what happened to her".

"I've already said haven't I, it was the Carters who had her in their car".

"Was she tied up in any way"?

"She was when she got out, but Jim went over and undid her. He spoke to her and pointed to the door".

"Did she go to the door on her own"?

"Oh yes, she had to go by herself, the doorman would have been alarmed if she went up with one of us".

"How do you know that"?

"Jim said".

"What did Jim say"?

"He said the girl would do as she was told because the brothers had her mate".

"What do you think he meant by that"?

"They would hurt her friend if she didn't do as she was told".

"And you were happy with that"?

"No. No, I thought they were bluffing you know just frightening her they wouldn't really do anything".

"Where was her friend"?

"I don't know no one told me anything".

"When did you go in the building"?

"Not me I stayed with the car it was Clinton and Jim followed the girl in with the brothers".

"Who went where"?

"I didn't see where they went but Macaulay came out first, the brothers came out almost straight away too, then Jim came out on his own about ten minutes later, then we left".

"Where was the girl"?

"I don't know I didn't see her again".

"Didn't you think that strange, what do you think happened to her"?

"I didn't really think about it, suppose I assumed Jim had left her tied up somewhere inside".

"So, you did not care what happened to her"?

"I was driving I never thought about her".

"Shame that, your mate left her tied up alright, he didn't tell you where"?

"No he never mentioned her".

"She's dead you know and all of you are responsible".

"Bloody hell the bastard he never said nothing, I was only driving the car I never touched her. Shithead Quarrel he must've killed her there was no need for him to do that. I never did nothing I didn't even know she was there until we arrived".

"We will find out later how much you were involved. Now why did you have to wait so long at the layby why not drive the van back straight away"?

"That's cause the others had their job to do".

"What others, what job"?

"I don't know who they were, Ginger somebody or other, I think Jim said they were saving us from trouble".

"What trouble"?

"I've no idea he said it was better not to worry".

"You say you went back to get the van, who drove"?

"That was Jim I drove the car".

" Did you see anybody else"?

"No, we went back to the layby and Clinton unloaded the van, at least I think it was him, I was parked down one end so couldn't see much. It was dark and he had on a big coat and strange hat so I can't be sure".

"What happened then"?

"I've already said haven't I"

"Tell me again".

Jim and I went to the station in the van to find another car, it wasn't there so we went to the farm place on the A33. The brothers were there waiting for their money from Jim, we burnt the van and left in our car".

"What money, how much"?

"Jim paid everyone half up front and the rest at the later meeting, when Clint had sold the stuff. My share was two grand I don't know about the others.

"Where did you go next"?

"Back to London of course it was the middle of the night, I was knackered".

"What about the missing car"?

George did not want to mention their visit to Ginger's house and finding the cops all round the car. He'd only tell them if they asked.

"I don't know, I just waited around at home till I went to the farm for my money. I suppose I won't see that again will I"?

"I shouldn't think so, but you have done well enough for now. Interview terminated...".

Jonny closed off the interview and stopped the tape, there was little more to be gained at this time with George, he needed to talk to the boss before they tackled the brothers and Jim Quarrel. He would come back to George when the others had been interviewed. It was going to be a long haul, but they were very close to closing this one.

"Well done June you opened the door with him, at least we have an idea who did what and when".

"Thank you, sir, I don't think he was involved in abducting or hurting the girl but was certainly complicit in the robbery".

"We'll charge him later when things are clearer, the chief will run it by the CPS in any case it will be their call not ours. I'm going to see her now, you go and take a break".

Chapter 46

"Thanks Jonny I'm of the same mind as you I don't think George had any part in the abduction and death of Verity, but he was certainly well aware he was involved in a robbery. Prepare the case against him and I will pass it to the CPS. Before then we need to deal with the other three".

"Right boss, June and I will deal with Manny Carter first then his brother Geoff, I'll run them at the same time in adjacent rooms, play one off against the other".

"That's fine I will take on this Jim Quarrel he is the best link to our finding Macaulay, if either of us learns anything significant well stop and have a conflab, okay".

Toni and Melanie entered the interview room to find Jim Quarrel and his solicitor Reise Goldman facing them. A uniformed constable entered behind them and stood by the door. Melanie started the tape, read out the charges and restated his rights then each spoke their names for the recording. Toni opened the proceedings.

"Mr Quarrel you are in a precarious situation, here you are facing charges with enough evidence against you to ensure you are put you away for life. Is there anything you want to say that might give us cause to rethink"?

"My client denies these charges and will complain that he was assaulted and arrested without due cause by one of your officers".

"A robbery took place at Westfields where a man was severely injured, a young girl was killed, and a number of valuable items were stolen. During that robbery another man was exposed to a dangerous substance and has since died. I know you were certainly responsible for much of that, unless you can show me otherwise we will pass the evidence to the CPS. You will then go to court where you will for sure be held in custody pending trial".

"Hold on there you are a bit premature, you haven't heard my client's statement yet, he was not the only one there that night and was only following orders, he was under duress having been threatened with his life if he did not comply".

"Okay, let us hear this tale of woe".

Jim Quarrel cleared his throat and began, he had forgotten the statement his solicitor had prepared he thought it was stupid to pretend he was afraid of an unknown man who made him do the job, he'd bargain with the copper, a name for a reduction in charges.

"Look, no one was meant to get hurt it just went a bit wrong. It wasn't me that took the girl I never touched her".

"Who was it made you do this who were you afraid would harm you?"

Mr Goldman leaned forward towards Jim and put his hand in front of his face to stop him talking.

"My client is making statements that conflict with the advice I have given, please can I have a moment alone before we continue".

Jim pushed his arm away and pointed his finger at his solicitor's nose.

"Bug off, I'm not interested in your advice just sit and listen you can sort out the legal details after I've done".

Reise Goldman sat back open hands extended in submission eyes looking skyward in resignation. 'Another bloody idiot' the words that came to mind.

"I'm not afraid of anyone, I knew what I was doing but I was under orders. If I tell you who from what do I get out of it"?

"I presume you mean Clinton Macaulay"?

"How the fuck do you know about him"?

"We had a tip that you would all be at the farm, where do you think that came from".

"Nah, Nah he wouldn't we were off and clear someone else must have known where we were going to meet".

"Yes they did, it was me. Funny Macaulay wasn't there though, I wonder where he is now, Sunny Spain maybe with all that money from the stolen jewels".

"Look I know where he might be".

"So, tell me".

"Not so fast, what do I get out of it"?

"Revenge maybe. Now, let us find out a little more of who did what that night, then we can talk about the charges. When you went to the door the girl had already gone inside what happened after that"?

"She had the voice print and card to open all the doors. We went to the office behind reception and she opened the safe".

"Why did she do that"?

"The Carters had her friend tied up in her gaff I suppose she was afraid for her, we had no intention of hurting her mate but she thought we would".

"Where were the Carters and Macaulay"?

"The brothers had gone in to keep the security guard out of the way. I thought they had just tied him up, today is the first time I knew they'd bashed him one. Macaulay just stood in the foyer by the door, he told me to take the girl upstairs to open the lab door, he would stand guard".

"Why tie the girl's hands behind her back and why the hood and face tape"?

"Just in case she tried to run or set off some alarm, we didn't want her seeing ours face either".

"What happened when you got to the lab".

"I took off her hood and loosened the tape, she said she didn't feel well, then she bloody feinted on me, I tried to make her come round but she was out cold. I just put the tape and hood back. Tied up her feet and put her in the cupboard. I didn't hurt her at all, I thought she would come round later, she wasn't tied very tight so she probably could wriggle loose. She was okay when I left her".

"What about the doors she didn't open".

"I gave them a few hard kicks they weren't too strong the locks broke and it was done, an alarm went off so I legged it".

Toni was not going to reveal how Verity had died at this time or the fact that there had been a radiation hazard, it seemed Quarrel was unaware of both. She wanted Macaulay first before revealing all her cards.

"Right so you all left empty handed, what was the point"?

"Clinton said the lab was where the best money was and that we should use someone else to go in as it was too dangerous".

"That was Ginger and Tommy right".

"Geeze you buggers know everything don't you, why all the bloody questions when you already have all the sodding answers. Of course it bloody well was"?

"So, you knew that it was so dangerous that you and Clinton couldn't go in, so you let some other poor bastard take the risk without telling them".

"No, it wasn't like that I didn't know really I just went by what Clinton told me".

"Okay I believe you, now I see he was the one who set it up and left you all in the lurch and has gone off with the money where is he now if not in Spain"?

"I expect the bastards hiding in his cottage".

Jim had blurted it out in his anger, this was to have been his bargaining chip to get a reduced sentence, he would hold out on the address at least till he got something from the coppers.

"And where is that exactly"?

"If I tell you what do I get"?

"You don't have to tell us we can easily find out but if you save us the time we might get to him before he buggers off. Maybe we will reconsider the murder charge".

"There was a cottage in Surrey we used to play there as kids, it belonged to Clint's auntie. She left it to her daughter, but I know he goes there whenever he can, the cousin doesn't use it, so he's sort of taken it over. He pays the bills and council tax so she doesn't mind. I'm not saying he's there like but he could be".

"What's the address"?

"What do I get"?

"We'll drop the murder charge to manslaughter".

"Can you give us a moment".

Toni nodded and got up from the table and walked to the corner. Jim turned to the solicitor where they spoke for several minutes.

"Ok, I will give you the address and will testify as a prosecution witness for dropping the charges relating to the death of the girl".

"Now you know I can't do that, but we will recommend leniency in sentencing, the best I can offer. Withhold this information, the murder charge will stay".

Jim knew that this was the best he could get for now, but also knew that the CPS might bend a little more for a good witness. He gave Toni the address. The interview was formally closed.

Toni went to where Jonny was interviewing with one of the Carter brothers. She entered the room where Geoff was being interviewed asked Jonny to halt proceedings for a few moments.

"How you getting on"?

"Not very far mostly 'no comment'. They are using the same solicitor so going from one to the other trying to play them off doesn't work".

Toni gave Jonny a summary of her interview with Quarrel and the likely address where they might find Macaulay.

"You get out there with June, inform the Surrey locals first though, their uniforms may come in handy if he tries to run. Mel and I will take over with these two, not that I expect much will come of it. You go and bring the bastard in I have a lot of questions for that one".

Toni and Mel entered the interview room where Manny Carter and his solicitor were waiting.

"I'll make this brief, due to your lack of cooperation I am going to terminate these interviews with you and your brother. I will pass our substantial evidence to the CPS, you will no doubt be charged with Abduction, Manslaughter, robbery with violence and causing grievous bodily harm, you will be taken to court where we will insist you are remanded in custody pending trial. You and I sir will move next door and inform Mr Geoff Carter of his similar situation".

Toni pointed her remarks at the solicitor who was about to speak but thought better of it. He didn't know what evidence they had so would wait for more information. Melanie terminated the interview formally. The uniformed officer led Manny back to the cells. The three moved next door and repeated the process with George. He reacted differently.

"Hey, you can't do that you can't keep me here my solicitor said he would get me out on police bail".

"He may have asked but we have refused, you will come up before a Judge tomorrow and then we'll see what happens. With these charges against you your chances of bail are less than zero so prepare yourself for a long, long time away".

He grabbed his solicitors arm yanking him round to face him.

"What are you going to do about this bitch she can't talk to me like that, you said you'd get us out".

The solicitor stepped back out of the clutch of Geoff's hands.

"I advised you to keep silent, so I suggest you do just that, as the officer said I applied for police bail which was refused at this stage I could do no more. I will seek legal counsel to represent you and your brother when you go to court".

Melanie again closed the interview and turned off the tape as Geoff was led away swearing at the solicitor and everyone else in his sight. Toni and Mel waited whilst the solicitor collected his files and put them in his briefcase.

"See you in court then".

Said Toni with a smile.

"Not me Detective I'll pass this pair on".

"I don't blame you, that tape will provide an interesting moment for the jury".

Chapter 47

The Surrey police car pulled up outside the cottage. Jonny was a passenger accompanied by two uniformed officers and a DI from the Surrey Constabulary. PC June Owens and their own uniform constable followed close behind. Toni's suggestion he went to Guilford Police station, as a courtesy before proceeding to the cottage had backfired. The cottage where they suspected Clinton Macaulay might be hiding, was on their patch and they wanted to make any arrest.

The Superintendent at the station insisted that they be accompanied at the scene so arrived mob handed. They knew Clinton might be dangerous, but this number of officers was a bit of over the top as their intention was to ask him to accompany them for questioning, no arrest to be made at this time. Still they were out of their area so had little choice but to comply.

The young Surrey Detective Inspector Michaelson was first at the door which he banged on loudly ignoring the doorbell.

"This is the police please open the door".

He boomed in a deep even louder voice. Hardly giving anyone inside the chance to answer he banged again, once again shouting for the occupants to open up. There was no response. He turned to his men and sent them around the back to see if anyone was visible. A short time later the front door opened an obviously inexperienced constable stood there his face ashen.

"I think you should see this sir".

The DI pushed by him without asking what he had found. Jonny held back, if this lot were going to contaminate a scene he wasn't going to be part of it.

The DI came out a few minutes later.

"There is a body in there can you see if this is your man"?

Indicating for Jonny to enter and look.

" Just a moment sir".

Jonny turned and went to his car he opened the boot and put on plastic shoe protectors and donned the usual neoprene gloves indicating for June to do the same. They returned to the cottage door and spoke to the waiting and somewhat bemused DI.

"Shall I call the doctor and SOCO sir or will you"?

"I'll do that you go and see who it is".

Jonny and June entered the room saw the body sitting in the chair apparently asleep. On moving to the front the bulging open eyes and dark marks encircling the neck were the obvious cause of death although they would have to wait for the medic to confirm. It looked like Macaulay although the photo they had was when he was younger it was close enough to identify him as their suspect here and now. Finger prints and DNA would be taken and a witness who knew him would confirm the identification later. Jonny did a quick appraisal of the room, moved into the small kitchen and utility area, it looked clean and tidy, he would leave it to the crime scene boys to evaluate any evidence they find. He came out and moved to the constable who had first discovered the body.

"How did you get in"?

"The back door was open sir".

"Open"?

"No what I meant it was closed but unlocked".

"Okay were you wearing gloves and what did you touch"?

"Only used the back door handle and the front inside door knob, I wasn't wearing gloves sorry sir, I wasn't thinking".

"Don't worry you weren't to know what was in there. Did you touch the body"?

"God no sir. I just looked, saw he was dead then came straight to the front door and let in the DI".

Jonny then went over to the car where DI Michaelson was on the radio. He turned to Jonny as he approached.

"I think it is our suspect Clinton Macaulay but will need to confirm that later sir. I have spoken to your constable who only touched the door handles, SOCO will need to take his prints and foot prints before he leaves".

He did not wish to embarrass the DI by mentioning that he would also have to do the same. The senior scene of crime officer would probably not be so sympathetic.

His first priority was to let the boss know. The Surrey CID was going to be all over this shutting out Jonny and June pretty quickly. They would need some strings pulling if the Surrey lot were going to hand this to them without a fight. His call to Toni explaining what he had found set in motion a chain of calls at a level well above Jonny's and Toni's grade. The inexperienced Michelson looked at Jonny standing his ground summoning up the courage to carry out what would be very unpopular orders that he had been given over the radio by his superintendent.

"The forensic boys are on their way as is the Doctor, you and your officers should leave the scene at once please Sergeant, we can handle this from now on, a report will of course be forwarded to you in due course".

"Jonny pursed his lips and smiled at him moving close, face to face".

"No way sir, this is, or was, our prime suspect in a murder and public security incident which we are about to conclude, we only contacted you as a matter of courtesy, not for you to step in and take over our case".

Exaggerating the level of his authority Jonny continued.

"My ACC has given me specific instructions and until I hear from him to the contrary I and my officers will remain on site".

Michelson stepped back.

"I have my instruction too Sergeant so please move away".

"We will wait over by our car but we're not going anywhere; I have just spoken to my Chief Inspector who will be here shortly, she has told me not to leave, you will no doubt be given a different action to follow very soon. There is nothing that we can do here until the forensics and doctor have finished".

Jonny didn't know if Toni would come down, but thought mentioning a more senior officers pending arrival would buy him some time. Michelson backed off nodding his understanding of the situation but still not willing to disobey his boss.

Jonny phoned Toni again.

"What is happening boss, I said you were on your way or they would have sent us packing, do we take control or not"?

"Hang in there Jonny I've passed it upstairs you'll just have to wait, if it is Macaulay there is not a lot we can do now he's dead, once they find out the others and their lawyers will put all the blame on him. We must keep this quiet for now, 'blame the dead guy', is not going to happen on my watch.

You just stay ready to take over, I'm on my way down I'll have full authority soon. I'll use their medic as he is almost there and are usually not interested in inter-police department squabbles, however I have cancelled their forensics team our own guys have been mobilised and will be with you asap".

Half an hour later a frowning Michaelson walked over to Jonny.

"I don't know what strings you pulled to get this to yourselves, but my Super's really hacked off and so am I. You can go ahead".

"Thank you sir, you can stay and observe how we go about things in Hampshire if you like".

"Piss off"!

"Before you go would you and your constable please leave your shoes for SOCO to eliminate your footprints from the crime scene, I'll see they are returned to you. You could wait of course. Oh, don't worry about leaving your finger prints sir, they are on file".

Jonny couldn't resist his taunting the detective, he just hoped he never had to deal with him at some later date, not likely but you never know. Not the type of guy he'd make friends with anyway. Let's get on with it.

Michaelson stormed off wearing his shoes, middle finger pointing in the air, if Hampshire SOCO wanted them, they'd have to come to him, no way was he going to leave them behind. Cheeky bastard sergeant, he'd have back at him one day.

"We're good to go June, our forensic boys are on the way, Chiefs coming down too we won't disturb anything until the docs been, he won't be long, ask the constable to close off the area front and back there should be enough tape in the boot".

The doctor was the first to arrive.

"DS Jonny Musgrove sir please follow me".

"Good day Sergeant, I'm Doctor King give me a moment whist I suit up".

He and Jonny walked into the house whilst June stood by the gate watching for the others.

"This way doc, I haven't touched anything, didn't feel the need to check for a pulse".

"I can see why, strangulation with a ligature seems to be the cause look at those marks right across the throat, autopsy will confirm that of course. Quite cold too, been dead well over a day I'd say, I'll do a liver temp anyway give us a better idea. Bruises on both arms, shins are marked too he was tied up at the time of death. Whatever was used has been removed, we should find some traces on his clothes that will tell us more. There did not seem to be much of a struggle. The multiple lines of bruises on his throat show he was restrained and released several times prior to the final event. Suggests torture perhaps. He urinated in the chair at some time, still quite damp so leads us to think less than a week".

The doc lifted his shirt and underwear and inserted a probe into the body.

"Only two degrees above ambient so more than two days less than a week, best I can do with time of death for now".

You can move him when you like, where's he going".

"Richmond, I expect, Dr. Taylors lot".

"Good she's got a good set up there, I'll be off then call me if you find anything that I can help with. Where shall I'll send my report, to Guildford"?

"No, not this time, Surrey police are no longer involved, so just to Doctor Debbie Taylor at Richmond and a copy to DCI Webb at Basingstoke please sir".

They left the cottage together with the doctor removing his protective clothing as he walked towards his car. Thank you and good byes were said and he was gone. Jonny removed his gloves as he was beginning to sweat in them but kept his shoe protectors on. He hoped SOCO and the guvnor would be here soon.

SOCO arrived and went straight to work, Toni turned up some time after. They had nearly finished when she arrived their task almost done and the body well on its way to Richmond.

"This is a rum do Jonny anything of interest yet"?

"Nothing really except, time of death is a bit uncertain, also strangled with some sort of ligature, doc says maybe the possibility of torture. SOCO have done a thorough search, no sign of the stones and no radio-active material anywhere in the house, some residual levels in the boot of his car though. It is almost certainly Clinton Macaulay from the photos, no reason to think otherwise. We don't have his prints on file so will need to find someone to ID him. No sign of forced entry. There are some remains of wiped up footprints inside the utility room that could have come from outside. The window is closed now but it may have been the way in, or maybe the back conservatory door, it was unlocked when we arrived. He could of course have let in his killer. The victim was tied up at some point, but all traces of the rope and ligature have gone. Several finger prints have been found all over the house SOCO are recording everything we will see what pops up when they have done".

Toni walked into the cottage to view the scene, sometimes she had a feeling that led her to look at the scenario somewhat differently to her colleagues. What was he doing here, why did he become a victim? What did he know or have that made someone want to kill him? The stones certainly, money maybe, or was it something completely unrelated to the Westfields saga. She looked around, this time felt nothing, hoping the autopsy would reveal more she left.

"Let's go Jonny nothing more to do here but lots to do back at the station".

The lone constable secured the door, reaffixed the tape and no crossing signs, then followed his bosses back to the station, he'd arrive in time to knock off at the end of his shift. No overtime today, not that he minded he was glad to be going home to some normality.

Chapter 48

Toni received a strange call from Mathew Walker and after his request to see her, she agreed to meet him in town, away from Westfields. She had long abandoned her interviews with the brothers, they had been charged and were remanded in custody. Matt wouldn't say what it was about just that it was important. She had been meaning to question him again as she still had reservations concerning his involvement so decided to take advantage of the moment and go straight away. He was sitting on one of the seats outside MacDonald's when she arrived, he arose and walked towards her.

"Hello detective let's walk a bit to somewhere less busy".

"We can go back to the police station if you like".

"No. No, I don't want to be seen talking to you, there is something going on and it worries me".

"Okay, if we keep going this way we can go into the theatre foyer, there are some seats and it will be quiet at this time of day".

He nodded and they walked in silence arriving at the theatre foyer a few minutes later. It was almost empty, a few people were looking at posters for forthcoming performances and a couple waiting to purchase tickets at the box office. The waiting area on the far side was unoccupied.

"Is it alright here"?

He agreed and they sat down next to each other on a long padded bench.

"Well Matt what is on your mind"?

"I'm not sure really, but we have had a delivery of some new stones so are able to start from where we left off. Only a couple of days ago it looked like we were going to close down".

"That's good isn't it, Mr Grimm has obviously found a supply from somewhere, they are resourceful and well-funded so I don't see the problem".

"That is just it, I spent months trying to find an alternative supplier, as it takes so long to process the stones from our current source, without success. These did not come from them I checked, they have our new order but it will not be ready for several weeks, if not months".

"Where do you think they came from"?

"I can't be sure, so don't say it was me that told you or I'd lose my job. I'm thinking they are the originals, you know the ones that were stolen".

"How can you know that, one stone is much like any other"?

"That's only true before they are processed, after being cut and polished they are unique, I measured the angles of cut on some of the ones I was given, they were identical to the originals, even if specified to a new supplier it is almost impossible to repeat the angle exactly".

"Are you sure that these could not have been manufactured, abroad for example, to the same specification"?

"I'm not saying it is impossible, but it is so difficult it would take weeks not days. There is one other thing that leaves me no doubt. One of the stones had two tiny scratches on the coating which, when assembled, matched exactly to the marks made by the clamps of our experiment. It had been used by us before".

This opened up a whole new line of enquiry that Toni would need to investigate; she wanted time to think.

"Look Matt this information is too important to make public at the moment and I wish to protect your position too. Carry on as if nothing was wrong for now and I will get back to you, Say nothing to anyone you hear".

"Okay, don't worry I won't breathe a word".

"By the way something I've been meaning to ask you, why did you stick that big yellow six on the notes file in the safe".

"Oh, that was to help Mr James, he liked to study our notes from time to time and could never find that file amongst all the others. His sight is so poor he has to use a huge magnifying glass to read them, he may be old and almost blind but his mind is as sharp as a razor and has guided us all the way through this project".

"But why a yellow six"?

"No reason, it was one I found in my drawer big and bright enough for Mr James to see easily, it could have been any number, just pot luck".

"Did you tell anyone about it"?

"Oh yes everyone knew, all the technicians would put their scribbled notes in there, the formal reports were put on computer and copied to memory sticks after encryption. The notes often helped us see the bigger picture and solve problems".

That's fine Matt thank you, I'll keep this conversation confidential for now at least".

Toni saw the notes file's role as somewhat similar to their own murder file; Mathew Walker's rank as a suspect had reduced considerably.

Chapter 49

William Grimm was nervous as he walked up the steps into Basingstoke police station, the request to visit had come from the Detective Chief Inspector who was dealing with the break in. He wondered why the visit was needed, normally the officers had visited his office when they needed to speak to him. He had been told that there had been a significant breakthrough in the case, maybe it was just an update but he had his doubts; he would need to keep his wits about him.

Please sit down William, I am sorry to bring you in like this but I'm snowed under here and can't get away. There has been considerable progress which I will explain later but first I have a few questions if you don't mind"?

"Not at all fire away".

"It seems likely we have apprehended some of the robbery suspects however we are some way off bringing charges as we have to gather evidence to prove our case. It seems likely that some of the equipment was indeed sold to one of your competitors although this will be difficult to prove, more of that later. The stolen jewels, or stones as you know them, have not been recovered. The suspect whom we know had them in his possession has been found but they are missing".

Toni did not let on that he had been found dead. She opened a folder and leaned forward to show William a picture of Clinton Macaulay.

"Do you know or have seen this man"?

William studied the picture for a few moments close enough to be sure.

"No I have never seen him before, is he one of those the men who broke in"?

Toni could see there was no glimmer of recognition or any sign that he was affected by seeing Macaulay's face. Her thoughts that William had killed Macaulay and taken the stones back were fading, but according to Matt he had acquired them or some of them at least. How did he do that?

"Maybe, we are still gathering information. I heard you are back in production is that what you call it"?

"We have restarted our trials programme, that's true. Our normal analysis work never stopped".

"Good news then but how, without the stones"?

"I managed to secure replacements from abroad".

Toni saw the tell-tale downward look as William spoke breaking eye contact which he had never done before, was it a lie or just nerves, she would press him further.

"Strange that, when all attempts to find this type of material had failed before, and here you are with just the right thing needed to carry on just popping up out of the blue. I'd like to see the invoices and the name of the supplier, perhaps our suspects had sold the stones to them and you have bought them back without realising it, now that would be a coincidence".

William just sat there not knowing what to say.

"Why don't you answer"?

"You never asked me a question just expounded a wild theory of what might or might not have happened".

Toni felt this response was well out of character.

"Well I'm asking it now, do you think that is what took place"?

"I have no idea but I doubt it, the Polish Company who supplied me had them in stock, they just required some adjustments to meet our specification, it was only six stones anyway we have to wait some considerable time to replace all that was lost, the invoices are somewhere in the office system, come and see them when you like".

William hated lying like this but was at this moment thankful to Alan Mortimer for having him create some documentation which would back up this false story, he hoped the police would not follow it further as the company in Poland he had used no longer existed.

Toni was not convinced, he would send Mel to check, in the meantime he was going to make William Grimm sweat a bit. Although he did not suspect him of killing Clinton he thought he, or maybe the Polish Company if they existed, had acquired the stones from the man that did the murder.

"William I'm still not sure what you say is what happened, if you did get them back by paying a ransom for example, you would have done nothing wrong, after all they were yours in the first place, but failing to tell us is a problem for you. Do you want to say anything more"?

"I don't think so, why do you keep pushing this, if I did what you said why wouldn't I tell you"?

"Because the man who took the stones from Westfields was found murdered yesterday and if they are now in your possession you are certainly not in a very good position".

The blood drained from Williams face and his jaw dropped. Finding out about the death of a stranger would not do that, Toni saw his reaction and knew that he was involved somehow.

"Now William, the interview so far has been informal no notes taken, I think a little more formality is called for as well as something a little closer to the truth don't you".

"Do I need a solicitor"?

"You didn't kill anyone did you"?

"No I certainly did not".

"Then all you have done is had dealings with the man that maybe did. If you cooperate then I can see you walking away with a slapped wrist, if that. You can of course have a solicitor if you wish but I am not going to caution you so you can just answer my questions voluntarily".

William agreed to go ahead but asked for a comfort break first, he needed a while to think. A uniformed officer accompanied him to the toilet.

He stood at the basin slowly washing his hands, mind racing. How should he respond when questioned? He couldn't believe it, had Mortimer murdered this man? He had no idea how Alan had come by the stones, but his impression was that he was certainly a dodgy character.

If the police investigate Alan and find he was involved, Westfields would lose their biggest investor and where would that leave him, maybe an accessory to murder. He would tell the truth but not reveal Alan's role, say it was a stranger who contacted him demanding payment for the stones, but everything else would be true.

Toni, Melanie, a uniformed constable and William Grimm were now in one of the interview rooms far less comfortable than her office. The presence of a uniformed officer in the doorway and the tape machine made this formal setting something that William had never experienced before. Telling a lie mattered here it became a matter of record. Melanie began the proceedings with the usual naming of those present and started the tape.

"William you understand that there are no charges being brought and this interview is just to gather information. A tape recording will be made and the officer will take notes do you understand and agree. You can of course have legal representation if you wish".

"That is fine I want to help in any way I can".

"Let us forget what you said earlier just tell me how you acquired the stones to enable you continue with the experiments".

William's heart was racing he had never been very good at lying and his strategy of bending the truth did not seem right. Someone had killed Vera and now this other man too, he would have to be open.

"Look what I said earlier was made up to protect someone, I'm sorry I lied as I really wanted to be honest about the stones being recovered but he made me think differently. Now I have learnt that someone has died I cannot continue with the deception. One of our investors learned of the robbery so came to see if he could help. He returned two days later with the very stones that had been stolen. He didn't say how he acquired them and I didn't ask, no money changed hands he just gave them to me and advised how I should cover up their return with the new supplier story. That's it, I set the teams working to restart the program".

"Now that more like what we expected to hear, who is this man, your investor".

"He is a major shareholder and has been for some years, he never normally interferes with our work. I can't believe he has done this maybe he asked someone else to recover them and didn't know about the death".

"That's quite possible but we can't know unless we speak to him, what is his name".

At this point William knew he could not add to the lie, maybe Alan wasn't a killer but he could not shield him any longer.

"His name is Alan Mortimer, he lives in London, I don't know where, his company is Conway Investments, also based in London. We send them monthly reports their address will be on file, I don't know it myself. He is such a nice fellow I don't believe he could kill anybody".

Toni couldn't believe her ears remembering the file Colin had sent over listing the Toby Jones investment enquiries. One of them was for Wesfields was he the secret investor. It couldn't be they were one and the same could it? More likely this Alan Mortimer maybe knows Toby Jones; was it possible that fate had handed her a connection. She told herself to calm down it was probably just a coincidence.

"Can you describe this Mortimer".

His description was nothing like Jones, so a coincidence after all, she'd have to wait and see.

"You know what William, that is all I need for now. You have done the right thing, I my need to come back to you again but that will be much less formal than now. My officers will phone your company for information please tell your staff to cooperate".

"Of course. Shall I stop the program and return all the stones to you".

"I don't think that will be necessary at this time we will see how we progress with the investigation, besides they're irradiated by now or some of them are aren't they"?

"That's true, they will be too dangerous to move, however the unused ones are back in the safe you can have them at any time".

"We'll see, goodbye Mr Grimm".

The detectives returned to the squad room and William left one confession out of the way, another, perhaps a more difficult one to face, was to his father.

"Mel you and Compton find out all you can about this Alan Mortimer, I'll get on to our old colleague DCI Dale in London to see what he can dig up. The post mortem on Clinton is this afternoon, I'll get Jonny to deal with that. We still have a lot of loose ends to cover on the robbery. This business with the Macaulay murder and Mortimer is whole new ball game".

Toni walked to the stairs and climbed slowly, she was tired and happy at the same time, her plan of action was clear but was going to run it by the Super beforehand. Superintendent Munroe was aware of the interview results but needed to be updated concerning the Macaulay Murder before she moved on. Her relationship with Colin Dale was more personal than official, she wanted to change that status and this murder was the key that would do that.

Her knock on the door produced the expected 'Come in' she entered and was invited to sit down.

"Well Toni it seems we are about done with this lot, shame about Macaulay though, muddies the waters a bit. Are we ready to go to the CPS with the others"?

"Not quite sir but it won't be long, lots of loose ends we need to be clear about, I want this one tight as a drum, no sneaky lawyer get outs that we haven't closed down".

"Quite right too, don't delay too long though, now what about this murder is it tied in to the robbery or a separate case"?

"There is a link I believe but I want to treat it separately for now. None of those in custody were involved. I have a line on a possible suspect who is linked because he has shares in Westfields. The director William Grimm has given us some information that indicates who may be involved, we are pursuing that line but I need your authorisation as it will involve using our friends at the Met".

"Hmm, is that necessary, I have already trod on toes with the Surrey lot over this, I don't fancy making more trouble especially with the London crowd".

"The suspect lives in London, his company is based there too. We will need to go there for the preliminary enquiries at least. We have friends there sir why not use them".

"You're referring to DCI Dale I presume, he may have been one of ours but his role in the Met is somewhat different now, he is ambitious; I wouldn't trust him or them too much, they'd steal this case from under your nose given half the chance".

"That may be so, I could do this unofficially if you like, but prefer us to be investigating above board".

She knew that Munroe would not risk an underhand investigation outside his jurisdiction. He would go the way she wanted.

"That is for certain Chief Inspector, no back-door information gathering please , without official records of evidence it is so difficult to use in court. I will contact my opposite number in the Met CID, in the meantime confine your investigations to Hampshire. What is the name of the suspect"?

"Alan Mortimer sir, I will send you an email with all the details as soon as I get downstairs".

"Toni, I appreciate your coming to me with this before going ahead, saves us both a lot of agro if it all goes south".

"Yes sir thank you".

Toni almost skipped down the stairs, at long last she was going to be able to work with Colin officially. This guy Mortimer may not be a killer but it opened the doors for her and Colin to pursue those other matters. The connection of Mortimer to Jones was tenuous but demanded closer scrutiny.

She had no idea know how close she was to those 'other matters', she'd find out soon enough.

Chapter 50

Alan was lying on his bed unable to sleep his mind would not settle until he went over his recent actions. Perhaps he had gone too far by returning the stones in person, he knew William and his father were honest so couldn't be sure if William would hide their return in the way he had suggested. He probably would not keep silent if confronted by the police: no matter.

If they came to question him here in London he had a readymade up story about paying a ransom to an unknown man one with a very different description to that of Macaulay. There was no real connection between him and the dead man and he had already created an alibi for around the time of his death, his clothes and rope had been disposed of, he felt secure, but maybe a word to the right man would let him know more.

The police almost certainly knew that Macaulay had the stones in his possession at some time. Clinton's quiet cottage in the middle of nowhere was not on their radar, or they would have been to arrest him before now. The chances of an early discovery were small.

His ambition to become the major shareholder were his next step. James Grimm would soon be too old to influence the decisions, he would lean on William who was more malleable, he would offer a good financial incentive to take on some of the old man's shareholding soon. The injection of cash could be used to buy more equipment and add another experimental laboratory. William would like that idea, progress towards the ultimate goal would suit both of them. Once the system was proven and worked in the laboratory the next phase of seeking approval from the MHRA and publicly announcing the discovery of a definitive treatment for these elusive cancers would see the value of Westfields shares doubling or even more overnight. Once approval was achieved the sky was the limit. William would not be able to resist when Alan painted this rosy picture.

Remembering his previous thought he picked up the phone and called his old 'friend'.

"Hello Fred, No. No don't speak just listen, give me an update on Westfields investigation, I'll call you in an hour ok".

An hour later he called Fred's mobile and received the information he wanted. There were four men in custody the fifth suspect Macaulay was dead, he knew that of course, they were not looking for anyone else with regard to the robbery. An investigation into the murder of Macaulay had begun, there was a London connection that was all that Fred could find out for now. There was no named suspect yet. He coaxed him to find out more and said he would call him tomorrow. The fact that there was an interest in London concerned him a bit but then Macaulay was a Londoner so that was probably why. He'd wait and see what tomorrow would bring. His next call was to his manager Kevin.

"Kevin I believe you may be visited by the police, it concerns Westfields, the break in I should think. I don't want them knowing where I live or they'll be disturbing me there so keep that to yourself. I'll go to the local police station if necessary. They will want to contact me so give them my new mobile number, you know the phone you organised for me. I want to keep this one private, you know just for us".

"There's not a problem is there sir, anything I can do to help".

"No problem it's just that they will probably want to interview anyone who has an interest in the Westfields company, so be up front if they ask about my investment. Be evasive if they ask about any of our other business, and don't mention my trips abroad, let them think I have been a permanent resident, tell them about my trip to Manchester though, but only if they ask, they will look for any reason to pry it is their nature to be nosey, part of their job".

"I can do that sir. I'll call you if they come round, a bit of advanced warning can be useful".

"That would be helpful Kevin thank you. Will you be in for a while yet I'm coming to the office, I have something you need to secure for me"?

"Of course, sir. I'll wait for you".

Alan made his way out of the apartment and called a taxi, the package, a nice little nest egg courtesy of that prick Macaulay, discreetly hidden in his overcoat inside pocket.

Chapter 51

DCI Colin Dale pulled up outside the offices of Conway Investments. His Superintendent had given him the task of tracking down Alan Mortimer. He had been given a briefing by the Super but was more than well informed by yesterday's unofficial conversation with Toni. He was met in a small outer office by a middle-aged lady, he showed her his warrant card and asked to see the manager.

"Please take a seat sir I will inform Mr Blackman that you wish to see him".

He smiled at her and remained standing. She knocked on the inner door and entered closing it behind her. A few seconds later she emerged holding the door ajar.

"Mr Blackman will see you now, please go in".

Kevin was standing behind his desk, held out his hand as Colin approached. They shook hands and he indicated that Colin should sit in the chair opposite. They both sat at the same time.

"I'm Kevin Blackman Detective, manager of Conway investments, would you like a tea, coffee"?

Colin declined, again showed his card and introduced himself. Kevin thought a Chief Inspector seemed to be too high a rank for the simple enquiry he was expecting, he must be careful not to give away anything that might get his boss into trouble.

"What can I do for you today"?

"I am just making general enquiries about Mr Alan Mortimer, I believe he is a major investor in Westfields the medical company in Basingstoke".

"A Chief Inspector, seems rather a senior position for such a mundane task, still I suppose after the break in at Westfields you need to find out as much as you can, what do you want to know"?

"I'm just helping out a colleague from the Hampshire police and I was nearby. Just tell me what you can about Mr Mortimer's investments and also where he lives, I would really like to speak to him directly".

"I don't know where he is at the moment, I can call him or give you his mobile number if you like. I'm sure he will come and meet you".

"That will be good, what is his address".

"I'm afraid I can't give you that. His home is a private matter and I've been instructed to tell no one. If you call him, he will tell you or meet you as I said".

"Okay, what about the investments"?

"Westfields is just one company of several he invested in some years ago, he has a non-controlling shareholding. He has little or nothing to do with the running of the business and only visits on rare occasions. It is a sound company with good long-term prospects, that's about all I can tell you, if you want financial figures you will need go to Westfields themselves".

"Have you ever been to Wesfields"?

"No, I manage Mr Mortimer's affairs from the office mostly. I never leave London, my dealings with Wesfields are by letter, and e-mail or sometimes by phone".

"When did Mr Mortimer last visit"?

"I'm not sure, I can look it up, it was the day after we learnt of the break in he went down just to provide moral support I think"?

"What about the second visit"?

"I don't think there was one, Mr Mortimer went up to Manchester for a business trip the same evening for two days and has been back in London ever since. He could have gone there I suppose but I wasn't informed".

"Do you know Mr Grimm"?

"I've spoken to Mr William on the phone a few times, purely about business of course but not recently".

"Who told you about the break in"?

"That was Mr Chaney, before he was found out, that was awful what he did Mr Mortimer told me about that, who would have believed it".

"Can you tell me what other companies Mr Mortimer has invested in"?

"All the investments are made by this company Conway Investments Ltd. None are personal by Mr Mortimer, or none that I know of. I am sorry Detective but I am not at liberty to speak about them without Mr Mortimer's permission. They are of course a matter of record at Companies House".

"I think that will be all for now Mr Blackman if you would give me that phone number".

Kevin wrote the number on the back of one of his business cards and handed it to Colin.

"Is there anything else I can help with"?

"That's it I think. No, there is one more question I almost forgot, where was Mr Mortimer on the nineteenth and twentieth".

Kevin looked in his diary.

"Oh yes, that was when he went to Manchester, he took the late train on the nineteenth and came back the morning of the twenty first, he stayed in the Sale Hilton, why do you want to know"?

"No reason really a lot was happening then and it's nice to know where everyone was, thank you again Mr Blackman if we need anything else, I'm sure Mr Mortimer will oblige".

A convenient alibi for Macaulay's murder. It will need checking was the first thought of Colin as he left the building, he would have a word with Toni before giving this number a ring. Bringing him into the station would be Colin's best bet, but sometimes Toni was more subtle, she would want to go to his home if she could. He'd go back to the station and start checking out Mortimer's visit to Manchester, then give her a ring.

Chapter 52

There was something about this Alan Mortimer that set Colin on edge. He couldn't put his finger on it but there was a definite vibe.

Alan Mortimer had volunteered to come to the police station but evaded the offer for Colin to come to his home. He had not been able to break the alibi as all enquiries by the local Manchester Police had confirmed his stay, with several witnesses having been in his company throughout the evening and the day. His cards showed payment for taxis, hotel bill and restaurant, before the return rail journey. He was never alone long enough to have made the return to the cottage and back again, so it looked like he was in the clear when it came to the murder, but they still needed to know how he had acquired the stones. With his alibi checking out Toni had decided to let Colin deal with the Mortimer interview in London.

"Mr Mortimer thank you for coming in, this is a purely voluntary meeting you understand a few questions to help our enquiries regarding the break in at Westfields. Do you mind if we record this meeting, it will make sure we are all clear about what is said? The constable will also take notes if that is okay"?

"No problem how can I help"

"I understand you made a visit to Wesfields just after the break in, what was the reason for that visit"?

"Well I was concerned of course for William, the night watchman and shocked at Verity's death, I wanted to see if there was anything I could do".

"The second visit you made a couple of days later, what was that for"?

"I never went back there again".

"You never met Mr Grimm"?

Alan now knew that William had been straight and informed the police he must have told them what had gone down.

"I never said that, I meant I never went back to Westfields however I did meet William in the town centre. I wanted to be discreet. I had recovered the stones and wanted to give them to him in private. I thought it best if he would conceal the fact as I thought you would take them away and stop the continuation of their work".

"Not very honest of you but the more important question, how did you acquire the stones".

"I don't think I want to answer that".

"You do realise that the stones were stolen, and the fact that you recently had them in your possession makes us suspect you may be involved. You must tell us how you came to get them".

"Of course I'm involved but only after they were stolen. If I tell you how I got them I will need protection as I was told to keep quiet or they would deal with me".

"I understand, you saying you were threatened, I get that, but you must tell us if we are to catch these people. You will only be safe if they are put away".

"I don't like it, but if I must. I was contacted by phone the very day after my visit and asked if I wanted to buy them back. I was very shocked at first but realised that the reason they were stolen was to ransom them. They had little value elsewhere but were of significant value to Westfields".

"Why did this man contact you why not the Grimms direct"?

"I don't know perhaps because he was from London and didn't want to go back to Basingstoke, he obviously knew of my connection to Wesfields; anyway, he asked for fifty but I said no to that, he eventually agreed to accept thirty thousand in cash. He then hung up".

"What happened next"?

"He phoned again an hour later and told me to go to a pub near Victoria Station with the money and wait.

He said if I called the police there would be serious consequences".

"What do you think was meant by that"?

"They would hurt either me or someone close, I don't know do I".

"What do mean by 'they' you said it was one man"?

"I felt he wasn't working alone. *'He' 'They'* What difference does it make I only spoke to one person".

"Okay. How come you had so large a sum available"?

"I didn't, I went to my bank and drew it out".

"That much so quick"?

"I'm a wealthy man and my bank is very obliging".

"Please continue".

"I went to the pub and sat where he said, I waited ten minutes maybe more, then this guy sat behind me, I didn't see him come in, I don't know where he came from, he was just there. He said not to turn around. I was shaking you know I've never had this sort of experience. He passed a bag to me through the back of the seat and told me to look inside. It was the stones, or I hoped it was they looked real enough. He told me to leave the envelope with the money on the seat and leave without looking back. He said if it was not all there or I went to the police, I was a dead man. I left in a real hurry I can tell you".

"Did you see this man's face".

"No way was I going to turn around and look, so no I did not see anyone just the voice. A man's voice with a London accent, I hid in a doorway and waited across the road to see who came out, no one did, I got scared and left".

"Why didn't you come to the police"?

"Why do you think".

"Okay what did you do next"?

"I took the stones to William, I didn't say how I got them but asked him to keep it quiet or go to the police I left that up to him. I don't know if I've broken the law by doing what I did, I was afraid of this man but still wanted to help, I didn't mean to do anything wrong".

Alan had spun his yarn and hoped the detective would accept the story. If they suspected him of the killing, he thought his false alibi would check out initially at least so most likely they would look elsewhere.

"What you did was understandable but if you had come to us we could have set a trap for this man, so yes what you did was wrong you have assisted a criminal".

"Does that mean I will be arrested"?

"Look you were under threat so had a good reason to avoid the police, but you do see there could have been a much better outcome if you had contacted us".

"I suppose so, I wasn't thinking at the time I'm sorry that I did that now, but it seemed I had no choice".

"Okay we'll leave it there for now, I may ask you to make a formal statement under caution if my superiors consider your actions had a criminal intent. My report will reflect your concern, so I expect you will just be given an official warning".

Alan thanked him and left, he had carried the first hurdle maybe there would be no more. If they took what he said at face value backed up by a confirmed alibi, the chances are they would not delve any deeper but go and look for his mystery man.

Colin was thinking differently however. It was all too pat, too well rehearsed, answering all the questions without a pause or a thought. No way this unknown man, if he even existed, would go to a meeting carrying incriminating evidence to a closed place, he would be suspicious of the police and check out Mortimer first. The nagging memory of something odd still causing an itch of doubt. He would send a copy of the tape to Toni, he would continue and dig deeper.

Toni listened to the tape along with Jonny.

"What do you think Jonny"?

"Same as you I expect guv, the buggers lying through his teeth".

"His alibi checks out though. So maybe there is some element of truth in his story. Let's look at it from his point of view. His interest in the Company means he will lose if they don't have these stones, so buying them back makes sense. I can't see any point in him being involved in the robbery, why steal something when you already own a part of it. The insurance that only gets them back to square one and returning the stones like he did means there is no claim other than for some lost equipment. It seem all he has done is to lose thirty thousand pounds".

"I still don't like it, if he didn't kill Macaulay himself, he could have had him topped to get the stones, that wouldn't have cost him anything except to pay off the hired killer, somewhat less than the thirty grand he said he paid for the stones I guess".

The pair of them bandied about different theories for half an hour but agreed that although they did not believe Mortimer's story there was no proof to the contrary so until there was some evidence they would proceed with the investigation, they both agreed however that chasing after the mysterious man was not going to happen at this stage they would look at what other evidence they had and proceed from there.

"Hello Colin, got your tape, what a load of bullshit wrapped up in some facts, still we can't disprove it at the moment or separate the truth from the lies, what did you think of him"?

"You know what, I wanted to lock him up there and then, but there is no evidence to show he did anything other than what he said. The convenient alibi suggests he could have used a contractor, but it all happened too fast for that. None of my snouts have heard of him and no hint of any contracts being put out. I really don't know what to think, but I'm going to check with his bank and find out a good deal more about our Alan Mortimer before I let this go. I hope I'm not being paranoid, seeing things that aren't there".

"No my friend your never far wrong. I'll send over Compton's search results, she has all his investments mapped out. You remember those files you sent me strangely enough some of Mortimer's investments matched enquiries made by your friend Joseph Mallard on behalf of Toby Jones, Compton brought it to my attention when she saw the Westfields name and thought they were part of our robbery enquiry. It is not a coincidence, there is a link somewhere we just have to find it. You carry on from your end, I'm going back to the Grimms one of them knows more and I want to find out what. Colin if the two of us feel the same about this Mortimer and I've never even met him, then he needs looking at with a fine tooth comb".

"That's a good find, say well done to Compton from me, you know what I'll have another go at Mallard and his lady friend. Be in touch soon. Bye Toni".

"Goodbye Colin and good luck".

Chapter 53

"Is that Detective Chief Inspector Webb"?

"Yes sir how can I help you"?

James Grimm had listened to his son's explanation of his actions regarding the stones. He understood but was sad that William had at shown a weakness of character in deciding to follow the influence of Mortimer, and worse to lie about it. His son's confession to the police and to him, showed at least some moral fibre remained and knew William had learnt a valuable lesson. There was still a nagging doubt that he must resolve.

"James Grimm here Inspector, I must talk to you".

"Yes sir, I recognise your voice do you want me to come to you"?

"Oh no, that will not be necessary, we can do this over the phone now, if you have a few moments, it's about Alan Mortimer".

"That's fine sir, please go on".

"He came to our offices the other day you know, I had never met him before, or I thought I hadn't. It was his voice you see I knew that voice, just like you knew it was me calling. He said we had never met but I was sure he was the fellow I met some years before, that half London half put on accent he had, it was very distinctive. William described him to me but it was nothing like the fellow I remembered, he had these ears you see, so I thought I must be wrong".

He had paused at that point for a breath and to gather himself, he felt foolish, his qualms were unfounded just relying on his memory of a voice from long ago.

Toni's heart leapt in her chest she could hardly contain herself she wanted him to go on but was frightened to hear what he may say next. She quickly switched on the phone's recorder, she would tell him after as she did not want to interrupt his flow.

"Anyway I kept listening, whenever he spoke and it came to me, where I'd met him that is. It was at an agency dinner. I could see quite well then, so knew what he looked like, he was seeking to invest in new companies he said, we chatted for a quite a while. When I described my man to William he said Mortimer looked nothing like I'd remembered. I thought my memory was playing tricks, so I am probably wasting your time".

"No this is most interesting I can assure you, you are not wasting anyone's time please go on sir".

"Well at the end of his visit I had recalled the name and when I told Mortimer, he recognised it. I could tell, his breathing you know, it changed. I've learnt to read sounds like that since I lost my vision. He pretended it must be his London accent and tried to laugh it off. He was definitely taken by surprise".

"What was the name you remembered sir"?

"Toby. It was, Toby Jones"

"Mr James you just made my day".

"I did. How"?

"All will be revealed sir, in good time. If it works out you will be the first to know. I will explain all and tell you a long, interesting, but sad story.

Chapter 54

Colin Dale and Toni Webb were again supping in their favourite pub, The Four Horseshoes. As soon as her conversation with James Grimm had ended she had called this meeting to discuss the way forward.

The cases against Chaney, Quarrel, George Brown and the brothers Carter were close to being fully prepared, her team, with Jonny in the lead, were working with the CPS to gather all the forensic evidence and statements together, in a final push ready for trial.

Finger prints of Macaulay matched the firearm print from a murder in London from years before, at least that old unsolved case could be concluded and maybe bring some family their closure and hopefully peace.

Charges against Tommy Green concerning Westfields were being dropped. He was showing signs of liver and kidney infections, effects from the radiation exposure. Toni thought this sickness would be punishment enough. The stolen goods found in his house were being dealt with as a minor crime.

The pair of Chief Inspectors sat convinced that Mortimer and Jones were one and the same; that he had murdered Macaulay or had paid someone to do it. Their meeting was to discuss a plan whereby they could prove it. The memory of a voice by an old blind man would not stand up in court, there had to be another way.

"Colin, are you sure the alibi holds water"?

"It seem so but I will go personally and check it out again if you like".

"Maybe, first just ask the Manchester guys again if there was any doubt".

"They won't like that. Mind you they wouldn't like me going up there and poking my nose in where they had already been".

"True, did they do a photo ID with the witnesses"?

"That I don't know, but the name and description of the man fitted, and so did all the card checks, train tickets and the like, all proved he was there".

"Send them a picture just to confirm before we look at the hired killer angle, we do have a picture don't we"?

"I haven't seen one, but I can get a copy from the CCTV when he came in to the station other day, it may not be very good, but I'll get it enhanced and passed up to Manchester".

"Good, that's a start. Compton has done a financial on him and on Conway investments. Two maybe three things stand out. One, he did draw out thirty thousand pounds on the day of the ransom exchange. Second, his accounts for several years have been audited with no problems, the company and personal taxes are all in order. His bank account is very healthy and shows just a regular income from the Company with the usual outgoings, except for this last withdrawal. Finally, he has shares in two other Companies that were investigated, as shown in the files you got from Joseph Mallard. He appears to be squeaky clean but we need to trace his history, If Toby Jones has a new name who was the original Alan Mortimer".

"I recon that's a job for Compton".

"She is snowed under with stuff for the CPS I can't use her now. I'll get June Owens on it".

"The young PC, I remember her. I thought she was uniform".

"She is, but has been helping Jonny as a second, the Super has asked her to transfer, she hasn't said yes yet, but she has been a great help and will want to move I'm sure".

"Don't work her too hard, the long hours may put her off".

"If that puts her off then she won't be much good in CID. We need more help and she is an ideal recruit".

"Right, back to the subject in hand, do we bring him in again and confront him with the Toby Jones identity swap"?

"I think not, if it is true, he will be forewarned before we have any real evidence. Again, if true he will have a well prepared story that will be hard to break. We still don't know one hundred percent that he is Toby Jones, just our gut feelings".

"Toni don't be despondent we will find the evidence, God knows we've waited long enough, remember the truth lies with the blind man".

They chatted a while longer, Toni went home but Colin had other things on his mind now, he couldn't wait another day to satisfy his need to be certain. He drove to the station and collected print outs of Alan Mortimer from the CCTV, they were not brilliant but would do the job; as an afterthought, he also took a photo of Joseph Mallard, a suspicious thought had crossed his mind.

The journey to Manchester took longer than expected, fortunately the district of Sale was south side of the city, so he arrived in good time. He had visions of being late and getting there when everyone had gone to bed. He certainly didn't want to stay the night, so was glad to find the hotel was still busy. His first stop was the man behind the reception desk.

"Good evening sir can I help you"?

"I am Chief Inspector Dale I need to ask a few questions".

"I'll get the manager sir".

"No, that won't be necessary, I am enquiring about a gentleman who stayed here on the nights of the nineteenth and twentieth of this month, a Mr Alan Mortimer, were you on duty"?

The man flicked through the register.

"No sir, that was Stephanie, she is currently working behind the bar, shall I get her for you"?

"No, that's okay thanks, I'll go there myself".

The man pointed out the direction of the bar.

"Before I go could I see the register"?

He spun the large book round so Colin could see; he took his mobile phone out and before the receptionist could object took a snap of the page where Alan's details and signature were clear".

The bar was only partially occupied with only one bar tender, a middle-aged lady with fine features and black hair, Colin assumed this would be Stephanie. Colin approached and showed his ID as he introduced himself.

"Not you lot again, I answered the questions the other copper asked the other day, I haven't remembered anything different or I would've called".

"I just want to clear up one small thing, this man Mortimer, your description is a little hazy, would you mind looking at a picture to see if this is the man".

"You mean Alan don't you, he had everyone calling him that, bought a few rounds during that evening, quite a loud guy. Come on show us your picture".

She took the print and squinted at it for a few seconds and handed it back.

"You've got the wrong feller there that's not Alan, looks similar but definitely not him".

Colin was excited now and although he'd broken all the rules about photo identification there would be other witnesses with whom he could follow the required process. He then handed her the photo of Joseph Mallard.

"That's him that's Alan, bit of a laugh he was too, got everyone going with his jokes".

"Thank you, Stephanie, you've made my day".

"No problem, you going to have a drink"

"Sorry, I'd love to, but I'm driving".

Toni answered her phone, it was barley six am and she was still not quite awake, this soon changed when she heard what Colin had done.

"You went to the hotel and re-interviewed a witness already covered by the Manchester Police without informing them, if they find out you'll get a kick up where it hurts from upstairs".

"Never mind about that we have him, his alibi is crap and you'll never guess what else".

Colin told her of his visit to the Sale Hilton and sat back with a big grin she couldn't see but matched with a spreading of her lips and a show of white teeth. She was still taking it in, no plan of action coming readily to mind just a feeling of joy.

"What next"?

"I'm going to bring Mallard and Mortimer in under caution. I will apply for a warrant to search Mallards office, car and home, if you can do the same for Mortimer you have plenty of grounds now. I will clear it with my Super for you to come here with your forensic guys to carry out the searches, I will interview Joseph you can tackle Alan, how does that sound".

"Are you sure your Super will go for that"?

"A chance to get Mallard for conspiracy to murder, he will love it".

"Great I'll get things started here, as soon as I have the warrants, I'll call you to make sure you are okay your end. Great work mate, if this guy is our Jones in disguise, I will........ I don't know what I will, but it will be a bit special I can tell you".

Chapter 55

Colin called Toni, he had both men in custody under caution. They both had solicitors with them, the clock was running before the deadline for issuing charges.

Toni was on her way as soon as the phone call ended. The journey to London took an age, or it seemed that way, just like when you were seven and it was Christmas Eve, time stood still on the only night of the year you wanted to go to bed early.

The results of the searches of both houses had revealed little evidence, finger prints, DNA, all as expected.

The DNA taken from skin and hair found at Alan's flat were being compared to samples found in Sandra Cooper's apartment from two years before. The analysis would take too long to be ready before the interviews started, maybe they wouldn't need that. One unexpected find in each apartment, if proved significant, would make a difference, Compton Busion was working on that now.

The Manchester police had carried out an official photo ID with three Hotel staff and two guests, after Superintendent Munroe had smoothed things over with his counterpart and both Colin and Toni had been given a dressing down for ignoring protocol.

"You two have left me owing the Manchester Super a big favour, you'd better make sure it is worthwhile".

Superintendent Walter Munroe was secretly pleased that Colin, with Toni's blessing, had been less that courteous in his actions, if he had gone the official route, they may have missed this crucial piece of evidence all together, for he doubted if the officers who had verified the alibi would readily admit to their mistake that quickly. Luckily the several witnesses, other than Stephanie, had identified Joseph Mallard as the man who had occupied the Sale Hotel room and bar on the nights in question. They all stated that he had used the name of Alan Mortimer more than once.

Toni and Colin discussed what they had in the way of hard evidence and ideas they had on how they would approach the interrogation. They agreed that Colin would take on Mallard first; Toni would observe to see what he revealed before going after Mortimer. You never know what Constable Compton would come up with before then.

Chapter 56

The Joseph Mallard Interview commenced by turning on the tape recorder and restating the caution. Next the usual verbal self introduction of those present; Detective Chief Inspector Colin Dale, Detective Sergeant John Musgrove, Mr Joseph Mallard and his solicitor Jesse Conrad. Colin began.

"Please Mr Mallard can you tell me where you were on the night of the nineteenth and twentieth of this month"?

Colin hoped the interview was not going to be one that consisted of 'no comment'. Joseph looked at his solicitor before he answered.

"I was at my office during the day and at home in the evenings as far as I recall".

"Is there anyone who can confirm that"?

"My secretary, Jenny Franks, who is my partner. She was with me for some of the time at least, we don't live in each other's pockets"..

"When did you go to Surrey"?

Joseph wondered what was going on. Surrey was the location of the cottage of the guy that he had found for Alan.

"I never went to Surrey at any time, well recently anyway, years ago maybe. What's this all about"?

"From the files we extracted from your computer it seems you did a search on the very place we are talking about, a cottage just outside Henswell in Surrey".

"That was for a client, I never went there".

"No client was mentioned in your file or any paperwork that we found, it looks like you did this search for yourself. How do you know Clinton Macaulay"?

Joseph was beginning to panic now, he turned to his solicitor telling him he did search for this Macaulay fellow but it was for a client. She advised him to tell them the truth.

"The search was for a client who wished to remain discreet. I never met the man or went to his cottage".

"Who was your client so we can confirm that"?

"No comment".

Colin thought here it comes the string of 'no comments. He would change tack.

"We'll leave that for now, can you explain the large sum of money we found in your flat"?

"That was payment for work I had done".

"Do you always get paid in cash"?

"Sometimes".

"Why not put it in the bank, I hope you declare these payments"?

"I never got around to it, I was busy, I would have done it later, and yes I declare everything".

"Was it payment from your mystery client payment for what you did at the Cottage in Surrey"?

"No it wasn't, and I told you I never went there".

"Well someone did, and if it wasn't your client it must have been you. Clinton Macaulay was murdered in that cottage and it seems that you had the means, a financial motive and no real alibi for the time in question. What do you say about that"?

"Please, I would like to speak to my solicitor in private before I answer".

"Detectives Dale and Musgrove are leaving the room in order that Mr Mallard can consult with his solicitor, the tape will be switched off at eleven twenty seven".

"You have him on the run there sir, and you haven't even used the big guns yet".

"I hope he gives up Mortimer, but he may just shut up shop. It's ironic, he has the perfect alibi but can't tell us without giving up his role in this murder conspiracy".

A knock on the door indicated that Joseph had finished and was ready to continue.

Colin and Jonny entered and restarted the proceedings. The solicitor spoke first.

"My client believes he may have got the dates confused and can prove he was nowhere near Surrey on the days in question, in order to do this he will have to betray a client confidence. He wishes to make a statement".

"On the days of the nineteenth to the twenty first I was in Manchester, I stayed at the Hilton hotel Sale. It may be difficult to prove as I was using another name, although if I went there the staff will recognise me".

"Why would you want to impersonate someone"?

"It was a job, a joke I thought for a client, I didn't know why"?

"And he paid you five thousand pounds to do that, some pretty big joke"?

"Yes, the money was not just for that, there were other things, I did a lot of work researching stuff, not just the trip to Manchester".

"What is the name of this client".

"No comment".

"Are you sure you don't want to tell us. We found a large sum of money in a suspect's house. These are new notes, recently issued by his bank, notes where the sequence of serial numbers match those of the ones we found in your apartment".

Joseph then knew they already had Toby, in custody and they had searched his apartment. God knows what else they had found. He had no idea what he might have said, but knowing what a devious bastard he was, he could not trust him one inch. Had Toby or Alan, whatever his name was now, murdered this guy, using him to create an alibi, he thought maybe yes. He had to be careful what he said but he wasn't going to take the can for a murder.

"All right it was Alan Mortimer, you already know, don't you"?

"More than you think, that false alibi you gave for Mr Mortimer, we have already broken, lucky for you, as you would have been charged with murder. I believe you were unaware that a murder was intended, however you will be charged with providing a false alibi and perverting the course of justice for now. One more question what is Mr Mortimer's real name"?

There it was the bombshell, Joseph did not know what to say, if he gave up Toby's name that would open up his previous dealings and lay him open to further charges. He would pretend he didn't know.

"I don't know any other name he was just Alan Mortimer to me".

"I suggest you think about that, any witness who helps with that line of enquiry and co-operates with the CPS may be treated leniently".

A lifeline, Joseph was now drowning in Toby's shit, and remembering how he had ditched Sandra, he decided to take care of number one. He would grab at that offer with both hands.

"I will consider that and see if can remember some names over the next day or so, I will consult with my solicitor first".

They completed the process of closing the interview, turned off the tape and left the room, Colin and Mel to consult with Toni, Joseph went back to the cells his solicitor in tow.

"You did great there Colin he will fess up Toby Jones I'm sure. My turn now, let's screw this bastard down".

Chapter 57

Toni was well aware how devious this man could be, if there was a way out he would have found it, or even planned it in advance. If he was to slip up it will be because he is over confident. She was still waiting on DNA and wanted to go in fully armed. She phoned Compton for the latest information, the bank had confirmed the money serial numbers were from their batch and it was issued to Alan Mortimer. SOCO had come up trumps too. Chemical analysis of the mud found in Mortimer's car tyres matched exactly to the mud in the layby close to the cottage. She would send DNA results as soon as they were to hand.

"Are you ready Melanie, let's do it".

"Interview commenced at fourteen ten on the thirtieth September, those present, Detective Chief Inspector Toni Webb. Constable Melanie Frazer. Mr Alan Mortimer. Mr Mortimer's solicitor Mr Arnold Gibbs. Please state your names for the recording".

Everyone did so in turn.

"Mr. Mortimer you remain under caution, do you understand".

"Yes".

"Mr. Mortimer can you tell me where were you on the nineteenth and twentieth of this month"?

"No comment".

"From where did you obtain the stolen stones"?

"No comment".

"You are facing very serious charges but I am not sure if you understand fully the caution. I know you have the right to be silent, but the failure to answer these questions will mean, that when you go to court and the prosecution makes a statement concerning your whereabouts, your counsel may not be able to defend you adequately".

"I do understand, but my solicitor said I should say nothing".

"That is generally good advice but in this case I would consider helping us in order to help yourself. I'll ask you again where were you on the nineteenth and twentieth of this month"?

Alan thought he had paid a lot of money for a perfectly good alibi so why not use it.

"I was in Manchester".

"That's better, can you prove that"?

"I stayed in the Sale Hilton, you can ask them".

"Did you go by car"?

"No, by train, my manager arranged it all for me, ask him".

"Did you go anywhere else whilst in Manchester, Surrey for example"?

"Now why would I do that"?

"We have information that suggests you might have been there on the day in question, have you ever been to a cottage in Surrey before"?

"No have never been there".

Toni did not pursue that lie, some information you keep till later, like when the prosecution offers the muddy tyre evidence in court.

"Now in an earlier interview you stated that you paid a ransom of thirty thousand pounds for the return of the stolen stones. Is that still your statement"?

"Yes".

"Where did you get the money"?

"I already told you, from my bank, you can check".

"We did and it is true that you withdrew that amount of money on the day you said, what is strange is we found twenty five thousand pounds hidden in your apartment. How do you account for that"?

"That's money I keep for emergencies".

"You mean you already had that money in your apartment".

"Yes of course".

"Then why not use it for the ransom"?

"It wasn't enough, so I drew out what I needed to pay the guy off".

"That seem reasonable to me. When you left the bank with all that money where did you go"?

"To meet the guy of course".

"Let me get this right you went straight to your meeting with the unknown man".

"Yes, are you stupid or something, I already said didn't I"?

"Then how do you explain that the serial numbers, of the notes we found in your apartment, match those that the bank confirmed they issued to you on the day in question"?

Alan was not sure what to say or do, he never even thought to check the notes numbers, there was no way he thought anyone would ever see that money, it was a safeguard to support his ransom story. Instead it was turning out to be a trap of his own making.

"No comment".

"Nothing to say again, well it seems like you never did meet the unknown man and pay the ransom, you still had the cash. I also wonder what happened to the other five thousand. We know Clinton Macaulay had the stones one day and you had them the next are you sure he wasn't the unknown man"?

"No comment".

"Seeing as how you are unable to comment on these events we'll move on. When we checked your alibi, that is your supposed visit to Manchester, we found several witnesses that identified the man, posing as Alan Mortimer, to be a Joseph Mallard and not yourself, how do you explain that".

"No comment".

"We also found five thousand pounds in Mr Mallard's apartment the balance of your thirty thousand pounds. We believe you paid him to pretend to be you, because the note's serial numbers are from the same group issued by your bank, that you falsely claimed to have been used to pay a ransom. How do you explain that"?

"No comment".

"This is getting a little monotonous. What is your real name"?

Alan's blood pressure took a leap upwards and his heart pounded. 'They can't know that, can they, bloody hell, keep calm'.

"What do you mean, Alan Mortimer of course".

"I mean what was your name before you changed it to Alan Mortimer"?

"No, no I am Alan Mortimer".

Toni decided to stretch the truth; the DNA results had not arrived but she was convinced they would prove positive, so took a chance.

"We have finger prints and DNA that say different".

What had he got himself into, why did he have to get involved with Westfields bloody problem, they would have sorted it out even without his intervention? Why did he not leave that Macaulay guy alone? He knew his vengeful nature had gotten the better of him, for that day he'd become the unforgiving and violent Toby Jones, not the calm controlled Alan Mortimer he wanted to be. Now he might have to pay. His temper was rising but decided to say no more.

"I believe your real name is David Charles Jones and not Alan Mortimer"?

His control was slipping, anger gripped his being, he stood leaned forward towards Toni, then pointed at his new face with both index fingers.

"Look at me you black bitch, do I look like Toby Jones"?

Unmoved by this racial outburst, Toni leaned towards him with a smile, face to face.

"Actually Toby you really do, especially when seen through the eyes of a blind man".

Toni charged him with the murder of Clinton Macaulay, in turn Colin charged him with various fraud offences relating to the sale of his property company of two years before. He was not charged with the conspiracy to murder Gerry Grey, a crime committed by Sandra Cooper about the same time. Both Toni and Colin knew this was orchestrated by Toby but they had insufficient evidence to satisfy the CPS. It mattered not, they had enough evidence to put him away for a very long time.

Toni went happily back to her Chineham house and Colin home to his family. For the first time in ages, they both slept well. that night.

Chapter 58

The DNA results proved positive, the samples found in Toby's flat from two years ago matched the samples taken from Sandra's flat and those taken from Alan on his arrest. He was sent for trial and remanded in custody.

Joseph Mallard gave evidence at the trial of David Charles Jones. He was found guilty of murder and given a life sentence, to serve a minimum of twenty five years. He lodged an appeal against his sentence. The trial for the charge of fraud was postponed to a later date, yet to be decided.

Joseph was given a three year sentence for his part in the perversion of the course of justice. This was suspended, following his cooperation with the CPS during the prosecution of Toby Jones.

He was barred from practicing as a private investigator for life. Fearful that Toby's vengeful nature might seek them out, even from within prison, Joseph and his girlfriend left England the next week, for pastures new and unknown.

Toby Jones died in prison, before the fraud trial. The inquest concluded it was an accidental death, according to the prison guards he tripped and fell from a balcony. There were no witnesses to that event.

The businesses and property registered in the name of Alan Mortimer were not proven to be obtained through illegal means, as there was no will or relatives found, they eventually reverted to the State.

Kevin Blackman was employed by the State Department and given authority to continue to manage Conway Investments. He was fortunate that no one knew about the forty thousand pounds Alan had given him for safe keeping, he had put it in his private safety deposit box. Kevin finally got married.

Superintendent Walter Munroe achieved his extra funding, so took on two new graduate constables. He was glad to accept June Owens and Keith Crane into the fold of the detectives. Melanie Frazer was promoted to Detective Sergeant and Jonny Musgrove became the new Detective Inspector.

He supplied Compton Busion with new computer equipment, a permanent assistant and an office of her own. She was encouraged to sit the sergeant's exam but declined. She liked her job as it was and didn't have time to study anyway.

The retired Sergeant Mann opened his post to find a small parcel full of cash, pay day was one thing Toby never forgot. The enclosed note said, 'till next time'. Now there never was going to be a 'next time'; he could at last sleep in peace.

Westfields continued ever more successfully with their experiments. They were very close to achieving their goal. Alan Mortimer's shareholding was voided by the courts and reverted back to James Grimm.

Toni finally moved upstairs to her new office and joined the 'paper pushers'. She was content in her new role where she could nurture her new team of detectives.

She bought her little house in Great Oaks, but still procrastinated over her pending divorce. 'Never mind' she thought, at least the Four Horseshoes would give her comfort.

Then begins a journey...

Made in the USA
Middletown, DE
10 January 2019